Wisdom

AND THE

Baobab Tree

a novel

Edward R. McMahon

Dewart Imprints LLC

ISBN: 979-8-9912627-0-5 (hardcover)
ISBN: 979-8-9912627-1-2 (paperback)
ISBN: 979-8-9912627-2-9 (ebook)

Book design by David Provolo

To Jason and Jodie:
I am so proud of you.

ACKNOWLEDGEMENTS

I would like to express my sincerest appreciation for all those who made this novel possible. My wife Fran provided invaluable support—and patience—over the life of this project, and made many spot-on suggestions. I also wish to thank Gail Spilsbury, my sherpa and mentor, who selflessly helped to steer me through the writing and production processes. Emily Lang gave me an education through her copy-editing prowess, as did Dave Provolo in book production and Tess Renault in final proofreading.

I am also very appreciative of Dick Matheson and other members of the Burlington, Vermont, Writers Workshop who shared useful comments to early drafts of this manuscript. David Carroll, Jean Page, Adamou Kombo, Thomas Melia, and Ambassador Niels Marquardt (ret.) also graciously agreed to provide helpful perspectives and suggestions to the draft.

And finally, my heartfelt thanks to so many of my colleagues who have worked to promote democracy and human rights in Africa; you have and will make a difference.

ANI - Agency for National Information
CDP - Center for Democratic Progress
DCM - Deputy Chief of Mission
IEC - Independent Election Commission
KDPR - Kombonian Democratic Popular Rally
KRP - Kombonian Revolutionary Party
PMLP - Popular Movement for the Liberation of Pohaneland
PR - Proportional Representation
RMK - Renewal Movement of Kombonia
SPB - Special Presidential Brigade
USAID - US Agency for International Development

Wisdom is like a baobab tree;
no one individual can embrace it.

Akan Proverb

Chapter 1

Setting the Scene

The night of Adam Edwards's arrival from the US had been a restless one in Kayemba City. As dusk enveloped the capital of the country of Kombonia in Central Africa, kerosene lanterns flickered lit. A smoky, smelly haze combining the scents of spices, waste, and charcoal wafted through the narrow streets, which were crowded with people, cars and livestock. By 9 p.m., however, an eerie calm took hold. A curfew imposed by the government resulted in an emptying of the streets and truckloads of soldiers careening around in pickup trucks, interrogating and arresting some of the few people who ventured out in the dark. By midnight, fearful residents heard mysterious explosions and the sounds of gunfire echoing off a hilly section of one of the poorer neighborhoods on the city's outskirts. This was not new; strange things had been happening for weeks, although the gunfire this night seemed longer and more intense.

The next morning the government's minister of information announced that a "small group of terrorists had been found and neutralized." However, this cursory explanation, from an official of a government whose credibility and truthfulness were seen as bankrupt by many citizens, did little to calm the jittery atmosphere. The reason behind the minister's explanation, depending upon one's point of view, was either to intimidate the population, or to demonstrate the government's steel-headed resolve to maintain order during a turbulent time.

By contrast, "street radio," as gossip is called in Kombonia, did a brisk business. A number of different alternative possibilities circulated. The first, with generally the least credence, was that only ordinary criminals had been active and that the security forces had acted against them. The second was that the gunfire was caused by a shadowy militia group known as the Popular Movement for the Liberation of Kombonia (PMLK), which was suspected of being allied with the Renewal Movement of Kombonia (RMK), a radical opposition grouping. The third, and most recent option, was linked to the alleged existence of a pro-government militia called "The Wolves of Kombonia." This group had made its presence known three weeks earlier, with an announcement of its intent to "defend the homeland vigorously from the termites who seek to devour all that our beloved President Mushi has achieved." Six members of the leading anti-government trade union were subsequently found beheaded with notes pinned to their chests stating that "the wolves have howled." Further complicating matters, and also reflecting the deep polarization between different ethnicities in Kombonia, some other backers of the ruling Kombonian Revolutionary Party (KRP) claimed online that the Wolves of Kombonia were in fact *agents provacateurs*, another opposition terror group created to discredit the government.

Kayemba City lies in a flat plain. This presented a problem to its British colonizers, who lacked a convenient hill upon which to construct a suitable Governor's mansion. Instead, they made do with a park-like setting in what was then Kayemba City's southern suburbs. There they constructed a replica of an English country manor, absurdly out of place in the Kombonian heat and dust, but nonetheless resplendent with carefully manicured, irrigated lawns and a long, curving drive. In 1963 President Ignatious Owemu, the country's first president after the British had reluctantly relinquished control, inherited the mansion, and made it the president's residence. Upon acceding to the presidency in 2002, Simon Mushi became its next tenant.

The grounds had deteriorated somewhat over time. The building, which housed both residential quarters and the president's offices, maintained an aura of faded grandeur. A useful by-product of its location, was that it was located away from the city center, and hence it was usually free from political protests. With the passage of time, however, Kayemba City's urban sprawl had come to encompass the area around the palace, with the accompanying juxtaposition of power and privilege against urban poverty—a phenomenon hardly limited to Kombonia, the developing world, or Washington, DC, for that matter.

Independence Avenue, the thoroughfare bordering the palace, was closed off at both ends with several army tanks barring passage. Smartly uniformed soldiers of the president's bodyguard force, the Special Presidential Brigade, or SPB, patrolled its grounds where they shared space somewhat incongruously with a flock of peacocks.

If one were admitted past the sharp-eyed, suspicious guards at the east end of Independence Avenue, one would pass peacocks grazing on the lawn and follow the drive up to the front door.

There a liveried attendant would open the door leading into a gilded hallway, with a reception room off to the right.

This particular morning, President Simon Mushi was in a paneled study on the second floor, his brow furrowed as he formulated his reply to a question posed by the only other person in the room, Martin Abdallah, the minister of the interior. Abdallah was the third most powerful man in the country, after President Mushi and Suleiman Nwanji, the defense minister.

What kind of man was Mushi? To begin with, he embodied many of the contradictions of contemporary Kombonia. He lived in an urban setting, but most of his extended family did not. He was educated, having attended Cambridge University, but only a tiny fraction of his fellow Kombonians had a university education. He was of the less-privileged Ome ethnic group, but had chosen to work—quite successfully—within a political and economic system dominated by the Tuyunu ethnicity. During his long tenure in power, he had taken some important, but still limited, measures to open up the political system. However, other than his own sub-clan, of which he was the unquestioned leader, he was viewed by many of his fellow Ome as a fraud, as a sellout to the Tuyunu.

Mushi was a minor member of Ome nobility. He had grown up with a sense of *noblesse oblige*, and found it possible to entwine his traditional responsibilities with those of "modernity," as he developed a career as one of the most successful lawyers in the country. Seeking to toss a bone to the Ome, President Owemu had requested that he serve as minister of justice in his government in 1988. After some thought, and recognizing the likely downsides in terms of his personal and financial security if he refused, Mushi accepted. He did so not only out of a sense of coercion, but also because he harbored a belief—rational or not—that the day was coming when an Ome could ascend to the presidency—and why not he?

Mushi's plan was long term. He had long felt that he had a mission to accomplish, one of creating a system of greater political openness than had ever existed. He was, after all, an Ome and his people—and he did think of them as "his" people—had only rarely tasted the fruits of political power. He saw, however, a need to move slowly. He, more so than many of his ethnic brethren, recognized that shifting the balance of political power could not be accomplished quickly. He was of course mindful of what had happened to poor President Melchior Ndadaye of Burundi. The first Hutu president of his country had only lasted three months in office before he was murdered by troops of the minority Tutsi ethnicity, who had previously held power. It was said that Ndadaye had warned his captors just before his death to "Think very carefully about what you are about to do." Those words haunted the future, as his murder set off an uncontrolled tailspin of violence.

Mushi had met Ndadaye in Cairo at one of the annual, expensive, and rarely effective regional meetings of African heads of state. Ndadaye had seemed quite positive that he could pull off the balancing act that was required of him; how wrong he had been, with tragic and destabilizing consequences for himself, his country, and the region.

So Mushi was very mindful that rapid reform could be tantamount to suicide. The Tuyunu elite had to be brought around slowly to the recognition that the world was changing, and that the centralization of political power in the hands of ethnic minorities was a recipe for instability and ostracization, both internally, within the region, and on the broader international level.

His plan was very risky and complex. He could not afford the luxury of following the advice of a Cambridge professor of politics who had seen in him a bright future and who had counselled, "Above all, do not promise different things to different audiences. You have to be constant in your message." Perhaps that could work in a place like England, but it would lead straight to political oblivion or worse in Kombonia.

He had, on this day, many different constituencies with which to deal. The Tuyunu elite, especially the military, were the ones who had effectively placed him in his position of power. That didn't mean he was trusted by them—merely that they thought he was sufficiently malleable to represent Tuyunu interests, while ensuring that his presence in the presidency would drain off enough Ome venom to obviate the possibility of an Ome revolt.

As adherence to the letter and spirit of constitutional law was not yet viewed as sacrosanct in Kombonia, Mushi was also keenly aware of his fragile relationship with the military. He had never served in it, and knew that its leaders saw themselves as a power unto themselves. They would have no compunction about staging a coup and terminating his presidency if they thought it necessary. He had heard the army chief of staff repeatedly proclaim, "We are the guarantors of national stability." To further complicate the situation, and add to the Tuyunu leadership's sense of insecurity, much of the military enlisted ranks were Ome. As a precaution, and only after much maneuvering with the army leadership, Mushi had finally succeeded in ensuring that his military guard—the SPB— included members of his Ome subclan as officers in its composition.

Mushi also had the restiveness of Ome sensitivities with which to deal. The economic situation was increasingly difficult, the country's infrastructure was deteriorating, and Kombonia was clearly affected by the moves for political reforms that had swept over not only Latin America, Eastern Europe, and Asia, but much of Africa as well. Most of the Ome wanted much more change than what Mushi had promoted. Kombonia's population also included other ethnicities, including the restive Pohane group in the west of the country who felt, not without justification, that they were regarded as the poor stepsiblings of both the Tuyunu and Ome.

Also, Kombonians of all backgrounds tended to think of their country as having a unique history and context, and that therefore the problems and challenges they faced were *sui generis*, particular to Kombonia. This rather insular view was, at least in part, a legacy of President Owemu's rule. He had limited Kombonia's foreign contacts, fearing threats to his power from other countries in the region, some of which counted in their populations' large numbers of Pohane and Ome. He also was suspicious of Western powers, whom he suspected of harboring designs of installing a more pliant government in power to be a more faithful friend in the Cold War against the communist bloc. His successor, President Mushi, did not particularly share these feelings of insecurity, but their impact lingered on in Kombonian perspectives of their own country and its place in the world.

These contrasting and conflicting elements—so important to understanding the country—not surprisingly led to a sizeable national identity crisis, notwithstanding much rhetoric about the "unity" of the Kombonian nation propounded by leading politicians. This underlying and uneasy sense of questioning of what it means to be Kombonian had been, until recently, swept under the rug and not addressed. Even now, with the winds of democracy rustling across Kombonia, it was a very sensitive subject; one that Kombonians had yet to feel comfortable about discussing or integrating into national discourse.

Mushi thus fully felt himself caught in the middle of the proverbial vise. People tended to think that he had more power than he did. He was seen, after all, as wearing the mantle of the all-powerful African leader. He knew how much that was not true. He had to tread carefully or the situation—which was one that he had largely created by instituting a measured political opening—could become unmanageable and spiral out of control. Beyond the unspoken threat of a military coup, violence such that had occurred the previous night, was growing, and not even Mushi was certain on a given day of its provenance. Political parties were calling for greater rights, the economy was a mess, and he had to deal with a parliament and political class that were increasingly more outspoken than in the past. And the European Community Ambassadors, as well as that pesky American woman ambassador, were continually pressing him to make further reforms. The World Bank and the International Monetary Fund were threatening to suspend further financial assistance unless he reduced the size of the civil service and devalued the currency.

There was one other important factor. Simon Mushi was a man, with the weaknesses as well as the strengths implied therein. He still enjoyed being president even more than he had thought he would. Notwithstanding the complexities and the constraints on his power, he found being Chief of State continually appealing. He liked the pomp and circumstance, the deference shown to him, the trappings of power. He found himself increasingly wondering what he would do if and when he were to become an ex-president. How would his immediate and extended family, subclan, and full ethnic group, all of whom benefitted from his presidential position and thus depended upon him, react to the prospect that he might no longer be president? Often, he would push these thoughts from his mind with the rationalization that just because he intended to reform Kombonian politics, it didn't mean that he would *ipso facto* have to leave power. After all, he would muse, look at the legacies of Presidents Rawlings in Ghana, Nujoma down in Namibia, or Chissano in Mozambique. They had secured the trifecta of garnering the international seal of good housekeeping, maintaining the support of their people, and making the transition from single party politics to multiparty democracy.

While all this didn't fundamentally alter his plan, its subtle, indirect effect was to buttress his sense that the process of democratic transition should not be hurried, and that if push came to shove, Tuyunu sensitivities needed to take primacy in his decision-making. In essence, he was more afraid of a military coup than of a popular uprising. He suspected that the previous night's violence was perpetrated by those in the military who were concerned about losing their privileges in the wake of a fully democratic transition.

All of these manifold elements of the reality that Mushi faced weighed on his mind as he responded to Abdallah's question about what to do in response to the previous night's violence. "We must make it clear that, whatever its origins, this will not be tolerated in Kombonia. Pass the word quietly that I am prepared to impose a state of emergency on the country if necessary."

"Very good, Mr. President." Abdallah turned to leave, but at the door he pivoted, to pose one last question. "Sir, the Americans have sent a representative here named Adam Edwards to open up an office of a human rights and democracy nongovernmental organization. They say that this is to help our democratic transition. To be frank, however, we suspect he could be a CIA agent working undercover. What should we do with him?"

Mushi pursed his lips. "This American organization should register with your ministry in order to function legally here, correct?" Abdallah nodded his assent.

"Then don't bother him yet. I think it would be best to wait and watch. I don't want to have a problem with the American ambassador, certainly not right now. If he does seek to register his organization, don't take action on the application. Instead, please inform me."

Chapter 2

Introducing Adam Edwards

Adam Edwards was pretty much a happy-go-lucky type of person. He liked to semi-joke that he was a Libra, which meant that he sought to avoid conflict, and focus on creating common ground between people and different perspectives whenever possible. While not exactly brilliant, he was of above average intelligence. And although he wasn't the best athlete around, he enjoyed sports growing up and had no trouble making friends. He was a good-looking, lanky guy, who grew to six feet four inches and 220 pounds, although he never perceived himself as being big or very imposing. He got a kick at times out of displaying class clown type tendencies in grade school.

Living in the Main Line suburbs of Philadelphia, his family was relatively wealthy. This privileged reality served to shield him from, and to mask, some of the stresses in life. So on balance, Adam had a happy childhood. He loved to seek out adventures and new challenges and came from the type of background that ensured that most of them would be positive. Having only a limited or superficial knowledge of the environment in which he was functioning did not particularly bother him, as he had fun adapting to and doing well in whatever circumstances he found himself in. In fact, he enjoyed the stimulus and challenge of finding himself in different places. He made friends with ease and was an adequate, if somewhat lazy, student.

In his later years, Adam came to realize that the seeds of some of his future problems were sown in his upbringing. Especially in his younger days, it was very important for him to be liked. He later realized that this came from some level of insecurity, of self-doubt. He took pains, for example, to avoid being tested in conflict, either physical, mental, or emotional. He sometimes felt that he would feel more at home with the Canadian stereotype of a polite, even-handed personality rather than the brasher and more outspoken American persona. He belatedly came to realize that this resulted, at least in part, from his upbringing in a pretty Wasp-ish family, in which major discord was suppressed, and the family skated on top of and around significant differences. His desire to conform was accentuated by the reality that his two siblings, a brother and a sister, had developmental challenges that included difficulty in normal social interactions. Overall, however, the truth was that he had had a good start in life and had been spared major trauma or challenges of the type that could deeply scar most people as they moved into adulthood. He was thus able to slide easily through many of the early phases of his life and did not find himself challenged or tested in terms of character very often.

One event that did have a profound impact on him was when his aunt took him to England when he was just twelve. His family had distant relatives and a network of friends there. His eyes widened as he first saw the English countryside from the window of the BOAC VC-10, visited the chalk cliffs of Dover, the Tower of London, and the ancestral Longleat estate where lions roamed freely. But what really fascinated his pre-adolescent mind, were the differences in everyday life. Why, he wondered, did people speak with different accents? Why did they drive on the other side of the road? Why did the toilets have chains to pull instead of handles?

Adam would find as he matured that these types of cross-cultural inquiries would evolve to more sophisticated lines of questioning. But the basic reality remained—he was stimulated by attempting to understand the basic differences between his home and the new environments. As such, he developed a yearning to put himself into different contexts. He eventually grew to appreciate that what captivated him was in fact being outside of his comfort zone, placing himself in venues and contexts in which he didn't fully understand all the dynamics and realities shaping events. In short, not really having a clue about what was going on. The challenge of navigating these unfamiliar waters was, to him, the stimulatory essence of life. He came to understand that he was not destined for a sedentary life, living on the same street, with the same people, and in the same country, in which time unfolded Groundhog Day–like: an unending drive through the Iowa cornfields. Was this contradictory to some of the other, more problematic aspects of his personality? Absolutely. But such contradictions often figure as part of the human condition.

Many of these deeper insights eluded Adam in his younger years. At Dartmouth, his carefree manner, quick wit, and fun-loving nature tended to obscure the fact that he cared about making a difference—having some kind of impact on the larger world—and that preferably such an effect would be positive and for the general betterment of humankind. This rather unfocused and naïve approach, which Adam eventually recognized and realized was not uncommon in youth beginning to look for their way in the world, led him, perhaps not surprisingly, to join the Peace Corps directly after graduation from college.

Adam was really excited about being accepted into the Peace Corps, and ecstatic when he learned that he would be posted to Thailand; an exotic country about which he knew very little. His departure from JFK Airport in New York was a festive affair, as various family members and friends showed up to see him off and share in his excitement about this next chapter in his life. After two weeks of initial training near Bangkok, he was sent to the regional capital of Chiang Mai in the north for more language immersion training. Then, the big day came when he set off to his "site": the village of Phukea Pong not far from the border with Laos, about four hours away by bus and then a motorized type of rickshaw. The village and surrounding area were home to about 4,000 people, most of whom earned their living through rice farming and river fishing.

It didn't take long to start getting to know his neighbors. Adam's arrival in the village was the object of considerable curiosity, and he found a swarm of children following his every move. He was also the object of polite curiosity by the village elders. The day after his appearance he was invited into the hut of the local chief, who began the introductions with a traditional form of greeting, the *wai,* pressing his hands to together and bowing slightly. Adam nervously reciprocated.

"We welcome you to our village and will do our best to ensure that you will do well and be happy here," he said courteously.

Adam responded in kind, hoping that his recently learned Thai language skills would see him through. Remembering his initial in-country training that emphasized making connections through contact with its children, Adam asked, "May I show all the children outside the hut a magic trick?" The chief assented, with a friendly twinkle in his eye.

Adam quickly stopped in his hut to collect a bag of Pop Rocks, a candy he had brought from the US that had been gasified with carbon dioxide under super-atmospheric pressure. When these sugar granules encountered moisture in someone's mouth the gas retained inside the carbon dioxide bubbles was released, causing a popping sensation as well as crackling and fizzing sounds. Adam excitedly opened the bag in the midst of the crowd of jostling children and handed out the candy.

To his consternation, the kids' jaws quickly became stuck and there were no popping sounds. Adam quickly realized that the tropical heat of Northern Thailand had deflated the carbon dioxide, leaving a treacly, residual mass of flavored sugar. Eventually the kids laughed and worked their way through the mess, but Adam was mortified at this failure for three reasons. First, he could only imagine what damage he had just done to the village's pediatric dental health. Second, he felt that he had just blown his chance to make a good first impression with the villagers. And third, he noticed the chief looking at him with a mixture of confusion and concern.

Seized by an inspiration, Adam raced back to his hut and grabbed a bag filled with another potential icebreaker. Reaching into it, he presented each of the two dozen or so kids with a rubber balloon. Taking one himself, he blew it up into the shape of a dachsund dog, tied it off, and presented it to the youngest looking toddler he could find. He then instructed the enraptured kids how to blow up, shape, and then tie off the balloons. This resulted in considerable merriment. The chief nodded sagely at this spectacle and said something to Adam that he would have occasion to recall many times in the future: "Our honored young visitor, you have just demonstrated a very important thing. It is not that you make a mistake; it is how you react to it. You have done well." Adam glowed with the praise while also feeling that he had just dodged a bullet.

Despite this warm welcome, after a couple of weeks Adam found that he missed contact with his newfound American Peace Corps friends; folks with whom he had trained, partied, and bonded with over their initial training period in-country. The nearest fellow volunteer was in another village about thirty miles away by dirt roads and paths, a tough haul if you only had a bike and a helmet—non-negotiable requirements for transportation in this area of Thailand. The challenge of travel was often exacerbated by the humid conditions that frequently exceeded 95 degrees. So, for the first time in his young life, Adam found that he had no choice but to make his life in the alien surroundings around him. At times he had to dig deep into himself to avoid loneliness and self-pity. In doing so, he eventually came to survive and flourish.

Adam's work assignment fell within the parameters of the Peace Corps in Thailand's "Youth in Development Project." Its purpose was to help local Thai youth develop the skills and attributes that would enable them to be healthy and engaged citizens contributing to their communities. In Phukea Pong, Adam tried a couple of different approaches to engaging the youth and found that he didn't have much success—he couldn't find an activity that would create a substantive connection. However, one day several months after his arrival as he was lazily kicking a soccer ball around a dusty field, he found himself joined by several young boys, eager to play. They met the next day, and then the next day to kick the ball around. Soon these play sessions became a constant, with a dozen boys coming regularly.

After about a week of this, Adam had a brainstorm. He asked the boys' de facto leader, Tanawat, whether they might like to act in a play. Tanawat's eyes lit up and he offered up an eager affirmative. Adam made this suggestion because he had noted both the kids' natural playfulness and a problem in the local health clinic. The latter was often short of blood, largely because donating blood was not a common practice in the region. Over the course of two weeks during the evenings Adam sat in his hut and wrote up a play about a village that had been hit hard by a natural disaster, which resulted in an increased need for blood available for transfusions. The boys eagerly learned their roles and began to perform the play in villages throughout the region, and then even in Chiang Mai. It proved to be a considerable success. Adam later wrote up a story about it to the Peace Corps headquarters in Bangkok as part of his regular activities reporting; in turn this was subsequently highlighted in the global Peace Corps newsletter as an example of a successful project, and for which Adam received a commendation.

This was the first significant experience in Adam's life where he developed and implemented a thoughtful solution to a societal problem. It was a new and empowering feeling for Adam, and he felt all the more proud about it as he had implemented it in a foreign culture, in a different language, and without the benefit of any peer feedback. He couldn't wait to come up with another, similar achievement.

After a couple of months in his tiny village, Adam began to realize that attempting to "change the world" in one fell swoop destined to leave him frustrated and discouraged. He thus decided to instead focus on becoming a part of the local community. Living like the locals forced Adam to adapt, rather than simply impose his way of thinking. It taught him to listen. He learned that conversations about behavior norms, and asking people for their opinions, could build understanding, trust, and empathy.

Adam's Peace Corps experience was not all roses. At times he was bored and listless. One of the weaknesses of the Peace Corps, he found, was that much time had to be spent figuring out what to do; his guidance from the Peace Corps had been limited in this regard. There was also the experience of starting up a relationship with a girl from another village, who quickly intimated her interest in marriage; an idea championed by her father, a village elder. Adam had an uncomfortable time extricating himself from that situation, which he eventually achieved by both giving the village elder a present of feed for his water buffalo and taking a well-timed vacation, during which he traveled by bus and motorbike through southern Thailand and Malaysia.

A little over a year into Adam's time in Thailand, the country held a general election. In an episode that wouldn't reverberate with him until a few years later, Adam volunteered to be a part of an election observation mission organized by the US embassy. He and a US Agency for International Development contractor, a member of the Defense Attaché's office, and another Peace Corps volunteer spent the day driving from polling place to polling place. The day proved exhausting but exhilarating to Adam and his colleagues as they saw nothing but orderly balloting processes and a population eager to exercise their right to vote. In fact, the atmosphere was festive at most election sites.

As Adam and his team exited one schoolhouse that doubled as a voting center, they found themselves surrounded by a group of boisterous children, none of whom measured higher than Adam's thigh. One of them craned his head all the way up to see Adam's head and then let loose with an exclamation in Thai which in turn was met with laughter from the assembled multitudes. The USAID contractor didn't speak Thai well enough to understand what had been said, so she turned to Adam to ask for a translation. Adam chuckled, "He asked his friends 'what does IT eat?'"

Adam had other fulfilling experiences. Near the village, at the border of a national park, elephants raided farms, leading farmers to poach and illegally kill the animals. This in turn brought occasional visits by the Thai police and security forces, who would respond by arresting a few villagers, largely to show their superiors that they were apparently dealing with the problem.

Adam heard the villagers frequently lamenting these problems and wanted to find a way to solve them, but he was met with a fatalistic reaction. Adam then recalled a summer spent at a summer camp in his youth where he helped on a beekeeping project. Inspired by this, and with the help and advice of the chief who had become something of an unofficial mentor, Adam spearheaded the construction of a "living fence" of beehives to scare away elephants and to provide income from honey and wax. Adam further worked to develop the site into an ecotourism activity for international and Thai visitors alike to witness the win-win solution that involved solving nature's problems with nature.

In the time-honored ethos of the Peace Corps, he found that he could match his strengths—in this case, both consensus-building skills and some knowledge of the bee world—to the community's needs (economic development) and attributes (available workforce and willingness to take direction from an outsider). He also solicited the villagers' input for activity design rather than attempting to make arbitrary decisions based on what he thought was best. Adam was influenced in his approach by not only his Peace Corps training, but because he had learned about a Western-funded nonprofit in Africa that had had much success in promoting local development by adopting a methodology based on the articulation of community-based needs, rather than the imposition of externally decided priorities.

For the first time, Adam thus realized that life was a never-ending series of compromises, and that the end result was often better than if the compromise hadn't occurred. Adam would later frequently remark that realizing this was when he became an adult.

Therefore, Adam's experience in Thailand was for a number of reasons an important step in his personal growth. It will never be known for sure whether any of his activities fundamentally changed lives, although Adam hopefully suspected that may have been the case for a few of his village friends. And it didn't mean that Adam emerged from his Peace Corps experience as a finished product, with little else to learn. What was clear, however, was that his Peace Corps service contributed to shaping him into a better global citizen through instilling the basis of a capacity to function within different cultures with humility and respect while listening to and understanding others.

Another impact of his time in Thailand was that it pushed the idea of a traditional business-oriented career even further from his mind, and also reinforced what he had already felt. He had a real, although still vague, sense of what he wanted to do in life—live and work amongst different cultures. Such a decision, however, did not make up for the lack of positive choices as to what he would do with the next steps of his life. When he returned to the US Adam spent six months of growing frustration pursuing usually ephemeral job leads, mostly for positions he didn't want, in New York and Washington, DC. During interim periods between job interviews, in order to not grow bored, he also did volunteer organizing and canvassing work for an ultimately unsuccessful Democratic Party congressional candidate in the Philadelphia suburbs in that year's November elections. He got used to having doors slammed in his face, and rejections from potential voters when he tried to hand out campaign flyers on the street. He also had some good experiences when he had substantive and productive conversations with people about the merits of his candidate.

In brief, his period of growth after graduation from college exposed him to the frustrations and challenges, but also the rewards, of getting involved at the grassroots level to promote meaningful change. As he sought out a future path for his life, he strongly felt tugged in this direction of doing something meaningful and cross-cultural. He just wasn't quite sure what it would turn out to be.

Chapter 3

The Center for Democratic Progress

Informed by his Peace Corps experience, Adam started looking for a job that could somehow push him toward his future. After a fruitless visit to an international development agency headquartered in Washington, DC, Adam noticed in the building lobby a directory panel containing an organization named The Center for Democratic Progress. He quickly googled it on his cell phone, which informed him that the organization supported democracy and human rights programs around the world. Intrigued, he rode the elevator up to the eighth floor and introduced himself to the receptionist, an effervescent young woman a year out of George Washington University.

"Hello. I know that this is sort of coming out of the blue, but I have an international background and would be very interested in learning more about what it is the Center does," he asked the receptionist.

She took a minute to look him over. "You know, I could just tell you to get an appointment with someone and come back another day. But you know what? I'm in a good mood. Let me see if Charles Mulcahy might have a couple of minutes to talk to you."

That happenstance decision forever changed his professional life. Mulcahy, a handsome former diplomat in his mid-thirties who directed CDP's programs in Africa, was indeed available and willing to chat. As he was escorted to his cluttered office, Adam noticed a beehive of activity with a lot of young staffers running about with intense looks on their faces.

As they entered his office, "So who the hell are you?" were the first words Mulcahy directed toward Adam, in a voice that somehow managed to be gruff and friendly at the same time. *I'm not sure if he is putting me on or not*, thought Adam, *but he sure has a noticeable manner about him*. Adam provided him with his resume. Mulcahy looked at it briefly and invited him to have a seat next to a coffee table.

"The first thing you need to know if you ever end up working here is that people care, they really care about what they are doing. The second thing is that no one is really sure what the hell exactly it is that they are doing. Makes for creativity and ingenuity. I often say that this place is one-third the State Department, one-third Common Cause and one-third a congressional campaign office two weeks before an election. Most of the people who work here are young, they have a bit of an attitude, and they are committed to promoting democracy. Beyond that it's like throwing mud on a wall and seeing what sticks. Whaddya think of them apples?"

Again, Adam was a bit nonplussed and wasn't quite sure how to respond. He took the safe route. "Perhaps you could explain to me a bit more exactly what it is that CDP is supposed to do?"

Mulcahy adopted a somewhat more serious demeanor and hunched his long frame over the coffee table. "So, we have a mandate from Congress to support the development of democratic institutions around the world. If you ask me, it reflects a very American combination of naïve do-gooder spirit and a ballsy energy that can help change the world."

Mulcahy leaned back and recrossed his legs. "Look at it this way. After the end of the Cold War and the growth of attempts to develop democracies, there was a clear need for the international community to provide advice and support. Things aren't going so well on the global democracy front, in case you haven't noticed. It is scary and unprecedented to move from a dictatorship to a democracy. That is even more true in this day and age when we are dealing with the populist and dictatorial leaders who think that they and they alone have all the answers. There isn't any book written on how to successfully democratize. Every situation is different, and yet human nature is similar the world around. People want democracy, and people can learn from others' experiences. That is what we try to provide—nuts-and-bolts information on how to get democratic institutions, political parties, elections, legislatures and the like, to function."

Adam was intrigued but he still wasn't sure that he understood. "Umm . . . how exactly do you go about doing this?"

Mulcahy absentmindedly fingered a nose hair as he thought of his response. "Well, think of a successful democracy as operating on four different levels, shaped sort of like a pyramid. At the bottom is the soil of civil society. By this I mean the existence of nongovernmental groups that can help get the word out about this democracy thing, and are prepared to try to help make the process work. In a more basic sense, this also refers to people who are prepared to sacrifice for democracy. Democracy wouldn't have emerged in the Philippines, for example, back in 1986 when President Marcos tried to rig an election if there hadn't been people willing to go into the streets day after day to risk their lives and make sure those fake results did not stand. Without this kind of spirit democracy won't happen.

Second, political parties. What kind of democracy can function either with no or one political party?"

Although somewhat intimidated by the fervor Mulcahy was employing in his discourse, Adam responded, "I guess it would be pretty hard. But what about some place like Tanzania? I think I have read that in that country there is a long history of placing limits on political freedoms while not totally closing down opposition parties."

Mulcahy smiled a knowing sort of smile. "Funny you should mention it," he said. "I've just been thinking about the region." He grabbed a set of papers off his desk and shoved them at Adam. "Here's a memo I've just done. Take a look at its summary."

A number of governments in East Africa all share a remarkable number of similarities. They:
- demonstrate ambivalent attitudes about democratic political structures and other elements of pluralism, including political parties and elections;
- eschew, ostensibly at least, the "old" way of conducting politics;
- claim to be against corruption and do generally avoid ostentatious lifestyles;
- permit press and civic organizations to operate, although often with some constraints; and
- have not overtly embraced the notion of the single party state.

Pulling the paper back, Mulcahy expounded further. "You see, the leaders of these countries explain their method of governing by claiming that, while they support freedom of expression and other political liberties, the old-style of multi-party politics, often led by corrupt and self-serving elites, has led to ethnically based civil conflict in the past. They are thus allegedly seeking to develop home-grown political institutions that can provide for pluralism while at the same time avoiding conflict. By the way, you may be aware that a variation of these limits on democracy has been happening recently in some West African countries that have been subject to military coups."

Adam's curiosity was peaked. "What does the international community feel about all this?"

Mulcahy shrugged, but his subsequent lengthy soliloquy suggested to Adam that this guy knew his stuff. "It has reacted ambivalently. The vision of committed leaders avoiding the excesses of the past while searching earnestly for solutions to the complex problems of development is refreshing. In addition, all countries cited above continue to be strategically important, at least from a regional perspective. The leaderships of Uganda, Ethiopia, and Eritrea have also embraced the free-market reforms and private enterprise support deemed so important by the IMF and the World Bank, and their countries have begun to make some economic progress. But the average person in the street is not happy about the economic sacrifices that come along with these reforms. There have been riots in Kenya, for example, about this in the past few months.

"The political reform side of the ledger is also wanting. Governments have not sought to create environments in which political party and civic organization development can take place. Let me give you a few examples. Decades after taking power, the Rwandan Patriotic Front continues to dominate politics there. Similarly, in Burundi a military-backed government is a de facto dictatorship, but the oppressed Hutu population seethes with anger. Nongovernmental organizations have long been suppressed in Eritrea. There has been a civil war in northern Ethiopia. It is awfully tough to foresee meaningful multiparty electoral competition in these countries.

"And yet, it is precisely the lack of political checks and balances which has led to post-independence Africa's sorry experience of political authoritarianism and single party, personalist, rule. So I think you can safely say—with ironic understatement—that legitimate concerns exist about the lack of emerging democratic structures, and whether their leaders are prepared to permit the development of a political culture allowing various parties to win and lose elections; what we call alternance in power."

As Adam was digesting all this Mulcahy jumped up and apologized. "Listen, I've got to run to a meeting now. There may be something coming up in Kombonia that we could talk about, but it'll have to wait a few days. Why don't you call me back next week? I may know more then."

Adam wandered out of the office, slightly shell-shocked. After all, earlier in the afternoon he hadn't even known of the existence of the CDP—was it a front for the CIA?—and now some guy who may or may not have a screw loose was telling him to call back the next week to find out about a possible job.

I'd best check with someone else about this organization. So that evening he called his college buddy Peter Johannson, who worked for a second-term Ohio Democratic congressman, to ask if he had heard of CDP. Johannson was a really smart and ambitious up-and-coming Capitol Hill staffer. "Sure, I have had the opportunity to work with CDP—they sent me to Slovakia a year and half ago on a training program to work with parliamentary staff there. It was super stimulating sharing nuts-and-bolts stuff on how to enact legislation. CDP did a good job—they were well prepared and trying to make a difference."

Exercising due diligence, he checked with another friend named Naomi Vogel, a Democratic party elections expert who had conducted some training Adam attended when working on the Pennsylvania congressional race, and someone he guessed might have had contact with CDP. Vogel let out a loud sigh when Adam asked him if he was aware of CDP. "Sheesh…do I ever know about them—they screwed me over. I was supposed to go on a trip with them to Haiti and they cancelled it at the last moment. Said it was due to political conditions in-country, but if that was the case, why couldn't they have gotten in touch with me sooner? Were they so clueless they didn't know the way things were headed? I was pissed—I had my bags packed and was ready to leave."

The following week, with some trepidation he called Mulcahy, who suggested that he come in and visit with himself and Janet Ross, CDP's vice president for administration and personnel. Before meeting with Ross, Adam felt that he had to be honest with Mulcahy.

"Look, I am really interested in pursuing the idea of a job here, but I have to admit that I am not exactly an expert on Kombonia. I don't know much about its history, for example."

Mulcahy chuckled and handed him a document. "Here, check this out. It is a briefing memo my staff prepared when we were putting together the proposal for our Kombonian project to the US Agency for International Development mission there." Adam took a few minutes to read it while waiting for the meeting with Ross, but he guessed that a two-and-a-half page memo hardly did justice to such a country's complex history and makeup.

Much of the session with the vice president was devoted to discussion of CDP's *modus operandi.* Ross, a warm, maternal figure in her fifties, began by providing additional context about how CDP functioned—perhaps, mused Adam, because she had suspected he might not received it in a fully coherent form from Mulcahy.

"People get involved with this organization in a number of different ways. There are some traditional staff level positions here at the Washington headquarters, but to be honest there aren't many. We've been through a period of tremendous growth. Our greatest period of budgetary growth in percentage terms started back in the 1990s when the first president Bush was in office. That growth—from $18.5 million a year in 1989 to $150 million a year by 2010 enabled us to move from implementing short-term, in-and-out type programming to opening up in-country field offices; we currently have them in about thirty countries. Since then, with the overall global decline in democracy, our budget has shrunk a bit but is still over $100 million a year."

"Forgive this basic question, but when you say programming— what exactly is it that you do?"

Ross let out a bit of a chuckle. "As perhaps Charles may have indicated, we're not always sure ourselves. What we try to do is to focus on institutions and political processes. If we see a need for a parliamentary program on committee systems, we'll do that. If we think a civic organization advocacy project would be more useful, we'll go in that direction. If it seems like an election commission needs advice on how to structure itself and function, we can help out there. To be honest, a lot depends on what we work out with our funders—especially USAID, and how events evolve on the ground."

"Do you often get checked up on about your work? What yardsticks do you use to measure success?" Adam was trying to understand what sort of accountability CDP might be subject to in its activities.

"So therein truly hangs a tale. This work is very difficult to quantify. It is not necessarily about how many civic organizations are created, bills are passed, or votes are cast. It is much more subtle, and deeper, than that. How do you evaluate if a country is developing a democratic political culture? What does that really mean? How do you measure it?"

"Excuse me," Adam queried, "but if you can't measure it, how can you justify asking for more money? Upon what do you base your results?"

"Well, for one thing we have to take what people say to mean something. We have testimonials a yard long from presidents, ministers, parliamentarians, party leaders, civic activists, and a whole range of people who have fought on the front lines for democracy telling us and others how much they have valued our work. Sometimes I think that the emotional support we give is as important, if not more so, than the technical information imparted. Other than that, we do try to develop some more numbers-oriented benchmarks for assessing the work, but it isn't easy."

"Why not?" Adam was a bit nervous about asking seemingly uninformed and naïve questions early on, but he reasoned that due to his newness, his CDP interlocutors might be prepared to cut him some slack.

"Because, as I said it is really tough to quantify our results. Look. Let's say we are trying to support a civic organization somewhere.

It would be easy to say that the program was a success because seven new organizations were formed. But how effective were they? Did their existence help democracy take root in that country? Or maybe we supported a training program for a newly elected parliament. Do we use the number of bills passed as a success yardstick? What if they were poorly drafted or useless legislation? You have to dig a lot deeper to assess the impact of this work, and it's not a simple task."

"So could you give me some examples of these civic organizations that you talk about?"

"Surely. Civic organizations can act to facilitate interaction between the different, and at times opposing, forces within society. Groups such as NAMFREL in the Philippines, PARTICIPA in Chile, the Bulgarian Association for Fair Elections and Human Rights, the Center for Democratic Studies in South Africa; these are all examples of nonpartisan organizations whose focus has been to act as watchdogs over the democratization process and to conduct democracy-related civic engagement programs."

Changing the subject, Ross mentioned Kombonia. "Let's talk about brass tacks. We are looking at the country of Kombonia in Africa. It is moving towards what might be the first democratic elections in their history, but it is far from a done deal. There is a lot of tension there. As you know, we have received funding from USAID to undertake a project. The next step for us is to send someone out there to advise us on what we should do specifically, and to probably be our field representative. You've done the Peace Corps gig. You've worked on political campaigns. You seem to fit into the CDP-type field representative personality. You have the profile of the type of person who could do this for us. Would you like us to consider you? If so, you'd need to give us a few references."

Adam gulped. *Whoa…I wasn't expecting this.* "Well, I'm flattered, but I really need to know more. What is the role of the field representative?"

"They basically run the show for us in the particular country. For example, if we are doing civic education with local nonprofits, that person is the primary point of contact, the liaison with the NGOs and local authorities, who organizes training programs, oversees the logistical and administrative side of things, the whole shebang. In larger programs we may have more than one expatriate field person, but in a place such as Kombonia where we don't have a huge amount of funding, we would just go with one person."

Until recently, Adam had been supremely unaware of the complexities of Kombonia's politics. In fact, to be honest, he had only been vaguely aware of the country's existence. Even though he was nervous about taking the job, he didn't let his lack of knowledge or experience daunt him. His Thai experience had nurtured his belief that he could do pretty well in whatever circumstances he found himself in.

"Ok. If you want me then I am your person." Adam mentioned several people whom he knew would give him positive reviews.

Chapter 4

Learning the Ropes

Three days later Mulcahy called to tell him he had been hired to be CDP's Kombonia field representative for a one-year period, at an annual salary of $80,000. Adam was ecstatic and got thoroughly sloshed that night with some college buddies in DC. Soon thereafter he started a whirlwind ten-day orientation period in CDP's over-crowded offices. He was introduced to the accounting people, who assured him that if he paid proper attention to managing the books there wouldn't be any problems; to other people on the Africa team, who told him that the toughest part of his job would be keeping track of financial and administrative issues; and to the human resources and field support people who promised to provide advice and help in opening the CDP office. He also met with CDP's election specialists, whose job was to provide technical support and information on the broad range of issues related to the casting of ballots.

One conversation in particular was to come back to him later. Patricia Morgan, the head of the elections office, mentioned ways to ensure that cheating did not occur during the official vote counting process. "We at CDP have developed a very innovative method for helping to ensure transparency in the vote tabulation," she explained. "It is called a Parallel Vote Tabulation—or PVT for short. At its core it is very simple. Let's say you have a country with 10,000 polling places. You can identify a sample of these polling places that accurately reflects the key social and political components of the country. If it is a good sample, if you have a nonpartisan civic election group in-country—sort of that country's equivalent of the League of Women Voters—you can send representatives only to those selected polling places.

"When each polling place announces its results, they send them to the election observer group's headquarters, and you can get a very accurate picture of what the real vote total is across the country. We have learned through experience that a good representative sample needs to include as little as seven and a half percent of the country's polling places to have a margin of error of two-to-three percent. So, in our fictitious country we only need to visit 750 polling places to quickly know what the results should be. The official election commission knows that we know, so if they end up announcing results very different from ours, there will be a lot of explaining to do."

Adam was learning a dizzying and, to him, mind-numbing amount of information about elections, email accounts, bank accounts, shipments of goods, how to manage relations with the press, telephone lines, house and office leases, portable generators, local staff, and a myriad of other substantive and logistical details. He couldn't help but gain a huge amount of respect for the amount of work required to set up and keep running a field office in Africa.

The deluge of information was exhilarating and stimulating, but at the same time made him feel rather lonely. During one of these crazy days, he found himself wishing there was someone else to help him. He was pretty sure that the information being dumped on him would probably be of much greater use if he could come back and learn it after a month in the field. *Good God*, he admitted to himself, *I don't even know what all of the right questions to ask are!*

It was during this period that Mulcahy took him aside and spoke to him in a low voice, "Ouch. We have some problems with the USAID mission in Kombonia. I just spoke this morning with the mission director, and he wants to know why we aren't out there undertaking programming. He's pissed because they have given us $500,000, and they are asking what there is to show for it yet.

"I tried to explain to him that we had to make sure that we were getting the right person. I didn't want to stress the fact that we really aren't sure what, if anything, we should specifically be doing now. This is going to be an important relationship for you to manage."

"I wanted to ask you about USAID," Adam said. "What exactly is CDP's relationship to them? How independent are we of them?"

"Good question. In fact, it is usually the first question we get asked. We try to be responsive to the US government since the reality is that they give us money. But we don't simply jump to attention, click our heels, and do what they want automatically. Our government funding is partly through grants and partly what are called cooperative agreements. Both mechanisms allow us to have a lot of leeway in making decisions about the type of work we are going to do.

"I should emphasize that we are not what is called a 'beltway bandit.' Those sorts of for-profit operations have a much closer and subservient relationship with the government. They work on contracts in which they are pretty much told what to do.

"That is not what we want to be doing in terms of promoting democracy. We don't want to be seen by people in the country where we work to be agents of the US government. That can make things go south quickly, especially if the USG has what it thinks are other, strategic interests in-country that might not mesh well with promoting democracy. We don't think that is the way it should be, but we aren't naïve.

"Also, we find it pretty ironic that people so often assume that governments should be doing most of the democratic development work. That gives the impression that they are still the main actors, whereas the whole point in a democracy is that there are independent actors; trade unions, churches, journalists' groups, farmers' organizations, even individual people; they all can and should legitimately play a role. We think we should be seen as one of those independent actors rather than as a government-run organization. We have our own can-do, problem-solving attitude and are proud of it.

"The second question people always toss out at us is whether we are ourselves promoting a partisan political agenda. After all, there is a lot of polarization around the world these days, and people are suspicious. So it can be a tough one sometimes, depending on the environment. But the reality is that we don't push this or that foreign policy; we are interested in supporting the institution of democracy itself.

"This work came about way back in the early 1980s when President Reagan gave a speech to the British Parliament where he called for the democracies of the world to figure out how to be supportive of movements in favor of human rights and representative government. Turns out the Democratic-led Congress liked the idea as well, and it authorized using US taxpayer money. Both sides realized that democracy leads to stability and can support US national interests." With a chuckle, Mulcahy added, "I guess that if you're a Republican, you'd say that democracy promotion efforts were created by Reagan, whereas if you are a Democrat you'd say that Congress established them. Maybe that is the secret sauce of bipartisanship—either side can claim ownership…"

Mulcahy then glanced at his watch and exclaimed in a mischievous tone, "Ooops—time for you to experience one of the world-famous CDP staff meetings." They headed into a large conference room that was filled with about forty CDP staffers. There was much milling about until one rather authoritative-looking man started the meeting's proceedings. Mulcahy whispered, "That's Fred Shapiro, our fearless president."

Shapiro asked various team leaders to update everyone on the status of various projects. Partway through these briefings, much of which was in language and terminology unintelligible to Adam, he did begin to notice a common thread. Everyone's projects either were 'highly successful,' 'going really well,' or 'right on the mark.' At one point, Adam whispered to Mulcahy, "Jesus—doesn't anyone's project ever fuck up?" Mulcahy looked at him with a twinkle in his eye and whispered back, "We'll talk later."

After the meeting Mulcahy and Adam walked back to the former's office. Mulcahy closed the door and semi-jokingly said, "You've got to understand that we have grade inflation around here. If we didn't toot our own horns a bit on the loud side, how do you think we'd ever get funding?"

His features then took on a cloudier expression. "Fuck-ups— you want them? We've got them in spades. We had a field rep go bonkers over an Ethiopian boyfriend and get kicked out of the country just before we had a high-level international delegation visiting there. We had some projects in southern Africa go so far over budget that they disappeared into a black hole. We had one jerk-off staffer write a memo containing some personal stuff about a particularly vain Asian autocrat that got leaked to the dictator himself…our asses got kicked out of that country faster than you can say Bob's your uncle."

Adam could only gulp. *Sheeeit…I hope no such fate befalls me.*

The next day Adam met Shapiro. It occurred almost by happenstance, as Mulcahy was giving Adam his final out-briefing. He suddenly smacked his palm on his forehead, exclaiming, "OMG, we've got to get Fred to lay hands on you before you're out of here." He looked at Adam and with a wry smile said, "If you haven't met Fred you can't fully understand the institutional culture of this place."

Mulcahy was positively laid back compared to Fred, a hyperactive, overweight man in his fifties, who quickly displayed an insightful, if continually roaming, mind. Although it was clear that Kombonia had not been very high up on his radar screen in recent months, he demonstrated a keen knowledge of the basic political dynamics of the country, as well as of democracy promotion in general.

Shapiro started out in a tone that was lecturing but not demeaning. "I tell all the new field reps that for democracy to take root, a lot has to happen. Elections have to be held. Accurate and up-to-date voting registers have to be drawn up. Political parties need to organize, and independent institutions such as the judiciary and the legislature have to be created or reinvigorated, and provided with resources to enable them to perform their roles.

"We as democracy practitioners must work on two different levels. One is helping to provide technical information and assistance regarding the functioning of democratic institutions. Another, perhaps more important, but very subtle and challenging issue is how to help these countries develop not just the form but also the spirit, the political culture of democracy. The understanding of the state of law, of a civic culture, of the legitimate competition of ideas in the political marketplace—these are all elements that are critical to the long-term survival of democracy."

Shapiro took a quick swig from a can of Diet Dr. Pepper and continued. "This is the soil from which democratic institutions can take root. A previous military coup d'état in Niger, for example, took place because the army lost patience with a protracted constitutional tug-of-war between the president and the parliament. On the one hand, this crisis resulted from ambiguities in the constitution regarding the division of powers between the presidency and the legislature; on the other it reflected a lack of willingness to compromise and a negative sum political culture, which is often a bitter legacy of authoritarian rule."

Adam felt like he should say something. "I guess in a lot of these situations the trick is to figure how to handle the military, so they don't feel like they need to stop the democratization process to protect their own interests."

Shapiro nodded in assent. "We have seen the tragedy in recent years of fledgling experiments in democracy being destroyed by the military. Niger, Mali, Myanmar…I could add to the list. But this isn't the only problem. One other point that we have learned is that elections are not only a prerequisite for democracy, but that they themselves must also take place in an environment of openness. We have seen many 'gray area' elections, which reflect some relative openness of the political process, but where there is no realistic possibility of the opposition candidate winning. There may be no outright rigging of the results, but what the international development people call the 'enabling environment' may be sufficiently skewed to affect the process. To properly understand the context in which elections are taking place, international observers have to be in-country and on the ground for a substantial period prior to election day."

Adam knew he was displaying his ignorance about the subject matter, but he couldn't help asking, "So what are the key issues that determine whether elections are free and fair?"

Shapiro chuckled while answering—it seemed to Adam that this was a guy who was really into his work. "That is the million-dollar question. There is no scientific way of determining whether an election is legitimate or not.....to be honest, the whole notion of 'legitimacy' is pretty damn vague and subjective. But there are a bunch of factors that go into whether an election is viewed as free and fair or rigged. To mess with an election, you don't have to simply stuff a ballot box; there are a lot more subtle ways to tilt the scales. It depends on the context of the place, but some of the relevant issues to be examined include the voter registration process, access to media, freedom of parties to develop and articulate a message, and independence of the election authorities. In fact, some tilting of scales happens in pretty much most elections, even in established democracies. The important thing is whether they are tilted enough to call into question the overall legitimacy of the polls."

Shapiro had a head of steam going and continued. "A few years ago, we were in the euphoria of democratization. We thought it was going to be quick and easy. Now we can ask ourselves—why did we think this? What would make us believe that this would be a simple process? Another key question that we may get more into is: OK, so we have to take a long-term perspective, and be in it for the long haul. How should we look at short-term events along the way? For how long should we keep on giving an authoritarian president like Kagame of Rwanda, for example, a free ride?"

Shapiro, to put it mildly, had dominated the conversation. Adam learned a lot from it but later, back in Mulcahy's office Adam complained wistfully, "I didn't get much of a word in edgewise." Mulcahy laughed ruefully and said, "Join the club, bud. Still, I think he liked you. He let you say one or two things."

Although he didn't know Mulcahy very well yet, Adam decided to take a chance and speak frankly. "Seems like a rather authoritarian personality to be head of a democracy promotion NGO."

This provoked a belly laugh from his new boss. "Woowwee— out of the mouths of babes. Some of us old-timers have been thinking the same thing. But to be fair, you know, you can't run this organization totally as a democracy. At the same time, it's true that some of us would like it to be a bit more in that direction. We'll see what happens. By the way, all of that stuff about what goes into making up legitimate elections—I'm pretty sure that is exactly what you'll be dealing with in Kombonia."

Chapter 5

Preparing for Kombonia

Adam did some serious beers one night at the Brickskeller, near Washington's trendy Dupont Circle area, with Walter Kocinski. Walter was a college buddy of his who had recently spent two years in Kombonia working for UNICEF, and was now working on Capitol Hill. They first reminisced about their college days together and their common origins—both came from well-off, upper-middle-class, Wasp-ish East Coast environments. Walter laughed when the talk turned to Africa. "You know, I didn't understand why I liked you so much until I spent some time in Africa and saw how people with similar backgrounds have a particular bond. We're the same—after all, you and I come from the same ethnic group!"

Regarding Kombonia, Walter had a lot to say. "That is a funky mother of a place, bro. Like some other countries in Africa it is kind of like stuck in the sixteenth century but also getting dragged into our current time. So your job would be to help the place move towards democracy, huh? I think you might need a one thousand-year project budget to do that," he chuckled semi-mirthfully.

"What do you mean that it is being 'dragged into,' as you say, the twenty-first century?"

Walter asked the bartender for another IPA and paused for a minute, scratching his chin. "Well, what else can you call a place where people herd cattle with one hand and use a smartphone with the other? Where straw huts in the middle of East Bumfuck have solar panels? Where the desert is full of used plastic shopping bags, blowing to nowhere? What would you call that?"

"I don't know. I'll confess that I don't know much about Kombonia. So, let's pretend that I am a senator going out there for a three-day fact-finding visit and you are a staffer with twenty minutes to brief him. What would I need to know?"

Walter again paused to collect his thoughts. "Whew…that's a tall order, but I'll try. OK, for starters, as you know, it is located in the northern part of East-Central Africa. That means that since like, forever, it has been something of a punching bag between different tribes along important trade routes. It's a place of contrasts. There is an arid, hilly, poor northern region that contains much of the land but a minority of the population. These lighter-skinned folks are more Islamic and are tough dudes who are very proud of their nomadic traditions. There's a relatively wealthier southern section which almost reaches the coast. Around four million people live in the three largest cities of the country, the capital of Kayemba City with maybe two million and Mululi and Toshana, which each have about one million. These cities have gotten bigger in recent years, but most of the population still lives in rural areas. The whole country has maybe twelve million people."

"Speaking of the population," Adam queried, "Who are they? Are there a bunch of different tribes, like in many other African countries?"

"Oh yeah. That's a big deal there. There are three main ethnic groups: the Ome, which have about a third of the population;

the Tuyunu with about a quarter; and the Pohane with maybe one-fifth. The thing to know is that the Tuyunu are the former nomadic people in the north, the Ome are more in the south, and the Pohane are in the western part of the country. This is a bit of a generalization, but they tend, shall we say, to not always play well in the sandbox together."

"OK, I'll bite—why not?"

Walter put his hands up in a tongue in cheek gesture of surrender. "Dude, I am not an expert on this shit…understanding Kombonia is like peeling back the proverbial onion skin…but I tell you what—I'll email you part of a briefing paper I shared with visitors when I was in Kombonia. Oh, and one other thing that I remember is that the per capita income is about $550 which, I think ranks it like 175th out of 196 countries in the world. Most of the population are peasants doing subsistence farming, although a few have better paying jobs in the small mining sector."

"So how do folks get along there?"

"Well, I'd say that relations between the different ethnic groups are tense, but violence has only occurred on rare occasions. Although there isn't a lot of intermarriage or geographic intermingling between the ethnic groups, the country hasn't blown up so far."

Adam shifted the questions to Walter's actual experience in-country. "I worked with the Kombonian Association for Democracy and Development, an organization that is dedicated to helping the nation develop democratic institutions. It is known mostly by its acronym of KADD. It is part of a very small and new civil society there—groups that are nonpartisan and have one or more issues that they push for in the public sphere."

"Are such groups needed for there to be democracy in Kombonia?"

"Well, let me put it this way. To use a the human body as an analogy, and bear with me here, let's say a country's political culture is like a knee. Civil society plays the role of the ligaments holding the knee together. In a place like Kombonia, which hasn't had these ligaments, bone can grind on bone, causing extreme pain. So without the civil society playing its role of facilitating, sort of lubricating, political discourse, political parties will have little way of interacting with each other except through direct confrontation."

"Well, I get what you mean, Walter, but I still wouldn't want to have you operating on me."

"Eff you too, buddy. But to get back to my story, we did an educational project helping young people understand what rights they have under the Kombonian constitution. KADD concentrates these kinds of programs concerning open and transparent government processes and citizen participation in government. But it's not that simple. One of the most cynical things done by the government has been to create groups that were allegedly independent and part of civil society, but that really supported the government."

Walter snorted. "And this has happened elsewhere…these things have even earned this Kafkaesque acronym—Government Organized Non-Governmental Organizations, or GONGOs. In Kombonia, for example, there is a group called the Citizens Group for Democracy and Progress that plays this role."

"I guess things are never simple," Adam responded vaguely, attempting to sound knowledgeable although in fact he had little clue to what Walter was saying. He sloshed his pint of beer around on the polished wood of the bar for a bit. "So you are pretty impressed with KADD?"

Walter raised his voice to be heard over the din of the growing crowd. "You're right on when you say that things aren't that simple. A bunch of the KADD folks mean well, but they don't always get along with each other. Some of those Tuyunu and Ome are like oil and water. And some—not all—of them are just in it for the job…they could be distributing sewage equipment for all they care; what is important is that they are getting a steady paycheck from the big, rich Western donors. And the head of the KADD —whew boy, can he be a piece of work!"

Adam, feeling a bit overwhelmed with all this information, could not even pretend to sound like he understood. "What the hell do you mean?"

"What I mean is this guy—his name is Albert Duwango, by the way—has an ego a mile long and a mile wide. For someone who espouses democracy, he sure acts like an authoritarian. It is hard to get a word in edgewise when he gets going. Jesus Christ, with him it is either his way or the highway."

Walter stopped, thought for a few seconds and then said in a more measured tone, "But the thing is that in Kombonia, you need someone who's got energy and courage and is willing to shake things up and stand up to power. After all, life's not always black-and-white. You're not going to get a George Washington or a Nelson Mandela every time. So Duwango may have some blemishes, but he and his group are the main folks in town in terms of civil society promoting democracy."

Adam wondered…and not for the last time—*what the hell am I getting myself into?*

And yet, and yet…a kind of dreamy, far-away look crossed Walter's face. "But you know what? Despite all that crap, despite the UNICEF bureaucratic BS, despite the USAID micromanagement stuff, despite garbage in the street, despite Duwango's weirdness, despite the Kombonian soldiers manning roadblocks with zero body fat and sunglasses hiding their killer eyes…there is something about that place that made me feel alive: the people, the music, the bush where the sky goes forever and the stars explode at nighttime. I don't know—I can't really explain it but it was the best fourteen months of my life. God, do I miss it. If I didn't have my girlfriend and a new job here in DC, I would be itching to be back out in the field in a heartbeat. But I guess life has to move on," he sighed.

Such an outpouring of emotion raised many more questions in Adam's mind than it resolved. He tried to articulate some of them, but found that the combination of the late night and all the beers he consumed had dulled his thought process. Later, in Kombonia, he would often think back to that evening and, as events unfolded, begin to understand what Walter had been talking about.

As his time to depart for Kombonia neared, Mulcahy strongly urged him to connect with Raymond Bearson, a professor of government at Boston University specializing in African Studies. He was a leading expert on both US politics and the region, with a particular focus on and understanding of Kombonia. Adam duly sent him an email, explaining who he was and asking if they could have a phone call chat so that he could gain first-hand some of Bearson's expertise and perspective on the country.

The professor replied quickly. "I'm pleased to hear of your interest in Kombonia and would be more than happy to share with you some views on it. And I can do you better than a phone call. You may be aware that next week it is Kombonia's National Day, the date when they became independent from Great Britain.

I know their ambassador here and am planning to come to DC to attend their celebration at the embassy—they usually invite the Kombonian community in Washington and others who have some connection to the country. If you'd like, perhaps we could connect for lunch and you could then come as my guest to the embassy for the celebration afterward."

Adam was thrilled by this response and met Bearson, a heavyset and bearded man of about 60 who combined a jovial mien with a keen intelligence, for lunch at the Tabard Inn near the Kombonian Embassy the following Wednesday. After they had settled in and ordered their salads Bearson started off with a surprise. "You know I am headed to central Africa this coming year—I'll be spending my sabbatical teaching and doing research in Burundi. So I'll be in the neighborhood."

Adam was pleased to hear that news. *The more people that I know and can hopefully rely upon the better.* "That is super. And listen you don't have to be concerned about telling me things I might already know about the country. Just share it all with me."

"Look, it is first really important to understand the history of the place. After the British sent troops in and took control in the late nineteenth century, a period of relative calm ensued. As was common in British African colonial policy, they didn't try to replace the existing tribal structures—they ruled through them. A colonial legislative council was established in 1921. Now, as the British tended to favor the more aristocratic and self-assured Tuyunu, they allowed a few Tuyunu chiefs to become members of the council. With the passage of time, though, and especially after World War II, increasing calls for self-government were articulated most vociferously by a largely Ome-based political party."

"So how did the British maintain control over the situation?"

Bearson coughed politely. "Well in doing so, they made things worse for the country. They opted against the costly and unpopular solution of garrisoning a large number of troops. Instead, they chose to arm the Tuyunu, and make them the backbone of their security forces. This could, they reasoned, act as a check against the restive Ome and Pohane groups."

"What happened then?"

"Well, the combination of increasing rumblings from Kombonia seeking to cast off British rule, the expense of maintaining a colony, and moves by other imperial powers to grant independence to their African territories all pushed the British toward relinquishing control over Kombonia in 1963. They bequeathed what was, on paper, a beautiful-looking democratic constitution modeled after Britain's. But almost immediately, however, things started to deteriorate. The first prime minister was Ome, but the existence of the Tuyunu-led military had the effect of inflaming ethnically based suspicions and tensions. So Kombonia had a number of short-lived civilian governments until a general named Paul Owemu, who was a Duba married to a Tuyunu, took power in a military coup in 1968."

Adam was soaking up this information sponge-like. He had in fact heard some of it before, but every meeting he had or report he read about the country was like a paintbrush stroke on the canvas of his mind, adding texture. They finished their lunch and it was time to head to the Kombonian Embassy. They entered the building, joined a reception line, and were greeted by Kombonian ambassador Jennifer Amwanku and other staff members. They then exited into the garden where the National Day ceremony would be held. Waiters passed around with trays of cold drinks, a welcome refreshment on the muggy and hot Washington summer day.

"What can you tell me about the ambassador?" Adam asked Bearson.

Bearson looked around before responding. "Don't make the mistake of underestimating her. She is very close to the minister of the interior and is sharp as a tack. And, of course, President Mushi is no fool—he knows that having a female ambassador in Washington buys him brownie points."

Soon thereafter, Ambassador Amwanku emerged and began to welcome the fifty-odd guests. About fifteen minutes into her remarks, as she was singing the praises of her country, two young people suddenly pushed their way through the crowd and ran up to the ambassador. Time seemed to stand still for a moment as the ambassador gaped, open-mouthed, at the interlopers. Then they opened up two sacks of white flour, dumping their contents all over her. They turned to the crowd with fists raised, shouting triumphantly, "Long Live the Pohane people!" A shocked silence reigned for a moment until the ambassador's security guards dragged the two away.

A buzz enveloped the crowd as people milled about; some hurriedly leaving the embassy, others animatedly exchanging perspectives about what they had just witnessed, while still others simply appearing confused and dazed. Amidst the tumult, Bearson looked concerned and said to Adam, "I think we should get out of here. Who knows what may happen next? Those folks were probably radicalized students, maybe even members of the terrorist group the Popular Front for the Liberation of Pohaneland. I don't think there would be any follow-up actions here, but you never know. We should play it safe."

"Fine, but you need to explain all this to me."

"OK, let's chat in the lobby at my hotel."

A half hour later, ensconced in wing chairs in the hotel lobby with calming beers at hand, Bearson explained. "Before we get to today's events let me just describe the history a bit more. Beyond the ethnic factors, there were a lot of reasons for the failure of Kombonia's initial experiment with democracy at independence." Bearson ticked the list off on his fingers. "They included low levels of literacy, low commodity prices for some of Kombonia's few exports, poor communications, and a limited experience and information on how democracies, in the form of contemporary states, actually function.

"In addition, some Kombonians opposed the system handed down by the British simply because it reminded them of colonial rule. And the experience that the people of Kombonia had had with imperial rule was hardly democratic—the wishes of the Kombonians had rarely taken forefront in British policy decisions about the colony. It was more about how Kombonia's agricultural and mineral resources could benefit Britain. These problems are hardly surprising when you consider that the total number of Kombonian university graduates numbered exactly twenty-three at independence."

Adam was stunned. "Oh my God, how you can run a country with less than two dozen college graduates?"

"Well, that wasn't all. The country lacked strong independent organizations such as trade unions, a vibrant press, human rights groups, and other bodies that collectively constitute what is often referred to as civil society, which as you know serves in many democracies as a check on government and gives voice to people's aspirations and needs.

"Another problem facing independent Kombonia has been corruption. There were few, if any, institutional checks on government ministers awarding contracts to unscrupulous operators willing to pay the largest kickback for government contracts. The judiciary was ripe with low-paid judges open to bribes. Also, judges rarely ruled against the government, aware that their well-being could be contingent upon toeing the line. Corruption was additionally facilitated by the care Owemu, and then Mushi, took to stay on the side of the West during the Cold War, resulting in generous levels of foreign assistance with few strings attached to it."

Adam didn't want to seem impatient, but he was very much focused in the moment on understanding what had just transpired at the embassy. "So, are these the motivations for those people who attacked the ambassador?"

"Not so fast. You have got to understand more of the backstory. People were unhappy with the failings of the first post-independence government, so General Owemu quickly assumed power, announced that he was the head of a military revolutionary council dedicated to the 'salvation of the Kombonian people,' replaced parliament with a rubber stamp legislative body, outlawed all parties except the KRP, and ruled as a dictator until his death in 2002. His government had been ostensibly socialist, a name which was in vogue for many newly independent African nations. In reality, Owemu governed with a shrewd pragmatism, utilizing the stick of an iron hand when needed, but also used carrots to good effect, handing out jobs and perks not only to supporters, but to also co-opt potential rivals or alternative sources of power.

"Upon his death Owemu was succeeded by his prime minister, Simon Mushi, an Ome who was seen as something of a sellout by many of his ethnic compatriots who did not come from his immediate subregion or clan. Mushi, under internal and external pressure, legalized opposition parties and organized elections in

2002. These elections resulted in Mushi being elected president and the KRP winning a seventy-five percent majority in the constituency elections to the National Assembly. Both the presidential and the National Assembly elections were for five-year terms, although more power resided in the presidency.

"Mushi adopted a lighter touch to governance than Owemu, and limited the number of political prisoners. He enjoyed a good reputation in the international community, but the print press was sharply divided into pro- and anti-government camps. Electronic media remained state controlled, although the internet spread throughout the country, especially with the advent of smartphones from 2008 on. The form of government is unitary. There are currently no political prisoners, and in recent years Mushi has sought to somewhat soften his government's image.

"With the legalization of opposition parties in 2000, two main ones emerged: the Kombonian Democratic Popular Rally (KDPR), led by Ignace Ruwoyo, and—here is where we get to today's events—the Renewal Movement of Kombonia (RMK), headed by a populist radical named Felix Obewame. While the KRP is largely Ome, the KDPR Tuyunu, and the RMK Pohane in make-up, they all do have a minority of other ethnic groups in its ranks, especially from areas where the various groups have intermingled. The KDPR was formed prior to the country's independence and existed underground, while the RMK was formed after the death of Owemu. Both opposition parties have claimed that elections since 2002 have been illegitimate, due to government-inspired fraud.

"In the most recent election, in 2019, domestic nonpartisan and international observers were equivocal in their statements about the election. The KDPR, however, took up its eighteen seats in the one-hundred member National Assembly, while the RMK, which received ten percent of the vote, continues to boycott parliamentary activities. Kombonia is now preparing for presidential and legislative elections in mid-December. It would be an understatement to suggest that political tensions are rising."

Adam tried to take this all in. "So, tell me more about the RMK."

"Well, it represents the Pohane people who feel that they have gotten the shaft since independence. Their region of the country is poorer, and their interests have tended to be overlooked. To put it in our terms, both the Tuyunu and Ome think of the Pohane as unsophisticated country bumpkins. They don't give them much respect. As you can imagine, that mightily pisses off the Pohane. And that, my friend, is the background to what you saw today at the embassy."

———

Two days later Adam received a briefing paper from Walter about the nongovernment sector in Kombonia. That evening he settled into his couch and poured a beer before he started to read. A couple of paragraphs caught his attention. *Ironically, the seeds of Kombonia's single party state downfall were sown by the system's very failings. The inability of the KRP to provide adequate services such as health and education led to the development of domestic and foreign-supported nongovernmental organizations. Restrictions on human rights and political freedoms fostered the creation of civic and professional organizations with an emphasis on strengthening the rule of law, civil society, and democratic political freedoms. These groups played important roles in articulating interests and mediating political change in nations where authoritarian rule has given way to plural-*

ism. Examples of these groups are human rights associations, democracy promotion groups, women's or regional associations, and advocacy groups. KADD has been a good example of this.

In response, the government has sought to control the nongovernmental space through various means. It denied requests for activity permission on vague grounds. It issued requirements that, to be officially registered, they had to submit to invasive, supervisory oversight and draconian requirements. Organizations were either denied permission to operate or ordered to dissolve. These were officially designed to ensure their proper functioning, but in reality, impeded their ability to function.

After he finished the briefing paper, Adam took a deep breath and exhaled…*Holy shit. OK—in for a dime, in for a dollar. We'll see what happens.* The next two weeks were spent in a hectic whirlwind of briefings, packing, medical appointments, saying goodbyes, and partying. Adam then found himself on a Lufthansa flight to Kayemba City via Frankfurt.

Chapter 6

Early Days In-Country

I shouldn't have let the phone call interrupt my prayers. Yusuf Abwangou let out a big sigh and adjusted his glasses to look at the notes he had taken. Yusuf was about thirty-five years old, a slight man whose physique belied energy and drive. A research professor in history at the University of Kombonia, Yusuf was also the number two person at KADD. He was committed to the cause of democracy in his country. This largely came from his mixed Tuyunu-Ome background; his father, an Ome, was a civil servant who met his mother when he was posted to the city of Moka, in the heart of Omeland, about three hundred kilometers north of Kayemba City. He felt a strong need to find ways to knit the country together because he had a visceral, almost literal sense of how delicate the national fabric was, and how easily it could be torn apart.

But this avocation wasn't easy to pursue. Being of a mixed race, Yusuf knew that he did not instinctively inspire the almost feral sense of loyalty that members of various ethnic groups usually exhibited toward their own. He knew that he was under intermittent surveillance by the Agency for National Information, the Kombonian government secret intelligence service. It was commonly known that the shadowy ANI routinely treated perceived opponents harshly; several times he had received mysterious phone calls warning him not to support the opposition.

And working for KADD was not always easy, either. His boss, Duwango, could be a demanding taskmaster, and act in ways that Yusuf and others found to be insulting and demeaning. But his attributes of energy, drive, and courage outweighed his negatives, so Yusuf stayed the course. He understood that Duwango had the needed type of personality for the initial founder of a nonprofit or, for that matter, private business. He had a clear vision and a bull-in-a-china-shop type mentality, achieving much through the sheer force of will. His approach was definitely one way to achieve meaningful change given the ossified and authoritarian political culture. But it was also dangerous. Duwango's life had been threatened repeatedly.

The object of Yusuf's current frustration was different. He had just received a call from Barry Johnson, the local USAID mission officer with responsibility for democracy and governance issues, who informed him that the mission had awarded a grant to a US nongovernmental organization called the Center for Democratic Progress to work on promoting democracy; and it was likely that they would reach out to KADD, given its important role in Kombonian civil society.

Yusuf was not happy, although he masked that in his response to Johnson, thanking him politely for the information and expressing the hope that KADD and CDP could find ways to work together. His real reaction was—why couldn't USAID give KADD the money directly? What a waste to bring in a foreign group that would not understand the complexities and realities of the Kombonian situation…it probably includes the typical naïve

American do-gooders who will just make the situation worse, he fretted.

Yusuf surmised that the Americans would know that there are two main ethnic groups. But would they understand that it would be a mistake to view Kombonia simply through this bipolar lens of ethnicity? Not for the first time, Yusuf ruminated on the lot of other, smaller groups existing in the country, including the Pohane, Duba, and Mafenke peoples, who tended to be seen as second-class citizens by the Ome and Tuyunu. In recent years the Pohane list of complaints about their status and disadvantaged position within the Kombonian political, social, and economic scene had grown. The Duba and Mafenke were relatively recent arrivals on the scene, having migrated from other parts of the continent in the past five hundred years. Small but economically influential groups of Asian Indian and Lebanese tradesmen also operated in the largest cities, and had come to serve as buffers and tools to be used by the governing powers.

And what about the rest of the country's history? Would the Americans understand the Kombonian population's lack of self-identity concerning their nation and its place in the region, in Africa, and in the world? After all, Yusuf mused, the country didn't even exist as a geographic entity until the colonial powers began to use Africa as their own personal chessboard in the second half of the nineteenth century, dividing it up to suit their plans and whims. From 1887 until 1963, Kombonia was a British colony. Even the former name of the country—Komboland—reflected its dual, and some would say schizophrenic, existence. Emperor Kombo was an eighth-century monarch who ruled during a particularly successful (i.e., expansionist) period in the Tuyunu people's history. And "land" was a favorite British colonial suffix that was deemed to sufficiently Anglicize the territory's name.

Yusuf's ruminations turned to the current period. The constitution required presidential and legislative elections by December of the current year. Not for the first time, Yusuf's stomach tightened as he considered a key problem—that the elections would be administered by the ministry of the interior. What could be done to ensure that the government did not cheat? Yusuf had spent a lot of time trying to identify a solution that would be successful and acceptable to the range of highly divided Kombonian political actors. He was, however, honest with himself; he had yet to develop a credible vision of how this could be achieved.

The best he could come up with was to place faith in the hope that the existing Kombonian Independent Election Commission (IEC) could stand up to the government and ruling party. Its track record from previous elections, though, was hardly inspiring. And would the authorities allow nongovernmental observers to verify the bona fides of the election? If so, could an independent and neutral organization like KADD, which wanted field observers to actually have the skills, resources, and people to deploy across the nation? In addition, would the ministry of interior be prepared to solicit or receive advice on the conduct of elections from the international community?

Yusuf worked his worry beads as he pondered these questions. He also wondered how much this CDP group would know about the background of the current governance crisis. He was also concerned that CDP could bring its own agenda and priorities to any collaboration. And he had previously seen that increased donor interest in a particular topic, if not handled carefully, could result in corrupting the integrity of domestic civil society groups interested in the issue. Whether consciously or not, they often began to orient their agendas and priorities to fit those of the donor, and squabble amongst themselves as to who should get the white man's money. All in all, Yusuf was a worried man.

The light began to shift, at first imperceptibly, from the bright sunshine as seen from 38,000 feet in a sleek airliner, to darkening hues of purple, and then to a dusky character. The sands began to disappear from view below. Adam Edwards shifted in his seat uncomfortably. *Jesus Christ, haven't I traveled enough to know to bring a change of underwear in my carry-on bag?*

It had been a long journey—seven and a half hours from DC to Frankfurt, with a layover there of three hours before his next seven-hour Lufthansa flight to Kayemba City. Now the plane was 45 minutes from landing at Kayemba City's Murife International Airport. The seemingly endless sands of the Sahara had given way to brown, and then, although it was now too dark to see it, green rolling pastureland.

Through his fatigue, Adam felt a growing sense of queasiness and tension, similar to what usually happened at the start of a great adventure. That is what he lived for, after all, the rush of doing something interesting, exciting, and exotic. *I guess Kombonia meets those qualifications.* The flight attendant passed by asking if anyone had any last drink requests. Adam's mouth was stale and washed up, but he couldn't refuse the offer of one last free beer.

The nose of the plane made a slight dip, signaling its initial descent. Adam wiped his hand over his tired face and yawned, a signal of nervousness, facing the abyss ahead. At this moment of vulnerability fueled by fatigue, Adam felt a spasm of queasy, unvarnished, and honest introspection—he knew that he didn't really know what he was getting himself into. He experienced a chilling doubt as to whether he was up to all the challenges that no doubt lay ahead.

Two weeks later, Adam looked back on his initial introduction to Kombonia with some satisfaction. Thank God he had been met at the airport by the USAID "expeditor," the person who made sure he survived the crush of deplaning passengers, the immigration and customs entry formalities, the chaos around the luggage carousel, and the hot and pungent airport terminal. Once he got to his hotel, he slept for twelve hours straight.

The first days in-country had been spent refreshing himself with the smells of a developing nation, reminiscent of, but at the same time different from, those of Thailand. The scent that permeated his nose as he wandered the streets of Kayemba City, getting his bearings, was the mixture of the sixteenth and twenty-first centuries to which his friend Walter had referred. Animal dung, fresh foods, sidewalk vendors, flowers, dust, concrete construction, gas exhaust; they all combined to remind him of the challenges of living and existing in a low-income country's capital city.

He began the process of finding a sufficiently large enough apartment to double as a field office. Aware of the flexible manner of making such arrangements in the developing world, Adam started to create a network of initial contacts around town. These included embassies and international development agencies, Kombonian nongovernmental organizations, and professional organizations. As a gregarious, outgoing type, Adam didn't find it hard to make initial acquaintances. In fact, he found himself in a whirlwind of activity over the first couple of weeks in Kayemba City. Operating in a series of outwardly expanding concentric circles of contacts, he began with initial meetings at the US Embassy and USAID mission. He then touched base with other donors active in Kombonia, including the British, French, and Germans. The European Union had a separate diplomatic representation, as did a scattering of others such as the Japanese, Italians, and Canadians.

Adam felt an initial euphoria about being in Kombonia and was encouraged by a warm feeling that he was going to do just fine there. He also knew, however, from Thailand that developing good, useful, and productive relationships with the host country's people could require significant time; a luxury he did not have with the elections approaching and tensions rising in the country. This challenge was especially true as he was aware that to do his job, he needed to maintain a certain level of emotional and intellectual detachment; that he couldn't become too close to the people else he get enmeshed in rivalries and conflicts that could keep him from doing his job. He had heard about a UN Special Representative in war-torn Burundi who had had no social engagements with Burundians during his two-year stay there because he was so concerned about possibly being seen as favoring one or another belligerent group in the country. Still, while Adam was, on one level, aware of the need to tread carefully in making connections, he scoffed at the extreme nature of the UN diplomat's level of self-isolation.

Adam went to a party the first Friday night he was in-country. The gathering was hosted by Sarah Bingham, a young and attractive former Peace Corps volunteer who was now the deputy director of the Peace Corps operation in Kombonia. Adam heard about the party during an initial courtesy phone call with Barry Johnson from USAID, who, as often happens in an expatriate environment, told him it was fine to come without an invitation. The party's occasion was the birthday of a staff member. Adam discovered that Sarah was well liked and popular amongst the international community, as well as being knowledgeable about Kombonia—a combination that he would find was not always the case within the international community. He made a note to himself that she could be a good person to get to know better.

They exchanged initial pleasantries at the party. Adam asked, "Is there a Hash House Harriers race group here?" The Hash House Harrier tradition runs deep in the expatriate community around the world. It is a typically eccentric British tradition, often performed on Sunday mornings, of groups racing along a trail marked by white hash marks, usually in the form of a powder or chalk. Runners are supposed to occasionally cry out, "On, On!" The race, which is usually several miles in length, typically concludes in a massive beer drinking session during which newcomers to the event usually are subjected to some form of bizarre initiation rites.

"Yes, there is indeed a Harrier chapter in the city; in fact I belong to it. Why don't you join it, if you are willing to go through the initiation ceremony," she suggested, with the slightest hint of flirtation. "The next race is a week from now."

Adam accepted, and in the sweltering 10 a.m. heat the following Sunday presented himself at the race starting point. It was, logically enough, in front of the British High Commission with its Union Jack fluttering proudly overhead as if the British had never left. About thirty runners, mostly expatriates, took off in a cacophony of yelps. The race wound past quizzical Kombonia City pedestrians, through the main market area, and then into a poorer, popular quarter of town. The racers dodged overloaded trucks, and pounded past open drains, single story concrete houses and shops, and the odd chicken wandering in the street until the route emerged into a semi-rural farming area. They then looped around and the route started to take them back toward the city center. Adam found himself huffing and puffing in his attempt to keep up with Sarah. At one point she turned her head to see him and laughed, "What's the matter with you, slowpoke?"

"You've been here longer—you are more acclimated to the altitude," Adam responded playfully.

"Sorry to inform you but Kayemba City is all of two hundred feet above sea level!" came the stiletto response. Adam tried to think of a rejoinder but he was too winded to respond.

The next Monday he had his first meeting with Harlan Stuart, the USAID mission director. He was ushered into his office after a seemingly endless twenty-minute journey through all of the security checkpoints that had become an integral part of official US government buildings overseas. Stuart was a self-assured AID veteran. His office was basically US government standard, although Adam would come to notice that it reflected the common Kombonian habit of having the air conditioner on full blast, with the thermostat set a few notches lower than really needed. Three USAID mission staffers whose welcoming smiles, it seemed to Adam, were merely perfunctory sat in the background. The chill that ran through his body was only partly due to the temperature as Stuart took an overtly solicitous and friendly tack which, through its overkill, came across to Adam as subtly demeaning and aggressive.

"Well, we sure are glad to have you here," Stuart began. "I hope everything is OK with your settling in. I'd like to formally welcome you to Kombonia as part of the USAID team. We have a lot on our plate in a bunch of different ways. The Kombonian agricultural output is in bad shape. We have a big infectious diseases portfolio here. The economy overall is not doing well. And on top of everything we now have this election and this political unrest to deal with."

Stuart fixed his gaze on Adam, as if measuring him up. "Yes, we certainly have a tough job here to do, and I am going to be counting on you to handle this democracy situation very carefully in your programming. As you probably know, we have important commercial interests in bauxite mining, as well as security interests related to combatting the spread of Islamic extremism here. After all, Al-Qaeda in Africa has been active in neighboring countries, and we have information suggesting that they are looking to do some bad things here.

"So our interests could be really adversely affected if the political situation gets out of hand. I know that CDP has a good reputation in its programming elsewhere so I sure hope—actually I am confident—that you and your colleagues will be up to the task."

Adam thought that Stuart had put a little too much emphasis on the 'sure,' a bit of needling, sending a message. His pulse quickened as his mind recognized that this seemed to be a test as to how much of a team player Adam was likely to be. Not wanting to get off to a bad start with Stuart and USAID, Adam decided to emphasize the appropriateness of his background to his current assignment, and to make clear he placed a high premium on good relations with the USAID mission.

"I want to assure you that you'll be happy with the way things will turn out, sir," he began, only to be interrupted.

"Well I am mightily pleased to hear that, yes indeed. We look forward to being in close contact with you. I think it would be best if you were to have meetings twice a week with Barry Johnson, our democracy and governance officer here. I'd also like to have weekly written progress reports." Then looking at his cell phone Stuart then abruptly ended the meeting.

Adam left perplexed and worried; feelings fueled by his lack of experience in how an independent and nonprofit organization like CDP, which received its funding from the US government, should relate to it in the field. *Stuart didn't really understand or perhaps even care about democratic development issues.* In fact, the more that Adam mused about the meeting over the next couple of days, the more he felt Stuart had given the impression he saw democracy in Kombonia as a nuisance, that somehow risked getting in the way of other US government objectives.

That unsettled feeling, compounded by the concern that USAID might intend to second-guess and micromanage his work, settled into the pit of his stomach and spawned a bunch of follow-on worries. Was it by chance Stuart had said that he was a part of the USAID "team"? Adam wasn't sure if he was being overly sensitive, or perhaps even slightly paranoid, but he wondered whether Stuart was just being welcoming, or sending a message that Adam was in fact subordinate to USAID? Was this the type of relationship that was supposed to develop between CDP personnel and USAID missions? How would it evolve? Should he try to establish greater distance? After all, CDP wasn't an official US government agency. What if Stuart was to tell him to do something he didn't want to?

All of these thoughts occurred against a vague feeling Adam had, even freshly arrived, that Kombonia's political tectonic plates might be headed toward a potentially fatal encounter. Every day street radio reported a few more deaths in outlying parts of Kayemba City…these were mysterious, chimera-like doings; no one ever seemed to have seen exactly what happened, how many people were killed or injured, or who was responsible.

Adam desperately needed someone in whom he could confide. He decided that Cornell Oates, the young public affairs officer in the embassy, was a person he could try to get to know better and who could possibly be a friend. Several nights later, he met Oates for dinner at a mediocre Indian restaurant run by a listless couple from Mumbai; it was nonetheless one of the few locations around town frequented by middle-class Kombonians and the expatriate community, eager for any type of variety in cuisine choices.

After small talk over a couple of beers, Adam lowered his voice a little bit, even though no one was within earshot and asked, "So what's this guy Stuart like, anyway?" Oates let out a chuckle and then looked at Adam, obviously deciding how much to confide in him. "What the hell," he said, "I'll tell you. Stuart is a royal asshole. He's a control freak, surrounds himself with sycophants and can make your life hell if you cross him."

Adam kneaded his forehead to try to release some of the tension he was feeling. "OK—so what's the bad news?" he asked in a semi-sarcastic, self-pitying way. "By the way, how does he get along with our ambassador?"

Oates let out a second laugh, deeper and more profound than the first. "Boy, you are sizing this place up quickly. They cannot stand each other. Chalk on a blackboard. If you are a sadist, it is fun to watch those two going head-to-head. I don't think both will last out their full tours here. Most people are on Ambassador Anderson's side. If you want my advice, keep your head down and don't do anything risky. There is a lot you don't know about this place yet, and it could reach up and bite you in the rear pretty quickly."

Just then Sarah blew in—seeing Adam she let out a big smile and headed to the table. Adam's pulse rate increased as she stood by him. "Hello Cornell. Have you guys been talking about me?"

Intrigued by Sarah but not knowing enough about the situation or the people there to feel comfortable airing dirty laundry, Adam made a noncommittal reply. "No, Cornell is just sharing his views about this place." Unfortunately, its only effect was to heighten Sarah's curiosity. "No, really—I want to know. What's up?" This time Oates replied. "If you must know, we were just discussing the relative merits of Mr. Stuart and Ambassador Anderson."

Sarah's deep blue eyes flashed in an immediate and unambiguous negative reaction, which seemed to Adam to be at variance with her previously measured demeanor. "Stuart is a real jerk. He would have made Mussolini proud." She appropriated an empty chair and directed herself toward Adam. She looked at him in a way that momentarily entranced him and said, "May I give you some advice? Don't let him push you around. Nothing good will come of it." Sarah then looked at her watch. "Ooops. OMG—sorry—gotta go. I forgot I have to make it to a reception for a visiting American jazz group."

The next day Adam called Mulcahy. He was increasingly concerned, and as he frankly admitted to himself, unsure of how to proceed. He was particularly worried about how to manage the relationship with USAID and Stuart. It took all day to connect—he got through on his sixth try; either the internet connection was unstable or Mulcahy was unavailable. Mulcahy eventually returned his calls at 11 p.m., just as he was about to sink off to sleep. Over the course of his time in Kombonia, Adam would never really learn to accommodate himself to the late-night phone calls from DC, which would usually wake him up a couple of times a week.

"I am really concerned about this guy Stuart. He seems like a micromanager and doesn't appear to care very much about democracy here."

Adam couldn't tell over the WhatsApp connection whether Mulcahy's tone was normal, or whether it was slightly disappointed and disapproving of Adam's need to seek guidance at this point. "This is one of the big deals that we often have to confront. Frankly, we want all the good things to be had out of a close relationship with USAID, and none of the constraints that such a situation could entail. We want to be in a have-your-cake-and-eat-it-too kind of position. If I were you, I would err on the side of independence, but without rocking the boat too much. CDP is not a government agency. Our ability to 'have an attitude,' to not get mealymouthed about things, is because we aren't trying to be diplomats. If something sucks, we want to be able to say that it sucks.

"The key is developing effective personal relationships. You could write into stone how something is supposed to go, and it wouldn't matter a bit if the people on the ground didn't think that way. Ironically, we tend to have our closest relationships with embassies and USAID missions where they do not set out to micromanage us, where mutual respect is developed. In those circumstances, we tend to share more information and be closer. You go and figure it out.

"So, it sounds like you potentially have a tough situation. If you want my advice, which I guess you do, I would try to work around Stuart. People in the embassy, including the ambassador, of course, could be allies. Most importantly, use your meetings with your direct USAID contact—isn't his name Barry somebody?—to try to develop trust with people like him and get them to feel comfortable with you without you selling out heart and soul to them."

Mulcahy paused in the flow of his monologue, a discourse that Adam deemed too valuable to try to interrupt. "By the way, you should know that Fred Shapiro is very sensitive about this independence from AID issue. To him and others around here, it is a matter of institutional culture. Fred doesn't want CDP to be looked upon as simply a tool of the USG. Remember, he has an organization's reputation to uphold. CDP has to differentiate itself from the other groups out there, and don't fool yourself—there is some competition; this is a growth industry. Also, he's got a Board of Directors to which he has to report. They are the ones who decide whether to hire or fire him, and they don't want him to be running a chicken-shit outfit here. And, to be fair to him, I really do think that he believes in the importance of our work a lot, as a matter of principle."

After three weeks in-country, Adam decided it was time to start dipping his toes more directly into the Kombonian waters, and started a round of introductory meetings with civil society groups. He found that there were several groups oriented toward promoting human rights and democracy. A couple of them with whom he met seemed to be headed up by impressive individuals, but he came away with a sense that there was not a lot of substance behind them; that they existed in the first instance to get donor funding. Some others struck Adam as being very careful about criticizing the government, and presented quite positive viewpoints on Kombonia's evolving political situation. He wondered if they were truly independent of the government—were they like the GONGO phenomenon he had heard about from Walter?

Especially after learning about Harlan Stuart and meeting with him, Adam was both curious and nervous for his initial in-person meeting with Barry Johnson, who would be both overseeing the cooperative agreement and Adam's main point of contact. Johnson was personable and welcoming enough, and apologized for having been briefly out of the country when Adam had met with Harlan Stuart, but the meeting assumed a herky-jerky character as he was called out of the office several times by other USAID personnel for quick chats on what appeared to Adam to be a range of disparate issues.

Somewhat distracted, Johnson's main interest seemed to be getting Adam to soon commit to undertaking a program activity. "You guys can't just be sitting around here," he said, noting that the cooperative agreement with CDP had been signed several months ago and that concrete results needed to start rolling in. "You know we need to be able to show to USAID in DC that there are returns on the investment we have put into this project. When your advance team came out here a year ago and presented your proposal, you guys were all about results, results, results. The metrics, the work plan, the performance and evaluation system are all there in our signed agreement. When are you guys going to get your asses in gear and help democracy here in Kombonia?"

Adam was a bit nonplussed by all this, as he was not yet fully certain in his own mind exactly what type of specific activity CDP should undertake. The agreement with USAID focused on trainings, the provision of technical information related to democratic governance, and the issuance of a sub-grant to a Kombonian civil society group, but it did not articulate in detail the substantive content of these activities; this was left up to the establishment of a workplan, which had a due date of forty-five days after Adam's arrival in-country.

With each passing day, the deadline increasingly hung over Adam's head. He ruminated on the possible options. Parliamentary training seemed to be premature as there was not yet a functioning democratically elected legislature. Similarly, it struck Adam that work to improve the quality of local government would require at least some level of political will in order to ensure that adequate resources were devoted to the task. He doubted that such a commitment really existed in the current Kombonian government, which he was hearing did an adequate job of taking care of its supporters but not much beyond that.

CDP's focus is probably going to be in some way related to elections. The next polls were due at the end of the year, and Adam could already tell that tension was growing as expectations were that the moderate opposition KDPR party under Ruwoyo would be mounting a strong challenge. At the same time, Adam was hearing considerable skepticism that the government would permit a real election to take place. As one KRP supporter later told him in an unguarded moment, "We aren't fools. We know what would happen if Ruwoyo took power. He and his people hate us. They would destroy us!"

At the obligatory beer drinking session following his second Hash House Harrier run, Adam again chatted with Sarah. They played the name game and found out that Sarah had a friend who had gone to Dartmouth, and whom Adam knew slightly. As they laughed over the shared connection, their eyes lingered together for a minute longer than needed. Embarrassed, Adam sought to change the subject and asked Sarah what she thought of the prospects for successful elections. Her answer was instructive. "Look, it doesn't matter whether this place is a democracy or a dictatorship. No ruling party ever wants to lose power. The question any autocrat—and believe me Mushi and his people are not exactly Jeffersonian democrats—has in this day and age is 'how far can I go in making the election look democratic, while ensuring that I won't lose?'

"As far as I can see, winning a legitimate election is more of an art than a science. It depends a lot on each country's context. I think that here in Kombonia the KRP will do all that it can to win, but that is not necessarily the end of the story. There is some pluralism in the political system here; just look at the different political parties, the British tradition of independence of the press and the judiciary. It isn't great here, but some of that stuff exists. And the international community will be looking at what is going on; they have some leverage through the aid they give here. I am not saying that the whole election thing won't be a disaster, but it might not. Who knows what will happen?"

Adam also had another check-in call with Mulcahy that left him unsettled. Mulcahy urged him to move quickly in determining specific program activities. Adam felt uneasy about being hurried along by the workplan deadline, especially as he realized how important the initial program would be in shaping perceptions of CDP and its future course in Kombonia. He wished, not for the first time, that he had more experience and background in this work. He did send an email to CDP's field representative in the nearby country of Benin whom he knew had arrived in-country a few months before. Adam thought his perspective could be useful on a range of issues including hiring local staff, setting up bank accounts, and identifying programming. To be honest, however, the information he got back was somewhat useful at a general level, but it didn't provide him with as much of a roadmap as he would have wanted regarding how to proceed. He was going to have to work much of it out himself.

Chapter 7

KADD and Marie

About six weeks into his Kombonian adventure Adam happily sat in on a seminar organized by the Cultural Affairs Office at the US Embassy. Its topic was the American electoral process and to Adam's pleasure featured a visiting American professor—Raymond Bearson. In his talk he explained some of the quirks and complexities of the American electoral system in detail; the room in the embassy library was jam-packed with teachers and students from the University of Kombonia and others who were very interested to hear about and discuss how elections were conducted in the US. Bearson's presentation elicited many questions from the audience; in fact, a lively discussion ensued about the appropriateness of and reason for the Electoral College. Some comments and questions included:

"We in Kombonia have trouble understanding why in the US, which calls itself a democracy, the president is in fact only elected by 538 people."

"Why is big business in America allowed to spend as much money as it wants on election campaigns?"

"How does someone like Donald Trump get elected president?"

Bearson acknowledged the legitimacy of these questions. "Look, each country has the right, and responsibility, to create systems that reflect its own historical, cultural, religious, ethnic, economic, and other realties that together constitute its own particular social and political culture. However, while no country has exactly the same system, it must reflect fundamental and universal underlying democratic values such as freedom of expression, assembly, and thought.

"I would be the first one to agree that the system needs some changes. And, in fact, this is the core of the democratic system—it is not represented by an unchanging set of institutions and procedures, and they can instead be adjusted and changed as needed. In this way, for example, nonlandowners, African Americans, women, and eighteen-to-twenty-one-year-olds had gained the right to vote. Change doesn't often occur quickly, but as opposed to dictatorships where rulers do not care about public opinion, it does happen."

A stir ran through the crowd as he made his last point. And since Kombonia's presidential elections were on the horizon, the discussion not surprisingly also focused on the Kombonian presidential election system. Bearson noted that, "In comparison to the US what you have here is simpler and more straight-forward—the winning candidate simply needs to have a plurality of the vote, totaling at least 40 percent of the ballots cast. If no candidate reaches this threshold, a run-off election is held two weeks later between the top two candidates."

"Yes, we know that," interjected a student, "but this percentage requirement was recently adopted by the ruling KRP majority in parliament. They claimed that it was a means to ensure that the eventual president would be supported by a significant number of Kombonian electors. But we Kombonians know that this change has been engineered by the ruling party to make it more difficult for an opposition figure to win." Again, a buzz of support for this opinion rippled through the attendees.

"That may be true," Bearson replied. "But, to be frank, given the lack of prior experience in democratic elections here, no one really knows what would be the effects of this provision."

During a coffee break, Adam introduced himself to a well-attired man of perhaps fifty.

"Hello, glad to meet you. My name is Adam Edwards."

The man looked him over before responding somewhat formally, "I believe the pleasure of this meeting is mine. I am Albert Duwango, president of the Kombonian Association for Democratic Development."

In an unfortunately jocular, sophomoric reflex, Adam blurted, "No KADDing?" Duwango looked at him with an expression of polite, disdainful inquisition. At that very moment Adam remembered hearing about Duwango from his pal Walter in Washington. In an attempt to repair the damage, and with his interest piqued, Adam queried, "What does your group do?"

"As you may know, we are just beginning in our efforts to create lasting democratic structures here in Kombonia. This requires groups such as ours to alert the people to their democratic responsibilities and to help make sure that democracy takes root."

Wow. This is just up my alley; these folks are a group with which I need to connect. "I think we need to talk. You see, I represent a US-based organization that has very similar goals to yours. I have come here to help support such efforts."

Duwango's eyes momentarily took on a far-away look. "Ah, you Americans. You want to do so much, so well, so quickly. But so often you raise hopes that can't be met. Still," he said, pulling himself back into the present, "you are right—we must talk. I have heard that USAID has given your organization a grant. Can you come by my office at 10 a.m. tomorrow morning?"

A bit nonplussed, Adam agreed nonetheless and got the address.

The next morning Adam duly showed up at a building in a compound not far from the city center, which was apparently guarded by several grazing goats. An elderly man wrapped in the cloth attire favored by the Pohane escorted Adam up a flight of stairs into Duwango's modern and well-equipped inner sanctum. Duwango switched off his computer and welcomed Adam.

After a brief amount of small talk, Duwango brusquely got down to business. "I am very pleased you are here," he intoned, somewhat pompously. "Let us see how we can most effectively work together." Gesturing toward a plump pile of folders, he said, "I have here a set of proposals for seminars and training programs to help Kombonians understand more about democracy. I would like you to look at them and tell me whether these are activities you can support. We could enter into a sub-grant agreement with your organization, through which you could provide financial support."

Whoa, Nellie. We are going just a bit too fast here. This guy wants to get to third base with me and I don't even know him yet.

"Listen," Adam replied. "I have only recently arrived. I am living out of a hotel. I don't have the lay of the land here particularly well yet. I have to communicate back to my home office what I think should be the specific details of my organization's programmatic activities here. And I don't even know much about you or what you do. Maybe we could just set up a working meeting to start a dialogue and get to know each other better."

Duwango looked down his nose, both literally and figuratively, at Adam; his face adopted a slightly patronizing and bemused look. "One of the first things you will need to understand is that time is not something we have a lot of in this country. You may think this is a slow-paced place here compared to your America but if democracy is to take root, a lot of work has to be done very quickly. There are some very important and influential people here who would like to turn the clock back to dictatorial rule, or at least keep democracy from fully being implemented in Kombonia. Elections will be upon us before we know it; who knows in which direction they will take the country?

"If you are to be effective in our context, you have to understand that we do not have the luxury of time or resources to create chapters everywhere." The tenor of Duwango's voice rose in intensity. "People are dying every night. We can't wait for the grassroots to push for change; that isn't how things happen here. We, the intellectuals and elites of the country, have to lead the rest of the people. We thus have to prioritize our activities. We have to move quickly. For the foreseeable future the elites will govern the country; they are the ones we have to first inculcate with democratic values."

Fair enough, but I wonder if there isn't a bit of self-justification here. I bet Duwango lacks not only the time, but also the inclination, to hang out with the masses. He probably feels much more comfortable operating within his own world. Such an attitude rubbed against Adam, partly because he was aware it had been a part of his own upbringing. To be honest though, it was also because of his belief that a test of character is to see how willing one is to venture beyond one's own familiar world.

Duwango pulled down a book from his bookshelf and opened it up for Adam to see. "You don't perhaps fully appreciate that, while Kombonia has a chance to become a democracy, the situation here is very complicated and there are powerful people who want to shut this down. This book is about Portugal, where a military coup overthrew the government in the early 1920s. There was a very weak and newborn democracy there, and the parliament was basically full of bickering people. Look at the cartoon." It showed the legislature in chaos, with everyone engaged in fisticuffs. Off to one side a hand was beginning to pull the curtain back—it had military braid on the cuff.

"This cartoon," Duwango emphasized, "appeared in a Portuguese newspaper four days before Antonio Salazar's 1926 military-backed coup, which crushed that country's young democracy for fifty years. Beware that does not happen here. If it does, the next time we talk we may both be involuntary guests of the government. I am the deputy executive director of the Standard Bank branch in Kombonia, but that doesn't keep me from seeing the insides of jails here."

Duwango's presentation had certainly given Adam food for thought. "Look," he suggested, changing the subject, "might it be possible for you to help me get set up here? I need to figure out a place to live and work."

"That is not a problem," replied Duwango. "Let me introduce you to my deputy Yusuf." He pressed an electronic buzzer on his desk and a few minutes later Yusuf appeared. "This is Yusuf Abwangou, the KADD executive director. He'll be able to help you." Adam introduced himself, to which Yusuf responded with a terse and formal acknowledgement.

Adam was intrigued by Duwango's obvious energy and charisma but felt that he might be too elitist. He followed up with a question for Duwango about the potential utility of KADD focusing on a bottom-up, rank-and-file-oriented approach to promoting democracy. Duwango reacted negatively, seemingly irritated by Adam's continued focus on the grassroots. "Listen, young man. As I have already told you, KADD has limited resources and must thus rigorously prioritize its activities. Moreover, for better or worse, elites run Kombonian society. KADD's highest priority should therefore be to target our activities in the direction of the elites, and work toward ensuring that they internalize the key elements of a democratic political culture."

Yusuf expressed polite disagreement. "Mr. President, I understand what you are saying, but it is also true that the more KADD and its activities are known and appreciated by the man in the street, the more likely KADD is to survive." Adam noted the deferential tone that Yusuf adopted to Duwango, but also his willingness to express his own viewpoints, even if they were at variance with his boss.

Adam was thrilled to connect for dinner with Bearson the night after his Embassy presentation. Since Adam knew that a big part of his job would be interacting with the media, the conversation started off with Adam asking Bearson's thoughts on the press in Kombonia.

"I'd characterize it as an active, although limited, media sector. The independent press has tended to not be subject to overt interference from the government. But I think that the situation is becoming tenser as elections approach. The official electronic media, Radio Kombonia, and the state television channel all demonstrate clear partisanship in favor of the KRP. Some ostensibly private media, such as TV/Radio Rema and Star FM, are also oriented in favor of the party. The independent media include electronic and print outlets such as Radio Public Africa, Radio Myanara, and TV Rebirth. This independent media has considerable support amongst the population. However, a new law requires journalists to reveal their sources; it has not yet been implemented, but it has resulted in further self-censure on the part of the media."

"What about the violence going on here?"

"Well, as you know, it has been rising recently. Much of it is shrouded in mystery, but I don't think it would be a stretch to see it as part of the maneuvering before the upcoming elections. In my humble opinion, a critically important aspect of the elections concerns whether the security forces, which opponents claim do not act in a neutral fashion, have the will and ability to control the KRP youth militia, which are rather ironically named 'The Peacemakers.' They exist to do the regime's dirty work in performing an extralegal, quasi-police function, especially in dealing with the opposition. Some of the opposition parties, especially the KDPR and RMK, have youth wings but they don't have the same capacity to intimidate. In some places the Peacemakers call the shots, and the police and other civil authorities must at times be subservient to them. According to a senior KRP official, the Peacemakers are simply a youth group; they receive training and serve as party supporters.

"Unlike previous situations where foreigners were viewed as being 'off-limits,' there are recent examples of relief workers and missionaries being killed under mysterious circumstances. There is unsubstantiated, widespread suspicion that these murders were committed by elements close to the KRP for intimidation purposes."

Adam then asked about conditions where autocratic governments in Africa had lost power—he thought such a perspective might be useful as Kombonia moved toward its controversial election.

"Well," Bearson opined, "in a number of cases, meaningful political change occurred after the president lost the allegiance of all or part of the security forces. In the case of Mali, for example, this took place, ironically, through a coup d'état led by progressive military officers who subsequently handed power over to a democratically elected government. In the other cases, the loss of control over the security forces was more subtle, but the effect was similar. In the Congo, security forces sent to arrest a leading trade union activist met resistance from other security forces, and withdrew. And in Benin, street protests about the economic decline forced security leaders to decide between upholding President Kerekou's regime and spilling the blood of fellow *Beninois* or responding to what was manifestly the will of the people and supporting fundamental political change."

"Who were the types of people leading these protests?"

"Well, I can tell you that participation included the establishment elites of the former regime who had gotten fed up with it, as well as the members of the reform coalitions associated with the social protests. Prominent political figures prepared to risk their well-being for change and student activists, ethnic and religious leaders, and public sector trade unionists were at the forefront."

"I wonder if these factors are present here in Kombonia," Adam mused.

Bearson chuckled and said, "That, my friend, is the $64 million question."

Adam was in touch several times with Yusuf over the next few days. What Adam had sensed as his initial reserve began to temper a bit. He began to get the glimmers of the reality that the Kombonian elites had a rather formalistic and stilted manner of interpersonal relations, different from the American penchant for informality.

The following week Yusuf accompanied him as he looked at possible office space locations. Adam decided to push the envelope a bit and asked Yusuf what it was like working for Duwango. Yusuf responded, "He is a man of considerable energy and intellect. He is courageous. He believes that the people of Kombonia deserve to be free from dictators and live in liberty. We hope so much that you can help us achieve that."

"How tough is it for KADD to operate?"

Yusuf let out a small snort. "In theory the right for NGOs to exist is permitted in Kombonian law. But the devil is in the details. To employ another metaphor, the rubber really meets the road around what NGOs must do to have any kind of real impact. I can cite to you many ways in which the government impedes the ability of groups like KADD to function." Here this includes burdensome registration requirements and restrictions regarding from whom we can get financial support. We were, frankly, surprised that the government has allowed you to work with us."

"Wow—Duwango seems like exactly what the country needs now."

"Perhaps. But maybe not everyone feels the same way," was Yusuf's cryptic response.

Adam was soon to get a sense of what Yusuf meant. A few days later, Adam entered Duwango's office, only to find him in a towering rage. "They have not followed my orders! Don't they understand that I am in charge of this organization?”

"What is going on?" Adam queried.

"The city of Motamba is about a two-hour drive south from here. Their chapter of KADD wants to do things their own way and organize a program separately from the national organization. That is very unwise and lacking in discipline. We have to work together—we do not have the resources or time to each work separately. Now I will have to go to Motamba and bring back order there."

"Is it really so bad that they want to exercise their own initiative?" asked Adam.

Duwango turned to him, his eyes flashing with anger. "No one should question my leadership! As your Benjamin Franklin said, 'We must all hang together or we shall all hang separately.' You do not understand things here. We who wish to bring democracy to the country are challenging the entrenched elites, and this must be done in a careful and strategic way. The government and its people want to divide us. We must be strong and united!"

Adam was taken aback by this outburst. It seemed to him that it reflected passion and commitment but also revealed a chillingly authoritarian streak. *Ironic that a champion of democracy would display such tendencies.* Later that evening, as he relaxed on the patio in his backyard garden with a beer in hand, he decided to give Duwango the benefit of the doubt—certainly the situation seemed tense and it was probably wise to speak with as much of a common organizational voice as possible. *Kombonia has pretty much zero experience with democracy; I guess it shouldn't be surprising that autocratic instincts and manners of functioning prevail. It will take time for the democratic political culture to change. The world is rarely black and white. It is usually various shades of gray. And we have to be attentive to them because it is the subtle changes in hue that instruct us whether things are going well, or badly.*

It was about this time that Adam had his first substantive meeting with the US ambassador, Ellen Anderson. The ambassador was clearly interested in gauging Adam and the CDP project for herself. She was a handsome middle-aged woman and a foreign service professional with over twenty-five years' experience in Africa.

She presented a number of shrewd observations and questions to Adam, but first shared some concerns about political parties in Africa in general. "Unfortunately, due to the tradition of single-party dictatorships in the region, many political parties tend to be personality oriented, elitist, regionally and/or ethnically based, and weak on policy prescriptions. Kombonia is no exception. Not surprisingly, many of these parties, especially those not in power, possess few financial assets and draw upon a limited pool of human resources. These hindrances often mean that parties lack the ability to closely examine the experiences of other new democracies and are shut out of wider international political currents."

Anderson then changed tack and asked, "I understand that you are planning on working with KADD. What do you think of their infrastructural and logistical capabilities to carry out your planned activities?"

Adam gulped since he was neither certain of what they would do nor of KADD's internal capacity. "They clearly are made up of good people. They have impressed me so far with their skills and planning processes. To be honest, we won't know for sure until things happen, but I am confident that this is going to work out well. It is in all of our best interests."

The ambassador nodded, as if somewhat assuaged by the answer. "What is the likely impact of KADD receiving this money from the US government? Couldn't reliance on our funding give opponents of democracy the argument that KADD is beholden to us and simply doing our bidding? After all, let's be frank. In some quarters KADD is perceived to be in opposition to the KRP."

"Well, I wonder if this isn't going to be a problem no matter what. The fact that civil society groups, like KADD, are independent and not answerable to the government certainly can make government supporters feel like it is biased and hostile. But it is KADD's job to do its job—whatever the government may think of it. And maybe someday the government will understand that in a democracy not every person or organization will be under its control."

"Hmmm," mused the ambassador, looking Adam over reflectively. "I agree with you, but it is easy for us to say things like that...it is not our heads on the figurative—or literal—chopping block. So let me ask you something else. Let's take another scenario. Couldn't the more radical opposition say that we are doing the government's bidding and just using KADD to whitewash what will be a fake election, since the government has no intention of allowing itself to lose?"

Adam gulped and came up with the best answer that he could muster on the spot. "Well, I guess we will just have to do our work so well that, if this is a legitimate election, our project will succeed in helping to lay the groundwork for it to be viewed as such by Kombonians of all political persuasions." Even to Adam that answer sounded like bullshit.

On a rainy Friday evening, at the end of his first month in Kombonia, Adam went to a party organized by Ralph Jeffries, the deputy chief of mission at the American Embassy. He proved to be a nice enough, but rather bland, bureaucrat. Adam was working on his third beer of the evening when a very attractive Kombolese woman entered, shedding her raincoat to reveal a well-formed body. She sauntered into the room with assurance. Adam sensed a challenge, something that invariably got his libido exercised. Half a beer later, Adam managed to snare her in conversation, introduce himself, and ask her name.

She took a second to look him over. "I am Marie Mfalla. So, what brings you here?"

Immediately smitten by her looks and direct manner, Adam leapt into the fray. Somehow the words popped into his mouth, as if manna sent from heaven. "I will give you four guesses, and for each wrong answer you give, you'll have to take a drink," he offered up playfully. "I am either a teacher, a journalist, a diplomat, or an aid worker."

Marie looked at him dryly and said in her excellent English, "Well since your shirttail is hanging out in the back, I doubt you are a diplomat. And there is not much of a market for first world teachers here. You could be a journalist, but somehow I don't think you are. So I am betting the odds are that you are an aid worker."

"I bow down in front of your superior judgement. Guilty as charged. I guess you don't need to have a drink unless you'd like to…could I get you something?"

At her request Adam poured a glass of white wine. "And what do you do?"

"Well, it looks like I am the journalist out of the two of us. I write for *The Clarion* newspaper—are you familiar with it?"

Adam had heard a bit about the newspaper—it had a reputation of supporting the opposition, but of a more moderate persuasion than some. It was rumored to be underwritten by wealthy opposition backers.

"Yes—I know it is an important paper. How'd you get involved with it?"

"That is a long story," Marie replied with a sparkle in her eye. This had its perhaps presumed effect on Adam of making him more intrigued and interested in this beautiful Kombonian woman, who carried herself with such assurance and sophistication.

"Well, you have to tell me something," Adam opined; it was his turn to act semi-flirtatiously.

Marie took another minute before replying. "My father worked as an economist for ECOWAS, the organization of West African regional states. He was based at its headquarters in Abuja, Nigeria, so I lived there for several years during secondary school. It was very interesting to live outside of Kombonia and learn about Nigeria. As a result, I got interested in government and policymaking, especially as our Kombonian rulers have had, to put it politely, many deficiencies in this regard. I studied journalism at the University of Kombonia here in Kayemba City and the rest, as you Americans say, is history."

Adam explained what his mission was in Kombonia, and Marie's eyes grew interested. "So, our paths must cross again." Adam had no problem with that prospect.

Over the next few days, he thought repeatedly of Marie. *Maybe I should get to know her better. I am sure that she could be a useful contact. Who am I kidding? I want to make love to her.*

After going back and forth in his own mind about the advisability, or lack thereof, of potentially mixing pleasure and business, he called her. She didn't seem surprised to hear his voice. "Well, hello Mr. Edwards," she said in a voice that sounded inviting to Adam's ears. "I definitely remember you from Mr. Jeffries's party. How is your time in Kayemba City going so far?"

"It's great, but I have a very steep learning curve here. I need to understand more about the politics of the country, especially since there are supposed to be elections coming up."

"Yes—that is true. May I be of assistance to you in your learning process?"

That was all Adam needed to get his propellers furiously spinning. "Well, come to think of it perhaps we could have dinner some time, and you could peel back some of the onion layers of Kombonia's politics."

A soft chuckle punctuated Marie's ambiguous reply. "I'd be delighted to see if I can help you out."

———

So, it came to be that ten days later, Adam and Marie connected for dinner at The Cedars of Barouk, a popular Lebanese restaurant. They sat in the candlelit outside courtyard; its soft ambiance intermittently marred by the crackling noise of electronic mosquito zapping machines doing their job. Adam found himself attracted by her allure, by her ease of interacting in an expatriate context, while demonstrating a native, underlying care for Kombonia.

Over a mezze plate of hummus, baba ghanoush, and falafel, Marie asked a series of questions about Adam, expressing wonderment at some of his tales of life in the US and Thailand. Her solicitousness made Adam feel very comfortable in his own skin, and good about himself. In turn she was responsive—up to a point—when he asked her more about her upbringing. She told him that her mother was Pohane and her father Ome, and that much of her family still lived in the western part of the country. She also expressed concern about the direction in which Kombonia was headed. At one point, she opined that, "This president pretends to be for the people, but what he is really doing is protecting his own interests, and those of his own ethnic group. I doubt very much that this is going to be a fair election. And Ruwoyo of the KDPR isn't much better. Obewame, the head of the Renewal Movement of Kombonia, is the best man for this job, but he won't win. Something big is going to have to happen for things to really change."

Marie was only getting warmed up with her critique of Kombonian society. "Here in Kombonia as, I must say, in much of the continent, women are treated as second-class citizens. One person who is somewhat of an exception to this rule is Mariam Osibe, the deputy leader of the KDPR. She is the highest-ranking woman in the party and has considerable support at the grass-roots level of the party and amongst the youth. While a protege of Ruwoyo's, she has recently become more critical of his approach. She believes the party should attack the government more, and be more active in recruiting members. She is also uncomfortable with the patriarchal and top-down nature of the party and its lack of substance in its policies. She would like to see the party make a proactive effort to extend its appeal across the political spectrum and to solicit grassroots perspectives on policy development. While she is not prepared to challenge Ruwoyo for his job, neither would she resist a groundswell of support in that direction."

Wow, this is my kind of woman—strong, beautiful, opinionated, and classy.

The evening ended with just a peck on the cheek, but at least Adam extracted a promise on Marie's part to see him again. Adam savored her lingering scent. *Oh man…especially given the political sensitivity of my job, falling for a Kombonian woman could be risky. But screw it.*

Chapter 8

Up-Country

After Adam had been in Kombonia for two months, he knew that the hammer was coming down—he had to make some decisions concerning the type of programming CDP should undertake. He didn't want to ask for it, but Johnson granted him a two-week extension on submitting the workplan, and that time had just about run out. Clearly there was much that could be done; the problem wasn't a lack of options, but choosing the right one. Adam's gut feeling was that the program would need to focus on elections in some fashion, since the next polls in December were clearly going to be a watershed in the country's political development. Before submitting the workplan to USAID, he decided to recommend to CDP headquarters that a political party training project be organized for all the major parties around the theme of elections. This, he felt, was where the action really was, and where CDP could assist Kombonia in threading the needle of developing a democracy in the midst of serious civil strife and a history of autocratic rule. He put these thoughts into a memo that he emailed to CDP and awaited the response. A couple of days later he got a phone call from Mulcahy.

"Yo, guy. I don't think the idea is a bad one. I've got some questions, though. Ready? How much will it cost? How would it be structured? What are the anticipated results? How could such a program affect the political environment? Would CDP be perceived as being neutral?"

Adam was a bit nonplussed by the staccato series of questions. He also had to admit to himself that he didn't have the answers to all of these queries, but he responded as best as he could. "Listen," he said, "the parties here need to be better organized. It seems like the level of political debate and meaningful dialogue between parties is pretty low. In fact, the situation is pretty zero-sum—everyone wants to be top dog and destroy the others. If we could get a program together to show the parties that they need to be responsive to their constituents, and at the same time teach them that there are rules of the game to play by, then if they lose an election they'll still know that they will have a chance at the next one. We'd be doing them a great service."

"OK, I think you need to do some more planning, but I understand where you are going with this and will support it back here," Mulcahy replied. "I do need to correct you on something—we don't 'teach' people—we share experiences. We need to keep away from the Big Brother syndrome that we know everything and have got it all figured out, and that it is simply a job of transmitting this knowledge. God knows that would be a recipe for disaster. Staying away from this negative 'instructor-student' dynamic has been one of the reasons that CDP has been successful."

Adam took note of this seemingly sage advice. The conversation also forced him to think through logistical and organizational details about the project. How would it be structured? Who would issue the invitations? Who would get them? How? Adam realized that as mundane as these issues might be, if he screwed up at this level, form would become as important as substance. Nothing good would happen if he couldn't show that he could organize this damn thing.

Adam also had to decide the specific topics to be addressed. This decision, of getting down to brass tacks about what direction he would be taking the project, worried him, a lot. He had his brief experience as a campaign staffer back in the Pennsylvania congressional race as a reference point, but he doubted that would translate well in the Kombonian reality. *I wish I could talk to a CDP veteran here, someone who has been down this road before, who I could lean on and bounce around ideas.* Signs of stress emerged as Adam began to comprehend the magnitude of the task ahead of him, and the paucity of his relevant life experience. He was being tested; he found his nails were getting chewed down, and restful nights of sleep eluded him.

So, what was actually going to happen? Adam needed to get going with making decisions about programming. Based on his knowledge of how CDP operated and his experience in Kombonia so far, including a couple of initial meetings with senior members of the three main political parties, Adam made the decision that CDP would conduct a political party training event as an initial activity. The aim of this training would be to share information and contacts between political party development experts from several democracies with their Kombonian counterparts.

Adam thought that the specific issues that needed to be addressed, and which would resonate in the Kombonian context, could include how parties a) organize themselves internally, b) develop messages to gain the public's support, and c) prepare for elections. He emailed Mulcahy with this decision and Mulcahy concurred. Adam also checked with Barry Johnson to make sure that these activities fit within the parameters of the cooperative agreement. Johnson gave him a green light while nervously expressing Eeyore-like the hope that the event would be successful.

———

With the passing of weeks, Adam became increasingly concerned about the need to travel outside of the capital city to expand his knowledge of Kombonia, while also preparing for the upcoming seminar. His destination would be Melinda, a town about one hundred miles north of Kayemba City, near the unofficial border between the Ome-and Tuyunu-majority parts of the country. He had chosen this venue for the training specifically for its symbolic multiparty character. He had thought of holding it in Kayemba City, but on balance decided that it would be best to have the first seminar up-country, away from the glare and distractions of the capital. Also, he admitted to himself, since he really had no idea of how it would transpire, it would probably be prudent for the seminar to take place in a more isolated location.

With these decisions made, Adam began to make arrangements for an advance mission, where he could identify the exact venue, make logistical arrangements, and brief himself on the realities up-country, not the least so that he could seem informed for the seminar faculty. This would consist of four political party leaders from other democracies who would share their experiences and highlight best practices that could be useful to the Kombonian participants. He planned to ask political parties to invite their senior leaders from the central and northern parts of the country to participate in the seminar.

For the advance mission, Adam decided to ask Yusuf to come.

He had toyed with the idea of inviting Marie, but reluctantly decided that their relationship had not sufficiently jelled yet, and that discretion would be the better part of valor, especially since this was his first such undertaking for CDP. Adam was to be accompanied by Festus Ompango, who he had hired as a general assistant and driver. Adam had thought a lot about this decision, since he knew that good choices in his foreign national staff were extremely important—much of what he learned about the country would be filtered through their eyes. Adam had decided on Festus, a lanky Owe about thirty years of age from a town about fifty miles north of Kayemba City. Festus struck Adam as being articulate and intelligent. He was more talkative than the other three people Adam had interviewed, but did not seem to be excitable or rash. Festus had also been recommended by Albert Duwango, and Adam thought it politic to give his recommendation a lot of weight. It was only later that he learned Festus was part of Duwango's extended family.

Adam also felt comfortable enough about KADD's nonpartisan profile to see the advantages of associating it with the project. As an initial step, he suggested to Yusuf that he would be welcome to make the planning trip with him. At first, Yusuf had been reluctant to accept.

"Come on, it will only be for four days," Adam urged him. "What's the matter?" Yusuf pleaded business and family responsibilities. Adam suggested that this mission could be useful for Yusuf in his work. After some more discussion, Yusuf said, "Please listen to me. I am not particularly excited about going to Melinda. The Tuyunu do not always look favorably upon Ome visitors, or those like me that they perceive to be Ome. Also, if I am to be away for four days, I need to get some kind of reimbursement."

The last request threw Adam for a bit of a loop. He had not received clear instructions from CDP about when he should pay professional colleagues and when he shouldn't. He was not sure, for example, whether the international experts coming in for the seminar should be paid. He knew that the budget didn't have a large personnel-salaries line item, but on the other hand, he didn't want to alienate important contacts such as Yusuf. And Adam also reacted against the idea that he would be helping to commercialize democratic development programming, and that providing money would feed into the dependency mentality he was beginning to understand existed in Kombonia. A number of times he had gotten a feeling that in answering his questions Kombonians responded with what they thought he wanted to hear, rather than with necessarily the accurate information. He hated to think how these relationships would be even more greatly skewed if he were to begin handing out money all over the place.

In the end, he decided to call Mulcahy again and get his advice. Adam was wary of hitting Mulcahy up for his counsel too frequently and on topics that he was concerned Mulcahy would find mundane, but he decided that he needed to go to the well on this one.

"Hey, big guy, these are the kinds of things we have to deal with all the time on an ad hoc basis," was the reply after Adam had laid out the situation. "Sure, we may not have a lot of money in that particular salaries line item, but if you think that there are other personnel-related line items that may come in under budget, then you can cover the cost that way."

Adam thought about this for a bit, and decided to offer Yusuf a $75 per day consulting fee, which Yusuf reluctantly accepted. He also told Yusuf, "There isn't much I can do about the Tuyunu issue, except to say that we'll be sticking together, and I wouldn't think anyone would want to do something that might have inter-national implications."

The day came and they loaded up in a Toyota four-wheel drive that Adam had leased from a Lebanese automobile dealer. Besides clothing, they had spare gas, water bottles, extra food, automobile parts, and a couple of boxes with CDP brochures. They left early in the morning and soon found themselves negotiating with livestock on the road north out of the capital. The road was fairly good for about the first twenty-five miles, but it deteriorated soon thereafter. In the late morning, they passed through a small village, like several others. The road ran down the middle of it. Most houses were made of dried mud with thatched roofs. Children were plentiful, and Adam had the feeling the village extended for a distance off the road. Several miles beyond the village Festus abruptly announced, with a small smile, "That village we just passed through was my home."

"Good God, man," blurted out Adam. "Why didn't you tell me? I would have told you we should stop!"

After a moment's hesitation Festus replied, "Oh, I get back there often enough, I don't have to stop there every time."

"Really?" inquired Adam skeptically. "How often do you go?"

Another silence, only longer this time. "Well, actually, I have been back once this year."

"That's not often," snorted Adam indignantly, secretly pleased that he could act solicitously toward the Ome man. "I'd like us to turn around and go back to the village so we can stop in to see your family."

"Oh no, let us please not do that." Festus's voice took on a note of alarm. Adam glanced at Yusuf, to see what he was making of the situation, but Yusuf's face was expressionless, and his eyes remained glued on the road ahead. It was clear that he had little desire to enter into the conversation.

"What's going on? Please tell me."

Festus looked over at Adam, nervously licked his lips, and then explained. "We have a tradition here that when you return to your home village from the big city everyone thinks that you are a success and that you must bring presents for all your family. I do not have the means to do so."

Adam thought about this for a minute. *Imagine not seeing your loved ones because you don't have enough money to buy presents. How sad.*

Their vehicle continued to alternatively lurch and roll smoothly toward Melinda, depending on the condition of the road. The flat landscape began to give way from heavy vegetation to bush and scrub. The signs of lack of rain became more apparent, and the land began to increasingly give hints of encroachment into the desert. And the people that they saw on the road carrying food, wood, or other commodities also began to acquire a more light-skinned hue. "Yes, they are Tuyunu," Yusuf said, breaking into Adam's thoughts. "They are the majority from here on up to the country's borders."

Adam decided to tackle the sensitive subject of ethnicity head-on with Yusuf. "What do you think about the Tuyunu?"

Yusuf sighed. "Well, I have two feelings. They are a part of our country. An important part. But we are also in the twenty-first century. We are part of a system of nation-states, both globally and here in Africa. We need to build up the fabric of our national consciousness. Not to make ethnicity go away, but to make sure that people think of themselves as Kombonian first, and then Ome, or Tuyunu, or Pohane, or whatever second. You can see how ethnicity and regionalism have torn apart other countries. We don't want that to happen here."

Adam asked, "Do the Tuyunu feel the same way?"

Yusuf was silent for a while. "I think so."

There's a lot he is not saying here. "Something tells me that you have more thoughts on this. What you've told me so far is all for the good, but…" he let his voice trail away questioningly. "It is commendable, but perhaps doesn't fully answer my first question."

Yusuf let out a dry chuckle in concurrence. "You are right. What I just told you is what I say as an educated member of the elite, a university professor, and someone of mixed ethnicity, although I have tended to be seen as more of an Ome, since that was the ethnicity of my father. If, however, I wear my Ome hat, I will tell you that I am scared of the Tuyunu. They are different than we are. Something else moves and motivates them. They are much more driven than we are. They do not wish to integrate themselves into our life. They want to dominate us, as they have done for so many years. I am suspicious of what they do, even when they cover it with what, on the surface, would seem to be acceptable justifications. To be honest, I watch my back if I am in the same room with a Tuyunu, sometimes literally, but always at least figuratively. All Ome do."

Adam noted that Festus's head was bobbing in agreement, even though he had remained silent through the conversation.

"Phew. OK, I guess you let that all hang out," Adam responded. "Let me ask you another question. How do you think the Tuyunu feel about the Ome?"

Yusuf gazed off into the bush and thought for a while. "They see the Ome as lazy, poorly educated in the important things in life. Christian—a different faith. To be ruled. So, they don't like them, and it is reciprocal."

"Do they feel threatened by the Ome?"

"To be honest, yes. I don't really have the opportunity to have many of these types of discussions with them. But yes, I think they do see the Ome as challenging them. The Ome birth rate, for example, is higher. And I know," Yusuf said with a small, sad smile, "what your next question will be. You want to know what can be done about this."

"Well, I suppose the thought was rolling around in my mind. No one wants there to be another Rwandan genocide. Do you think its root causes are somewhat similar to what exists here?"

Yusuf let out a long exhalation. "The same could probably be said for thirty countries in sub-Saharan Africa, but thankfully they have not lived through that nightmare—at least not yet. We have to find ways and political structures that can respond to the fears of both sides. There are many, many other dynamics at play in this country other than those we have talked about so far. Each group has its clans, with their own feelings about each other. The military is a separate institution. The economic crisis creates different stresses. You, the international community, create a different dynamic. We have other ethnic groups to consider and a tense regional context. We have to create a political system that can accommodate all of these factors."

"Wow—I guess that is sort of a full plate. But isn't what you have so far a good start?"

"That is exactly what it is—just a start. Our system is a hybrid of the English and the American systems. Actually, it is worse than that. It is similar to the French tradition of a strong executive branch and a weak parliament, with powers between the two not clearly delimited. Maybe a country like France, with a long tradition of democracy, can deal with this, but I tell you in a place like Kombonia, with our background, if it isn't properly managed, it will be the end of us."

"So, again, what can you do about it?"

"We have to adapt. Just like Darwinism. Survival of the fittest means survival of those who can adapt to their environments. We need to make sure that our institutions reflect the reality of our country."

"What do you mean specifically?" Adam was really into this now.

"I'm not sure," Yusuf admitted. "But I think we need to look at issues such as decentralization of power. We have a highly centralized system of political administration. We need to look at ways to give the Tuyunu, and the Ome for that matter, more local autonomy. We need to have an electoral system that more accurately reflects the reality of the country. Maybe we should have a senate, or a Kombonian version of the House of Lords with traditional rulers and others with specific regional or sectoral interests. Together with the Chamber of Deputies these would serve to represent the nation."

All this was a lot for Adam to digest, but he needed to articulate one more thought. "Everything you've talked about so far relates to specific, tangible institutions and the legalistic form of democracy. But what about its spirit? Doesn't democracy need to have this as well—a positive notion of how people and political figures of different opinions should act toward each other, of how compromise and conciliation need to be part of a democratic political culture?"

"I agree with you, but I also agree with your James Madison, who said that 'if men were angels no government would be necessary.' Instead, we must recognize that man's nature is inherently untrustworthy, and that it is more important to focus on the institutions, rather than the people who will inhabit them."

Adam was impressed by the discussion and by Yusuf's obvious intelligence and evenhandedness, but any further conversation was interrupted by their entry into the outskirts of Melinda. The feel of this city was very different from Kayemba City. While the latter had something of an aura of national import about it, Melinda seemed to be poorer and dustier, and had more of the feel of an oversized market town. Festus drove them to the Villa Arrivederci Roma Hotel, which turned out to be a nicely appointed four-story hotel. Its greatest attribute appeared to be an open-air restaurant and bar on the roof run by its Italian husband and wife owners, which allowed diners to consume their pasta at a relaxing remove from the sights and sounds of the city below. Yusuf and Adam ate there that evening, and Adam was struck by the beauty of the scene and the smells and the noises, including the traditional Moslem call to prayer from the minarets. Off in the distance shimmered the beginnings of the Sahara.

The next day they set about their work. They first looked at possible sites for a multiday seminar for 70 people. The third site they visited, a teacher-training college on the edge of town, seemed to have enough space and proximity for lodging. It also had electricity, which was no small matter. Adam was assured that they could cater lunches for the seminar participants.

During their meeting with the training college administrator, Adam noticed that Yusuf, although polite, seemed to be bored and impatient. This attitude deepened as they visited two other hotels to ask about availability and cost, as well as to inspect the premises. Afterward, Adam could not disguise his growing irritation and asked Yusuf, "What is going on here? You don't seem to be very engaged."

Yusuf produced a pained expression on his face. It was clear he didn't enjoy dealing with the subject. "This is not something that I should be doing. I am a university professor, not a hotel clerk."

Adam felt his temper heating up. "Listen, don't go haughty on me here. One thing I have learned is that if the logistics for a project don't work, the substance won't work. We could have the goddamn greatest seminar in the world and it won't matter a shit if everyone gets sick from the food, if the lights don't work, if the transportation is late, or if the hotels suck. This is real life and we have to deal with these things."

Yusuf protested. "But someone else should be doing this."

"Maybe," Adam responded. "But guess what? We don't have anyone to specifically do these kinds of things, and I'm not sure we have the money for that kind of person. Now, perhaps I could get Festus to do some of this, but I'm not ready to entrust much of the organizing to him yet. And besides, he will have his hands full with driving, errands, and basic office administration. Look," Adam pleaded, "I'm new to this, it's my first project with CDP, and I've got to do everything I can to make sure it goes right. I need your help." Yusuf begrudgingly agreed.

Later in the evening, Adam leaned on the hotel's rooftop wall and surveyed the myriads of faraway pinpricks of light crowding the cloudless night sky. Adam was always struck by how many stars there were in the African sky, away from the lights and pollution of the big cities. *The complexity of Kombonia mirrors that of the universe. Also, understanding Kombonia requires the same tools to understand life. You have to reach out of the comfy confines of your own safety blanket, stretch your hands out, and dare to reach for the stars.*

Adam had another beer, lit a rare cigarette, and continued to gaze at the panorama. The ambiance fed his continued self-reflection. He appreciated having learned Thai in his Peace Corps experience, because when he spoke it, it was as if another part of himself that he didn't know existed opened up. It was like looking at things through someone else's eyes. And with that you can also look back on yourself and learn more about who you are. Adam's last musing, before he said goodbye to the magical sight of the sky and headed down to his rather spartan hotel room, was that of the astronauts who have marveled at what they learned about the Earth, while looking at it from far away.

The next morning Adam and Yusuf met with Mohammed Ismail, leader of the Melinda office of the KDPR party. "You are most welcome here," Ismail said formally after offering them cups of thick, black coffee, which Adam politely declined. Coffee to him tasted like acid. He found meetings in Kayemba City easier since tea was offered more frequently.

Their encounter was short. Ismail responded positively to Adam's suggestion of a seminar on political party organization, and said that he would ensure participation of a delegation from his party. They then went off to visit other people. Later in the day, a message was left at the hotel asking Adam to visit Ismail. Leaving Yusuf to rest at the hotel, Adam returned to the KDPR party headquarters and was ushered back into Ismail's office.

"You know, we would be pleased to serve as your hosts for this program," began Ismail.

Adam, sensitive to the need to remain impartial in Kombonian politics, diplomatically responded, "Thank you so much for the offer, but I believe we should work through KADD, which has ties with all of the political parties. But we look forward to remaining in close contact with you as planning progresses, and throughout the project."

Ismail took a moment before answering. "I must be frank with you. We are very concerned about the participation of KADD in this program. Are you aware that this organization does not have any membership here in Melinda, or elsewhere in the north, for that matter? It is well known that KADD supports the KRP party, although of course they would not openly admit to it. This presents us with some problems. Because you are new in our country perhaps you do not fully appreciate this point. What do you plan to do about this?"

Adam swallowed hard. "Mr. Ismail, I am sure that you have your reasons for making this allegation. I must tell you, however, that we believe KADD to be a reputable organization. It has received funding from the donors to undertake its civic education work in a nonpartisan fashion, and we are not aware that there have been any problems in this regard."

"Then, young man, there is much that you need to learn. What makes you think that the donor countries really understand what is transpiring in Kombonia? Is your thinking influenced because Kombonia is strategically located as a route from the inland to the sea, and you do not want to anger the ruling party? Can you really understand that KADD undertakes its programs to benefit them? You need to be very, very careful. Now, we are prepared to cooperate with your program, at least for the time being, because we prefer to believe that you do not have a hidden agenda. But we will be watching your actions very, very carefully. We may be a landlocked country, but we are familiar with the expression, 'you are fishing in very deep waters.'"

He returned to his hotel much more troubled than when he had left, and shrugged off Yusuf's inquiry as to the substance of the meeting.

Chapter 9

Political Parties

The political situation was growing more tense by the day. Chillingly, social media was also becoming more extremist in views expressed across the political spectrum. The Wolves of Kombonia, for example, issued an online statement warning that, "The people of Kombonia will resist with all their might against any attempts to destabilize the country and reverse the gains made by the KRP over the past two decades."

One hot evening in mid-April, a half-dozen people in their twenties and thirties gathered around a table in an ill-lit, poorly ventilated room in a house located in a low-income section of Kayemba City. They called themselves the Popular Movement for the Liberation of Pohaneland, or the PMLP. A sense of palpable anger emanated from them. A large man stared intensely at the others and hissed, "We must go further than the RMK. Obewame would sell us out if the price was right. He is willing to stop short of full independence. We must put more pressure on Mushi and the oppressors."

As his compatriots murmured assent the leader continued. "We will tell the people of Kombonia that we have run out of patience with the self-interested maneuvers of the political elite."

"I think we should go further than that!" exclaimed another, with suppressed rage flashing in her eyes. "We should say that the oppressors must be brought down by the people. And to be heard we must do more than that. We will have to kill more of them than we have already."

The leader responded. "Those are brave words from you, MM. But I agree with you. Do we all concur that we must step up our campaign of violence?" No one dissented.

Soon thereafter the KDPR leader Ruwoyo declared himself a candidate for the presidency, which surprised no one. Obewame also gave a fire-eating speech in which he too declared his candidacy, although he stated up front his belief that the election would be rigged and that the result was a foregone conclusion. Obewame's decision to run had been contested by some of the most radical members of the party, sympathetic to the PMLP, who wanted to see him boycott what they were convinced would be a sham process. They had urged him to move toward issuing a declaration of independence announcing the separation of the Pohane region from the rest of the country. The state-run media, in response, suggested that it was clear that Obewame was preparing his party for his defeat at the polls.

Later in April, Adam got his next introduction to political parties, Kombonian-style. He scheduled a round of meetings to get acquainted with leaders of the main parties. A few days after Adam had what he felt was a rather anodyne meeting with the Kayemba City leader of the KDPR, a messenger arrived with an invitation from Ruwoyo to dine at his Kayemba City residence the following week. Adam accepted with alacrity.

Before going to the dinner, Adam made a point of asking around to learn more about Ruwoyo. He learned that Ignace Ruwoyo had been leader of the party since the party's founder (who was also his father) so anointed him on his deathbed in 1998. Like President Mushi, Ruwoyo was a tribal elder by birth in an Ome clan, but his was one of the most prominent. He served in the military and achieved the rank of major, but his growing political consciousness had marked him as an undesirable by the military leadership; he had been forced to take early retirement. He became a lawyer, worked abroad for three years as legal counsel for Shell Oil's operations in Africa, and also devoted himself to the KDPR and its search for power.

Marie had a lot to say about Ruwoyo. "When he took control of the party its membership had been declining and was in need of refocus and rejuvenation. By reenergizing the party's attacks on Mushi, and by somewhat grandiosely taking credit for the reintroduction of multiparty politics, he succeeded in restoring a measure of purpose and energy to the party, and presenting it as a credible alternative to the KRP."

"Sounds good. What's not to like about him?"

"He has been subject to criticism by some of the younger and more radical party militants who believe that the party should ally itself more closely with the RMK. They also oppose his somewhat more privileged background and big-business orientation. Some party members also did not like his decision to have the party's elected MPs take up their seats in parliament instead of boycotting it in protest to the KRP's authoritarianism, as the RMK parliamentary delegation had done. And they criticize a perceived lack of internal democracy within the party."

"What kind of election strategy do you think he will have?"

Marie shrugged. "It seems to be to keep a firm grip on the party, and maintaining the KDPR's middle-of-the-road opposition stance. He is also looking for ways to attract both RMK and KRP supporters."

It was clear to Adam from the various responses he got that the man engendered strong reactions. Some felt that he was a messiah, who could deliver the country from the ruin toward which it was rapidly headed. Others saw him as a charlatan who was only concerned about himself. Yet others felt that he was in some ways a mirror image of Mushi, presenting a firm external image, while being prepared to maneuver and compromise, if needed. The variety of viewpoints suggested to Adam that, in reality, he might be something of a chameleon, carefully guarding his counsel, and playing his cards close to his vest.

Relatedly, Adam had also noted that despite his best efforts, he could get absolutely no one to intelligently discourse on any policy differences between the three major parties; the question itself was sometimes met with a lack of apparent comprehension. For example, when Adam asked party officials what the key components of their platforms were, he got the feeling of being in an echo chamber—all would invariably mention generic 'motherhood-and-apple pie' type issues like support for human rights and a mixed economy.

The first thing Adam noticed as his car neared Ruwoyo's residence for dinner was the number of police and armed guards in the vicinity of his compound in a comfortable, upper-middle-class part of the town. *I wonder whose side these people would be on, if push came to shove?* He entered and was met by a group of men who ushered him in to meet Ruwoyo, a strikingly handsome man of indeterminate years. He was invited to sit next to Ruwoyo, and they exchanged greetings. Adam presumed that this would lead into a longer meeting, but instead, Ruwoyo stood up as did everyone else in the room, in union, a split second later. It seemed like a maneuver that had occurred many times before. A procession led into Ruwoyo's dining room, which was also quite large and well furnished, although the atmosphere was marred, to Adam's taste, by both a television blaring at one end, and the omnipresent rumbling of an air conditioner. Dinner was served with heaping dishes of yams, rice, fufu, lamb, and chicken-style drumsticks.

Adam found conversation with his dinner mates somewhat laborious. At one point he asked the KDPR official seated next to him what the drumsticks were named. "They are called Cutting-Grass." Adam's quizzical reaction elicited further definition. "You know, the rodent which eats grass." Adam's appetite plummeted as he realized the delicacy was what he knew as bush rat.

The meal finally ended at about 10 p.m. Adam started looking for a graceful exit, glad that the rather painful and regretfully shallow experience was coming to an end. Instead, he found himself ushered into an office with chairs for ten people. Ruwoyo entered with what Adam assumed was his inner circle of confidants.

"I think that we should get to know each other better," Ruwoyo intoned. "Let me discuss with you where we find ourselves today in this country." A twenty-minute monologue followed in which Ruwoyo explained his own origins and, as he put it, "gradual political awakening." Intertwined with this personal story was a lecture on Kombonian history as seen through the lens of a member of the Ome elite, one in which, of course, the Ome people suffered at the hands of others. At one point he grew animated in discussing President Mushi. "The man just wants to stay in power. And he wants to do it not only for himself, but for all his cronies and hang-ers-on," Ruwoyo snorted. "What would he do if he was no longer president? He'd be a joke. He'd be unemployed! He will never, ever voluntarily let that occur. We will have to make that happen. Mark my words."

Ruwoyo's exclamations were met with nods of assent and murmured agreement by the others in the room. The scene reminded Adam somewhat of the call-and-reply cadence of speak-ing employed in many African American churches back home, just lacking the theological content. *Although, maybe for most of these folks, supporting Ruwoyo is a sort of religion.*

By the time Adam left, it was 1 a.m. He had to rouse Festus, who was asleep in the car. On the way back to his apartment, Adam mused about Ruwoyo's force of personality and authoritarian aura. Adam could not shake the nagging sense that were Ruwoyo to become president, the country's accession into the ranks of democ-racies might be short lived.

A few days later, he received an invitation to attend the RMK's annual national convention. Adam found it interesting that the RMK had noted his presence in-country, and had thought to invite him. This meeting was taking place against a backdrop of ris-ing tension throughout the country due to its continued economic decline, increased popular attention that the next set of national assembly and presidential elections were less than eight months away, and rumors of a growth in support for the RMK and its leader, although the party's more radical wing was placing pressure on Obewame to take an unambiguously hard stand.

Adam briefly debated whether he should attend the conven-tion, since he had not been invited to attend any other party's con-vention and did not want to appear to be a supporter of any particular party. On balance he decided that he should, though. This was partly based on a sense that he needed to build some bridges with a party that could play an important role in the upcoming election. Also, he was certain that exposure to CDP training could help orient the party toward democratic values and practices. And he felt that he had started to develop a relationship with Ruwoyo and the senior KDPR leadership, which, he felt, required a certain counter balance. Finally, however, there was another, more personal, consideration. He knew Marie would be delighted, as indeed she was, when he called her to say that he was going.

"Excellent!" She responded. "Now you will start to understand some of the depth of feeling against Mushi and his cronies." Adam felt a certain smugness and excitement at having played the Obewame card with Marie.

On the Saturday of the conference, Adam made his way to the event, which was being held in a Chinese-built sports stadium on the outskirts of Kayemba City. Although it was still early—10 a.m.—the heat of the day was already oppressive. The area around the stadium was full of RMK supporters and, despite the tension in the country, the crowd assumed a festive feeling. Flags with the orange and black colors of the party waved about, and supporters did a brisk trade in hawking RMK T-shirts bearing Obewame's image.

Adam made his way through the dust and crowds into the stadium. A throng of perhaps 5,000 was already filling it as others continued to stream in. As a sports fan, Adam had asked around about the origins of the stadium and learned that this was a typical example of Chinese foreign aid—the construction of a popular and very noticeable example of China's "friendship" with the country under question. He also noticed upon entering the stadium the questionable quality of the Chinese construction; pieces of concrete were already chipping off the ten-year-old edifice.

Adam had assumed that he would simply attend the rally. However, as one of the few white people in the crowd, he was noticed by an usher who brought him to an RMK official who beamed when he learned who Adam was. "Ah, yes sir, we have been told to expect you. Please—accompany me this way." Adam again wondered who had worked to ensure his presence. Pushing supporters out of his way, the man led Adam to a tented area on the stadium field, near the speaker's platform. Feeling increasingly uncomfortable and wary of the preferential treatment being afforded him, Adam nonetheless took his seat on a plastic chair and made some uncomfortable small talk with others near him, who were clearly interested and intrigued by the *duzumu* (white man in the Ome language) in their midst.

The usher brought him a warm bottle of Coke as he waited for a seemingly interminable time for the event to begin. He let his mind wander. He found himself wondering if he should drink from the bottle, since he had been told that the rust on poorly washed bottles could cause tetanus. He decided to throw caution to the winds and chugged it. He also thought of a recent dream in which he found himself alone, lazily canoeing on a river on a hot summer day. The current started, slowly at first, to pick up speed. Part of him recognized that this could mean danger ahead, but mostly he was enjoying the experience so much that he did not let himself fully consider the implications of the situation. Adam had woken up from the dream with an accelerated heartbeat, as it concluded with the canoe falling over a massive waterfall.

Adam was jerked out of his reverie when music erupted from the stadium's loudspeakers and a large scrum of people began to ooze their way toward the platform. A speaker urged the crowd, with little success, to quiet down. A groundswell of applause, however, met the next speaker who then proceeded to introduce Obewame in reverential terms, as the second coming of the Messiah, who would slay the forces of evil and bring a new day to Kombonia.

Finally, Obewame, a small and compact man of an indeterminant age with an oversized voice, took the stage to rapturous applause. He began to speak, first in a lilting and soft cadence, which then grew in tone and fervor as he recited the story of the RMK and his role in it. He characterized the current system as dictatorial. He earned loud cheers when he proclaimed the people of Kombonia would be denied neither democracy, nor the victory at the polls that they deserved. Obewame then hushed the crowd and, dramatically waving his index finger, exclaimed that if the RMK was cheated out of victory, then the KRP would be responsible for what would happen next. The crowd went wild with enthusiastic cheers and applause—it was clear that they understood the veiled hint of secession underlining his comments.

Then, further displaying his gift for populist oratory, Obewame succeeded in further whipping up the crowd as he spread his arms wide and shouted into the microphone, "And do you know what?"

"What??" came back the thunderous response.

"Our huge success is being noticed around the world!" A fresh wave of cheers erupted from the crowd. "The international community supports us and our party!! As evidence," he thundered, directing his finger toward Adam, "we have a representative from the great nation of the United States here today amongst us: Mr. Adam Edwards! Mr. Edwards, please join me on the stage!"

Adam's stomach flipped; the warm Coke burbled back up his esophagus in a rush of nausea. He knew that in no way was he supposed to appear to display partisanship toward any particular party; in an instant the full and awful realization of his decision to attend the event hit him. But he was trapped, figuratively and literally. He jumped out of his seat to try to head toward an exit, but a mass of excited RMK supporters, thinking that he had lost his way en route to the stage, surged forward and, in a mosh pit–like fashion, passed his supine figure across their shoulders to the podium. Tossed onto it, Adam had to crawl on his hands and knees in front of a delighted Obewame before he had enough leverage to stand up. Adam then had no choice but to shake Obewame's hand and wave to the crowd. Then Obewame ushered him to the podium, and introduced him, in a stentorian tone, "Please tell us, the supporters of the RMK, what message do you bring to us from the American president and the people of your great country!"

Awash in humiliation, Adam was acutely aware of a certain looseness in his bowels. *How do I get out of this?* He stepped up to the microphone. "The American people support Kombonia's desire for democracy." Huge cheers. "We look forward to a peaceful and legitimate election." More rapturous applause. "And to Kombonia having a prosperous and hopeful future!" The stadium erupted in an orgy of approbation. The remarks in and of themselves were mere blather, but it didn't matter. The damage had been done.

The next half hour was one of the longest in his life as he tried, at first politely, to leave the event. He eventually resorted to shouting and using his sharp elbows to force his way out past backslapping RMK supporters cheering him on.

Eventually he got back to his house where he collapsed on the verandah, every inch of his clothing soaked in sweat. All he could focus on was the horror of what had transpired. He put his head in his hands and for a long time contemplated the experience, his lapse of judgment, and the future. He knew there would be consequences for his mistake, and he felt humiliated and manipulated. *How stupid could I have been to have fallen into Obewame's trap?* Fortunately or not, he had no other plans for the rest of the day and started drinking gin and tonics at 2:00 o'clock in the afternoon. He passed out by 5 p.m.

"Well, good job there, Mr. RMK." Harlan Stuart spewed sarcasm as he waved a copy of the RMK party newspaper with a picture of Adam and Obewame on the front cover. Adam had been summoned the following Monday to Stuart's office. "I didn't realize that you were a card-carrying member of the party. I have just heard from the ambassador. She is pissed. And so am I. Why shouldn't we put you on the first plane out of here?"

"I am so sorry," Adam blubbered miserably. "It was a huge mistake. I didn't realize what was going on."

"You didn't realize what was going on," Stuart mimicked in baby talk. "Well, what the fuck did you think was going to happen? These people here are playing a blood sport. Any one of them will chew you up and spit you out just like Obewame has done. It looks like you are in over your head here. Now get out of here. We'll talk later about what is going to happen to you."

Adam went back to his office and called Mulcahy, even though it was early in the morning his time. He explained what had happened. Mulcahy groaned. "Holy shit man, you have got to clean up your act. How could you have done that? How are you going to fix this mess? You tell me—what is your plan?"

"I have got to do something before I meet with Stuart again. Look—I have learned my lesson. I will put out a statement emphasizing CDP's neutrality. I will turn down any other invitations like this. I will set up a program with a variety of various political party representatives to start to get beyond this. I will tell Obewame that this was unacceptable and if it happens again his party will not be invited to any other CDP programs."

Mulcahy expressed doubt about the last point. "Listen dude, that particular horse has already left the barn. I doubt Obewame really cares about your reaction. You have served his purpose. And you need the RMK, as well as the KDPR and the KRP, to have a meaningful program in-country. Obewame would call your bluff in an instant. Don't go there."

The same day President Mushi called Phillip Aziz, his chief of staff, aside after a cabinet meeting. "I have heard that there is an American NGO interested in our political situation. Apparently its representative, whom I have previously heard about, made a fool of himself at the RMK rally on Saturday. I want you to look into it, and let me know if you think this is a group that we want operating in our country. You should know, by the way, that Minister Abdallah is not in favor of them."

Aziz, a sharp-witted and self-effacing individual, came from a mixed ethnic background. He was a discrete and effective bureaucratic actor; a cross between a "Mandarin"—a substantive and knowledgeable adviser—and a "Richelieu"—a suave, ruthless backroom operator. Where his own fundamental beliefs and interests lay was not clear to anyone beyond the fact that his track record was one of loyalty to Mushi, whom he had served as chief of staff for eight years. He responded quietly, "Yes, sir. I will look into it."

Chapter 10

Seminar (Part I)

The question of Adam's future hung in suspense as the news in Kombonia was dominated by another spasm of violence, with a strike by the biggest independent trade union over rising prices and government corruption. Also, Harlan Stuart's attention was diverted by a visit from a senior USAID official and a crisis in the USAID mission's HIV/AIDS program—apparently a local official had been lining his own pockets with some of the funding dedicated for community self-help projects.

So, with the passage of each day, Adam had additional time to regain his emotional balance and hope that the stadium nightmare might slip away into the mists of time. He also dove into a myriad of details in preparation for the inaugural CDP event, finding it a good way to help distance himself from the memories of the RMK rally. He hired a couple of university students to help with the logistics while Festus worked overtime, racing around the city picking up supplies, copying documents, and arranging logistics.

The program took on immediacy when Adam went to the airport to pick up the four international political party experts that he, with assistance from CDP headquarters, had identified and invited to serve as the faculty for the program. The first to arrive was Clement Ndongwe, a young and rising member of one of the leading opposition parties in Malawi. The other three arrived on the same Lufthansa flight from Frankfurt that Adam had taken. They included Matyas Fuchs, a veteran Hungarian opposition party leader; Kartika, a hijab-wearing leading voice for women's rights in the Indonesian ruling party; and Lisa Rentjens, a senior Belgian member of parliament and secretary-general of the Flemish Christian Social party, a small member of the governing coalition.

After arriving in Kayemba City, the internationals moved directly into a day-long series of briefings about the country and the program. These included a long session on Kombonian politics led by Yusuf and Victor Mbuya, a colleague of Yusuf's from the political science department at the University of Kombonia. The presentations and ensuing discussions between the Kombonians and the internationals were lively—Yusuf's and Victor's perspectives on the democratic transition gave the internationals a comprehensive and objective overview of the country's political evolution since the advent of multipartyism in 1992. They also provided background information on the Kombonian political parties. That night Adam reported back to Mulcahy in DC that things seemed to be going well—the initial briefing gave the internationals a chance to interact with each other and to start developing a shared group dynamic.

The internationals also began to acquire a sense of some of the challenges confronting Kombonian political parties, including the lack of genuine ideological differences and their ethnic and regional support. Other key issues included challenges in raising money for parties, limited access to state-controlled media by opposition parties, and a frequent lack of party discipline. This was evidenced by what were charitably referred to as "inducements" offered by parties, especially the KRP, to have their opponents switch their loyalty; a phenomenon locally known as "political hopscotch." The internationals were not especially surprised by this problem, which Fuchs noted was fairly common in countries such as his seeking to develop a multiparty system after years of single-party domination.

The next day the internationals and the CDP staff traveled to Melinda in three separate vehicles. Adam rode with Yusuf and Rentjens. As they sat in a jarring four-by-four drive on an unpaved track through the arid Kombonian bush, Adam mentioned Walter Kocinski's somewhat flippant comment back in Washington about democracy requiring 1,000 years to take root in a place like Kombonia.

Yusuf grunted in reaction, and said, "Your friend is partly correct. The challenge really is how to shape your so-called modern democratic institutions to reflect the reality of Kombonia. As you know, for example, we have many different ethnic groups…and a violent history between them. It seems to me that your American and British emphasis on the rights of the individual, coming from your political philosophers such as John Locke, appears out of place here in Africa in general and particularly here in Kombonia. Our tradition is based much more on our own community, which is mostly defined along ethnic lines. Being part of it is important. It is how we stay alive when times are difficult; by helping each other and being helped as needed. In fact, in some French-speaking countries here in Africa there are groups that could be called 'civic organizations,' which protect the rights of members of their own ethnic groups. I think the term used for them in French-speaking countries captures the idea—they are called *mutuelles*."

"Hmmm…so what you're saying is really interesting," Adam replied, impressed as usual by Yusuf's knowledge and range of information. "But how does this emphasis on community, as opposed to the individual, play out in terms of how democracy should function and be structured?"

Yusuf took a minute to chew on a stick of *werek*, from a gum tree, a method many Kombonians used to clean their teeth. "Well, take elections for example." You Anglo-Saxons use terms like 'battle,' 'fight,' and 'defeat' with regard to them. That makes us uneasy because we have a long history of tension and fighting between ethnic groups. This could easily lead to bloodshed—which, after all, is already occurring even now, months before the election. We want democracy to bring our country together, not divide it."

"OK," Adam concurred, "but democracy is about winning and losing. You can't get away from that."

"My friend," Yusuf replied somberly, "if that is all that democracy is about, then countries like Kombonia have no democratic future. We cannot simply have winners and losers. We cannot afford that luxury, especially since we place emphasis on our community, rather than the individual. For us, that system would mean whole sectors of society are winners or losers, not just this or that person. That would tear this country apart. You can see, right now, how tense things are. If we don't figure how to create a set of democratic structures and processes that are appropriate for Kombonia, we will be destroyed. This is why people are so tense. So much is at stake."

"Are you saying that what we are doing here could contribute to this place blowing up?" Adam asked in a frustrated, and to be honest, somewhat petulant tone. He was getting pissed off at Yusuf's academic tone and somewhat contrarian method of communicating.

Yusuf chose his words carefully. "What I am saying is that we have to be very cautious in choosing our democratic institutions.

They must benefit as many people as possible. Do not forget that we had a formal democracy 'given' to us by the British at independence. But it did not last long. The British somehow thought that they could simply transplant their beautiful House of Commons here, and all would be well. Well, we are not Britain. We are Kombonia, even though, I admit, its heritage looms over us in strange ways—you may have noticed for example, that our judges still wear wigs, as in Britain.

"Let me give you an example of how we need different institutions than Britain's. As you know, the British—and you Americans, too—use what you call the 'first-past-the-post' method for your legislative elections. Other people call it the 'majoritarian' system. Whomever receives more votes than the other candidates wins. Simple, and democratic right? You also have it for your presidential elections, if you put aside your rather, shall we say, 'unique' electoral college process.

"So, the British gave us this method. What we have seen is that it pits candidates against each other in the 'fight.' They are, in a sense, Roman gladiators battling until one person is left standing. Well, we are uncomfortable with this. We could see this ripping apart the country. We agree that elections are important and are a key part of democracy, but we want them to be more peaceful, less confrontational. That is why some of who have knowledge about these issues have thought that these elections—for what we hope with all our hearts will be the first truly democratic Kombonian parliament in the country's history—should be done using a proportional representation system, or PR. In that system you vote for a party, not for an individual. It is thus less personal, less individualistic. Also, we know that your system limits the number of parties represented. By using PR, more viewpoints can end up being represented in parliament. It minimizes the number of losers. It would be good for Kombonia."

At this point Rentjens, who had been quietly but intensely following the conversation, spoke up. "You know people sometimes ask me about our situation in Belgium. You see, we have two main groups, the Flemish and the Walloons, who basically can't stand each other. We use PR, and it helps. But we have also basically created a parallel governance system where there are many various levels and there is much duplication of effort, with separate parties and administrative structures existing in the two regions. I often hear criticisms of what we have created; it is too complicated, unwieldy, and expensive. And do you know what? All of these points are valid. But they miss the main point: they are cheaper than a civil war."

Yusuf nodded in agreement. "You are so right. But where would we here get the money to pay for all of that?"

Later that night, Yusuf returned to the theme of democracy in the African context. After they had had a couple of beers, Yusuf fixed his gaze on Adam and Rentjens and said in his rather formalistic manner, "There is something else you need to know, my friends. You Westerners think you are bringing democracy to Africa. You think we are primitive and have only had tribal chiefs in our history, deciding everything. I know that CDP and people like you have a more nuanced view of this, but overall, it is true that you think we have no experience with democracy. Well, let me tell you something. Do you know what the baobab tree is?"

Rentjens allowed as to how she had heard that it was a large tree found in Africa.

"Well, that is not all. It is often in the center of a village since it casts a wide, soothing shade. People often meet underneath it to socialize and talk, and seek compromises and settle disputes. It represents the bridging of differences and the fostering of unity. It is also known as the palaver, or discussion, tree. The idea of compromise- and consensus-building is known in the Tswana language of southern Africa as *kgotla*. More broadly, it has always been a key part of our African heritage. Now, I ask you—are not the concepts of the palaver tree and *kgotla*—where people are free to speak to one another, to air out and solve problems—are they not what your Congress in Washington or the Houses of Parliament in London do? Do they not reflect a fundamental aspect of a democratic political culture?

"And, while I am on the subject, do you know anything about the Oromo people in Ethiopia?"

Somewhat nonplussed by the seeming change in topic, Adam had to admit that his knowledge of them was limited or, to be honest, almost nonexistent.

"The Oromo have a tradition whereby their ruler changes every seven years. A council of elders chooses who is to be the new leader. They do this to ensure that no one ruler becomes entrenched in power. Does that sound familiar to your Western notion of presidential term limits? This system, which is called *gaada*, also has a division of power among executive, legislative, and judicial branches, balanced opposition among different political parties, and power sharing between offices to prevent power from falling into the hands of despots. So please do not think we are illiterate waifs, with no references to point us toward democracy in your more, quote, 'modern sense.'"

With the pressure of the job, Adam found himself beginning to develop a habit of continually reviewing in his mind each action that needed to happen from day one through the conclusion of a project—like one of those old-fashioned movie picture precursors, where a spinning drum with peepholes magically conferred the impression of movement. It was amazing how reviewing the same hour period of time could continually reveal previously hidden details that needed attending.

So on the first day of the seminar, Adam woke early, not having slept well. He kept running the almost minute-by-minute set of logistical details through his mind. Were there name cards and pens? Was the overhead projector functioning? Were the international presenters adequately briefed? In what order should he introduce the seminar participants? Had the right type and amount of food been ordered? Was there enough space in breakout rooms for group work? What would happen if people who had not been invited wished to attend? And on and on.

One issue that Adam had wrestled with in planning the event was which parties should be invited to send representatives, and how many. After all, there were more than one hundred registered parties in the country. Many of them were "suitcase parties" created by one or two individuals, usually wealthy, which had little chance of garnering significant support. Often the rationale for such parties was simply that they could sell their support to a larger party, or perhaps their existence was a vanity project on the part of the founder.

Adam had spent time worrying about how to limit the number

of parties represented at the seminar. Aware of the highly sensitive nature of the issue, he had decided that the criterion for seminar participation should be those parties that had elected representatives to the National Assembly whether or not they were participating in parliament. Adam thought that this was a shrewd way to include the RMK since it was an important party, even though it had opted not to take up its seats in the parliament.

At the opening session's coffee break, as participants, staff, and internationals milled about, Adam found himself next to a man outfitted in a traditional chieftain's garb, including a beautiful multihued cloth, beads, and a fly whisk. Adam was somewhat startled when he welcomed Adam in a deep voice redolent with a cultured British accent. Adam complimented him on his English, to which he replied in a friendly, but slightly sanctimonious, manner, "Yes, well, I did attend Jesus College at Cambridge, you know." He also introduced himself as Edwin Kombula, chief of the "paramount" Ome subclan, as he described it.

Adam then took the opportunity to ask him what the role of a traditional chief is in contemporary Kombonia. Kombula's response was quick. "We play a very important part in this country's life—in many different ways. The people believe in us; they see us as embodying their past and present. We are a source of knowledge, experience, and authority. Even people who move to Kayemba City still follow the traditions of our people."

Adam asked whether there was a conflict between the traditional way of governance and the formal institutions of the modern state.

"We think not, as long as the government respects and does not interfere with us. We are interested in helping our people learn how to govern themselves. But we also want to keep our traditions and ways of doing things."

"Yes sir, but what about the future?" came a surprising interjection from a younger seminar participant idling nearby. His name tag indicated that he was from the KDPR.

"My son," the chief replied in an icy voice, "perhaps you will learn that the future cannot arrive unless you know the past and who you are. And what impertinence is," he added archly.

Seeking to move beyond the resulting uncomfortable silence, Adam queried the chief, "How do you draw the line on what power you have, as opposed to the government?"

"Well, you see, there are many topics which have to be taken care of by the national government, like foreign relations, and keeping peace and order throughout the country. But there are many issues where we have good communication with the government representatives in our region; such as where to locate health clinics, what roads need to be maintained, how to ensure that our farmers get fertilizer. So, we have to work this out based on dialogue and mutual respect."

Later in the coffee break, Adam asked the younger participant what he thought of the leader. He snorted. "He and his type are simply in the pay of the KRP. They are toadies. Did you know that the government pays them to be agreeable and not create waves? The younger people do not follow them so much anymore—they are discredited."

The seminar program was divided into five distinct components. Prior to the official opening, the internationals, along with CDP staff, held preliminary meetings with all invited parties. Then, after the opening ceremonies, the seminar's initial day was to include the first plenary session, which allowed the internationals to present their respective organizations and field questions from participants. In the afternoon, discussion groups would explore in more detail the nature, functioning, and activities of each political international movement. The following day was to be taken up by interactive workshops, where they would use hypothetical case studies to examine issues related to party organization, platform development, and coalition building. Finally, in accordance with the Kombonian penchant for formality, an official closing ceremony would be held.

Approximately eighty people attended the opening ceremonies, including members of the diplomatic corps and the government, representatives of nongovernmental organizations, the press, and seminar participants. Local televised, radio, and print media coverage was provided for the opening and closing ceremonies. Adam was unpleasantly surprised when, as participants gathered for the opening, Festus informed him that the journalists were asking for payment to cover the event.

"What the hell!" he exclaimed. "Don't they have any self-respect? Do they just allow themselves to get purchased like this? What about the independence of the media? There should be a separation between media and those being covered!"

The omnipresent Yusuf heard this exchange and hurried over to calm Adam down. "Listen to me," he said. "These people hardly get any pay. It is common practice that if you want your event to be covered, you have to give them something. Otherwise there won't be much of any media here except that which is allied to the government."

"But that means they cannot be objective in their coverage!"

"Perhaps. But would it be better for there to be no coverage at all?"

Adam didn't like it at all but relented. "Well, OK, if we absolutely have to, we will give them $10 a day. But I still think this is bullshit!"

After the opening ceremonies, which featured a lengthy recitation of Kombonia's progress toward democracy from the KRP's perspective by the Minister for the Promotion of Democracy and Human Rights, the initial plenary working session was presented by Adam. He was to provide an overview of the issues to be addressed and, as he tried to refocus from the journalist pay issue, was nervous and excited to get going with the program. He had thought it important to provide the first substantive presentation himself, to set the tone for the rest of the program. Little did he know that he was in for a surprise. After an initial round of introductions Adam looked out over the audience of about fifty participants, cleared his throat, and began.

"Welcome to you all. It is an honor and a privilege for my colleagues and I"—he gestured to the international team—"to be here to consider with you how political parties can function and compete in a democratic political environment. First, let's step back and ask a basic question: Are there prerequisites for democracy in terms of education level, income, and development of civil society? Not necessarily…we can look at the Indian subcontinent to see that. India, Bangladesh, and Sri Lanka all have democratic traditions, although admittedly their democratic consolidation faces challenges." Adam sought here to subtly suggest that even countries with impoverished parts of the population, such as Kombonia, could develop democratic institutions.

"In general, there are three types of democratic transitions. First, an autocracy can open up and democratize the country, such as what has happened in countries as different and varied as Mexico, Ghana, and Mozambique. Second, a popular revolution can overthrow a dictatorship and install a democracy; this happened in what was then Czechoslovakia, as well as in the Philippines. Third, an ongoing struggle between autocracy/dictatorship and democracy can take place. The struggle lasts as long as the autocrats believe they can win. Once the recognition occurs that this is not possible, they then negotiate. Part of this is due to a slow collapse in the will of the autocrats/dictators to impose themselves on a population that grew increasingly tired of their proclivity for civil strife. This has happened in countries including South Africa and Poland." *This should give you folks food for thought as to how your democracy could evolve.*

"As important, if not more so, in these emerging democracies was the ability of their political party leaders to do three things: construct effective coalitions, build their party's legitimacy, and create a positive vision of the future. This workshop today is about these three topics. Note that they all begin with action verbs. You can control what you do. You cannot control what the others will do. But by doing the three things above, you will be able to come out the winners. It may not be today or tomorrow, but it will happen." *Damn, not a bad pep talk if I say so myself.*

Toward the end of his presentation, however, Adam began to feel that the body language of the participants and overall vibe in the room were a bit odd and disconnected to his discourse. He did not feel much energy from the participants, whose expressions remained uniformly passive despite his attempts to engender some type of positive reaction. *What is going wrong here? Am I not getting through to them?* He found it increasingly distracting and difficult to continue with his remarks, and noticed that his armpits were starting to become sticky, and he was perspiring on his face.

He then did what he often did in challenging situations, where he felt under pressure. He resorted to humor in order to break the communication logjam, expressing the first funny thought that entered his mind. He remarked upon the staid miens of the party representatives, asked them to relax, and joked, "You all remind me of the Soviet Politburo!"

This certainly got their attention; there was an immediate rustling in the room as participants stirred about. Adam was momentarily pleased that he had shaken things up and was get-ting a reaction until he realized, with a growing feeling of horror, that the response was not a happy one. Indeed, one participant's hand shot up, and he said in a tone of suppressed anger, "You have just insulted us. We have come here out of respect to hear what you have to say, and you treat us in this fashion?? How dare you do that!"

Oh my God my armpits are wet and I think I am about to vomit. I can't believe I have screwed up again. In order to buy time and get a handle on what had just happened, Adam quickly suggested, "Let's have a coffee break." During this pause, he sought out a number of the participants milling about in a state of near revolt. One of them, an opposition party member, hissed, "Do not ever compare us to a communist dictatorship. We are ready to die for the freedom which has been denied to us."

Adam gulped. "I am so, so sorry. I did not mean to insult you. Please answer me one question, though. When I was speaking, before I made this mistake, I got the impression that participants were not interested in what I was saying. Was that true?"

"Not at all sir!" came the emphatic reply. "What you were saying is very important and relevant to us. But you need to understand that we Kombonians tend to be somewhat reserved until we feel that we know people—this is especially true regarding someone like yourself who is not from here."

Adam realized, with bitter amusement, that he at least seemed to have created common ground between the united and opposition parties, since a representative of the latter separately buttonholed Adam and said in a rather haughty manner, "Mr. Edwards, the government of this country is doing all that it can to forge a democracy here. And yet you have just compared us to a totalitarian autocracy. Why don't you go home since you clearly do not understand the reality of the situation here?"

Seeking a calmer port in the storm, Adam beseeched a member of the British foreign aid agency, who was present observing the seminar, what to do. With a bemused world-weary tone, he opined, "You, my good man, have shall we say royally fucked up? You Americans so often think that everyone thinks the way you do. The Kombonians do not understand your informal sense of humor. They do not get that you weren't insulting them. You need to learn about not only Kombonian history but also their more formal way of doing things. And you had better make amends to them quickly."

By now, Adam's shirt was thoroughly soaked through, and his dignity and self-confidence were once again, as after the RMK rally fiasco, in tatters. Perhaps paradoxically, the humbling reality of having seemingly hit rock bottom made his next task easier. After the coffee break, he asked for the participants' attention and simply said, "I recognize that I have offended you. I did not mean to do this, but that is what I did. I am very, very sorry for having done so. I pledge to you that I will learn from this incident, and that no disrespect was intended." The reaction of the participants could only be characterized as begrudging in nature, but at least Adam was not faced with a walkout. *I will never ever again resort to adlibbed humor to defuse a tense cross-cultural situation.* He had learned the hard way how risky it can be to assume that humor would translate well.

Chapter 11

Seminar (Part II)

The seminar's atmosphere improved after Adam made his apology. The proceedings then shifted to the workshops directed by the international faculty offering technical training and advice. They exchanged experiences with their Kombonian counterparts on a range of issues, including party organization, coalition building, and party platform development. The workshops were conducted in a roundtable environment, with comments and suggestions recorded on large flip charts. Participants were divided into three groups, each of which rotated between the three workshops.

The party organization workshop was led by Rentjens and Ndongwe. They encouraged participants to plan for practical activities that could be undertaken by parties in a non-electoral period to expand their membership base, establish clear party structures, and recruit candidates. A timeline of activities was developed in a hypothetical run-up to the elections.

Rentjens spoke first to the group of twenty. She noted that, "Parties have to mobilize outside of their geographic and social bases. You need a 'big tent' approach to political organizing, targeting appeals to interest groups, and thereby broadening a party's constituency."

"What are the best ways to do that?" asked a skeptical member of the KDPR. "Do you understand the challenge we have of doing this, given our limited resources?"

Ndongwe was emphatic in his reply. "As a matter of fact, I do. We have had the same problem in Malawi. We have found that you need to take some soundings, to develop an idea of what the issues motivating people are, and which topics you can use to appeal to them. A few years ago, our party leadership thought they knew what people in northern Malawi were concerned about. But when we learned about focus groups and how to use them to find out what people were thinking, we received a rude surprise. They weren't so interested in the national-level issues that preoccupied our leadership; they were much more interested in local and day-to-day issues. We made sure to place a lot of emphasis on solving those problems at the time of the next campaign, and received greater support than previously."

Fuchs's platform-development workshop sessions focused on how party policies are shaped, especially from a process-oriented perspective. He began by asking the participants to write down the three issues about which their parties were most concerned.

Fuchs then shared the input, noting that, "There are three themes that seem to stand out in your replies. First, poverty reduction and economic development; second, respect for human rights; and third, limiting corruption."

Most participants nodded their assent.

"So, these are very worthy issues. But have you noticed that all parties are raising the same issues, and that they tend to be very general? How do you differentiate your party from others?"

"We need to show that we can solve these problems better than other parties."

"Yes," Fuchs replied, "but isn't it also important to make sure that you know what the people want, so there is broad-based input into platform development?"

One participant, a woman in a brightly colored garb and head-dress, asked, "How do you do this? Is it not the parties' purpose to, in effect, 'deliver the goods' to our core supporters? Others will then come along if they see that we can be effective. So we don't have the resources or even the need to appeal to everyone."

"Well, I'd suggest that parties in Kombonia may need to move beyond narrow political cleavages and be more inclusive. You can, for example, establish roving commissions to gather grassroots input. These should be broad-based. The name of the game, after all, is to generate enough support to be the winner. Usually that doesn't come from simply appealing to your core supporters or hoping that others will simply be attracted like magnets to your party. You have to build outward."

The coalition-building scenario/exercise led by Kartika focused on the importance of party ideology and policies as determinants in plans for forming a coalition with another party. She posed a key question: "Under what conditions and rationale would your party consider joining in coalitions, or otherwise collaborate with other parties?" Subsidiary questions included: Collaborate with whom? And on what bases?

Political ethics were discussed, including whether interparty relationships should be founded on fundamental common interests, or whether they could be viewed more as marriages of convenience. One participant observed, "If parties existed on solely ideological and policy bases, there wouldn't be more than five or six in the country. In reality they are more personality based."

Another participant concurred. "That's right—parties in

Kombonia seem more like organizations created to defend politicians' selfish interests, the interests of a region and/or a particular ethnic group rather than to defend a political ideology. While many parties say they adhere to an ideology, in practice they seem more like mechanisms for short-term political and financial gain."

Adam, who had woken up refreshed after a surprisingly deep sleep, was sitting in on this workshop and was very pleased, as he saw that the participants were moving beyond their own narrow party perspectives, and thinking more objectively about how parties can and should function in a democracy. *Damn—this thing may actually be working!*

Adam and the internationals then unveiled their hypothetical exercise, which presented participants with a set of issues that Kombonian political parties could usefully focus upon as the country neared elections. With help from the CDP Washington office and Yusuf, Adam had written and distributed to each participant a case study centered around the fictitious country of Kwoupou, which was encountering a political crisis somewhat similar to Kombonia. Some of the key themes involved the internal structure of parties, coalition building, dealing with resource constraints, grassroots and interest group input, message development, mechanics of campaigning, and election administration.

The hypothetical scenario turned out to be a huge success. Initially hesitant and unused to pedagogy including fictitious scenarios, the participants warmed to the idea and were able to address the same challenges to political party development that they faced on a daily basis in a constructive manner.

Seminar participants were asked to imagine themselves as members of various political parties in Kwoupou. Adam had had the good idea of assigning participants an identity in a Kwoupian party different from their Kombonian reality. Thus, actual KRP participants were assigned membership in opposition parties, while members of the KDPR and RMK became members of the ruling party. The idea was to familiarize the participants with the perspectives, orientations, and imperatives of their real-life opponents in order to be 'in their shoes,' better understand them, and hopefully promote mutual understanding.

Later in the afternoon, Adam couldn't constrain his excitement and relief that the session was going so well, especially in light of the previous day's debacle, and told Yusuf, "Man, I am so psyched that things seem to be going so well here!"

Yusuf, who was usually on the demure side, actually shared his elation. "I agree. What makes me very happy is that I have seen the ability of participants from the different parties, who are usually at each others' throats, to work together in these workshops."

By the close of the day, the participants had entered fully into the spirit of the exercise, even parading through the plenary meeting hall with a handmade Kwoupian flag and singing a hastily written and composed Kwoupian national anthem.

The next day, the participants built on the previous days' experiences to develop a series of multipartisan recommendations on how the functioning of Kombonian politics could be improved for all. One key political-organization issue raised by opposition-party participants was the need to distinguish state resources from party resources. Cognizant of the tradition of party-state collusion in Kombonia, participants recommended that state resources should not be employed to benefit a party as it develops its campaign strategy and/or organizational capacities. In addition, participants identified several specific activities that could be emphasized during the non-electoral period. These included analysis of human, material, and financial resources, identification of target groups, and outreach to traditional leaders of opinion as a means of preparing the party, before the electoral period, to become a 'campaign machine.' Finally, participants also focused on the need to expand a party's base of support by having local and regional input into the selection of candidates.

The platform-development workshop recognized the need to consider different societal groups when determining the issues that would form the focus of a party's platform. To poll the issues important to these groups, participants proposed contacting and interviewing the groups' leaders. At the same time, they recognized that arriving at a balance between these disparate groups and the party's traditional bases of support would be essential. Party structures, namely subcommittees, should be established to examine platform-specific issues and reflect the different components of society. The committees would be firstly composed of high-profile party members, and then others representing various segments of society.

The coalition-building case study was the last workshop report to be presented and also raised the most questions from participants. The workshop members emphasized that skills and ability to create coalitions could be the difference between the success or failure of a democracy. This would be especially true in the absence of one party gaining a majority. At the same time, they recognized the problems inherent in adversaries having to negotiate contructively with each other. Concerns were raised about the possibility of one party trying to 'purchase' the loyalty of other party members. There was further discussion about how far parties should forsake their interests and policies to form a coalition at any price. These topics reflected the participants' wrestling with the tough questions of how to deal with nuts and bolts of democratic governance.

One participant summed up the proceedings when he told Adam, "You know this business of democracy is so complex—the devil is truly in the details."

Adam concurred and added, "It is indeed tough but the alternative—dictatorship—is much worse."

"You do not have to remind we Kombonians of that."

The seminar's conclusion took longer than Adam would have liked. Realizing that an attachment to formal procedures and protocol was a part of the way Kombonians did things, Adam understood the need to 'go with the flow' on this, and was patient. Everyone assembled in the main auditorium, dressed in their finest clothes.

Adam made closing comments. "I am so pleased that participants have successfully worked together across party lines. This reflects an important element of a democratic culture—that political actors can be opponents, but not enemies."

Kartika then addressed the group. Speaking with some emotion, she stated, "I do not know how much my new Kombonian friends have benefited from my presence, but I am profoundly aware that I have learned and gained so much from my interactions with you. I will take much valuable knowledge back to Indonesia with me."

After some discussion amongst themselves, the participants decided that one representative from each party should also make a closing statement. A KRP representative stated, "Despite the small problem that you encountered on the first day, somehow you and your colleagues have helped us put aside our fixation on the current political situation here—as understandable as that is—and provided the opportunity for a mutual reflection on what is needed to compete with other parties in a democratic way. We appreciate that very, very much."

A KDPR representative gave heartfelt thanks. "I didn't think I would have much to learn from you. What could you, coming from America, Hungary, Indonesia, Belgium, or Malawi know that could help us here in our Kombonian context? After all, you don't know, really know, the Kombonian reality. But then when you started to speak—of the government limiting newsprint, misusing resources, subtly manipulating the process—I began to forget where you came from; you were talking about things that concern us here, too. I started to realize that we speak a common language. We share this, and I suspect many other things in common. This makes me think that we have these connections around the world, that after all human nature is not that different."

Adam's eyes glistened as he listened, feeling, for the first time, the power of being able to share, to communicate across cultures, to have an impact. It made all the crap worth it.

An interminable reception then ensued. Adam was exhausted by all the ceremony formalities, but more fundamentally by the stress of the entire seminar. *Organizing an event like this in an unfamiliar culture and difficult environment takes it out of you.* There were especially challenging logistics—copying machines were at a minimum, to cite just one example—beyond the substance of ensuring that the presentations and activities were meaningful and relevant to the participants. And that was before taking the whole 'Soviet Politburo' self-inflicted wound into account.

Immediately afterward Adam received another unpleasant surprise when he heard a commotion occurring in the conference center entryway. A table had been set up where participants could receive reimbursements for their travel expenses to and from the seminar. Angry voices were erupting, and the atmosphere was quickly getting tense. One of the CDP program assistants, Anthony, rushed up with a panicked look on his face. "Oh Mr. Edwards, we've got a problem; these people are asking for their per diem payments for attending the seminar! They want money!"

Adam was taken aback by this news that participants were expecting some sort of payment. His reaction was a flash of anger—first the damn press and now the participants themselves...CDP was busting its chops to help these people, and all they wanted was money! His next feeling was the panic of helplessness—*what should we do??* He rushed off to find Yusuf, who was in a deep conversation with a couple of participants.

Pulling him aside, Adam said urgently, "Do you know what is going on here? Why the hell are these people trying to extort us? Why didn't we know about this earlier?"

Yusuf took a deep breath and told Adam, "First, please calm down. You are the leader here. You may be scared inside, but above all, do not show it. Second, yes, these people want some money. But you need to understand this is the way that things are done in our country. Any time an international organization comes here and organizes a seminar, they pay participants a per diem to attend."

"That sucks!" Adam exclaimed. "Is that why they are here—to get money? Don't they care about democracy?"

"A desire for money and democracy is not exclusive, my friend," Yusuf counseled. "Many of these people are not well off. They have had to take time off from their work, and the women have had to leave their children. This is not something that can easily be done. Things are not black and white in this regard."

Adam did a slow burn. "So, you think we should pay money—

for which we have not budgeted—to placate these people. This is just like the freaking journalists!"

Yusuf gave a slow nod of assent.

"How much?"

"Five dollars a day should be sufficient."

Fighting back his anger, Adam told Anthony that the participants should each get that amount of money. One hundred participants multiplied by $5 multiplied by three days…$1,500 that would have to come out of the budget somewhere, assuming that the USAID accountants would permit a shift in line items. *What a way to do business.*

In the rush to leave Melinda and return to Kayemba City, Adam didn't notice a slim, attractive Kombonian woman hanging out near the front entrance to the hotel. She had her eyes on him, however. Adam was haggling with the hotel desk clerk over the bill, while other members of his team were waiting for him in the four-wheel drive. Finally, he finished with the hotel and hustled out toward the car, only to be stopped by the woman.

"Your friend didn't pay me." She seethed with indignance. "You should pay me."

"Excuse me?" replied Adam hurriedly, "I am trying to get to my vehicle, and I have no idea what you are talking about."

"Your friend, the big man from Malawi who just left a while ago."

It dawned upon Adam that she was referring to Ndongwe, but he still didn't know what she was talking about. "What do you mean?" he queried.

"We did it, but he didn't pay me. You pay me money now or else," she demanded.

Shocked, Adam half-choked as the meaning of the woman's words sank in. He didn't want to find out what "or else" meant.

"Oh my God," he exclaimed. "You mean to tell me that you are a…and he and you…" The words didn't need to be spoken. The woman nodded. *That bastard. He is now headed toward Kayemba City leaving me to sort out this type of mess.* Desperately, Adam glanced at the full four-wheel drive, with curious faces pressed to the window. A gaggle of young children with outstretched hands, and other interested locals, was starting to form; their curiosity fed by the atmosphere of confrontation that was beginning to permeate the setting.

Oh my God, I've got to get out of this situation quickly! Fuck it—I'll pay and deal with Ndongwe later. I hope the House Committee on Appropriations and the USAID Inspector General's office never hear about this. This is too effing much.

Adam pulled out $15 in Kombonian currency, shoved it at the woman, and hurried toward his vehicle.

***

Not surprisingly, Adam let out a huge sigh of relief as Melinda faded in their rearview mirror. Before leaving, Adam had asked Festus if there was a different route they could follow so he could see more of Kombonia. The latter consulted with the hotel desk clerk and returned with the news that they could take a loop to the west of Melinda, which would then join up at the main road about halfway back to Kayemba City.

The road, although unpaved, was pretty good. In high spirits and enjoying the release of tension from the seminar, Adam queried Festus, "Hey, I have heard that in some countries in the region, like Benin and Togo, they practice voodoo."

"Indeed," Festus replied. "In fact where I am from in the south, voodoo is important—it protects us from bad things." Adam noticed that Yusuf tried to shush Festus up, apparently disapproving of such talk.

Although Adam didn't think Festus was pulling his leg, he wasn't sure, so he decided just for the heck of it to follow up. "What do you mean that it protects you? I thought that the whole point of voodoo is that someone can cast an evil spell on you and make bad things happen."

"Ah, Mr. Adam," came the wizened reply. "That is only part of the story. There is protection against an evil spell. If you are fortunate, you can have a *contre*."

Adam was definitely paying attention now. "Excuse me, but what the hell is a *contre*?"

"That is a French word, used in former French colonies like Togo. It means 'against.' It is a good spell which kills the bad spell. For example, one of my villagers once stole a cow from a village a few miles away, and the victim cast a spell on our entire village. Luckily, however," Festus brightened, "my family has not been affected because we have a *contre*."

"So how do you get a *contre*? Why doesn't just everyone have one—sort of like a vaccine protection?" Adam's tongue was firmly pressed against his cheek.

"It was given to my forefathers and has been passed down through the generations," Festus responded vaguely, thus avoiding the specificity that Adam had sought.

Adam decided that Festus was totally serious. By now Yusuf's face had frozen into a self-contained shell, something Adam noticed that happened when Kombonians often sought to mask their emotions. Perhaps, Adam thought, a perverse legacy of the stiff upper lip of the English education tradition. Not for the first time, and nor for the last, Adam was struck by the realization that he had a lot to learn about this place. *Maybe I should try to acquire some magic while I am here…kind of like a traditional insurance policy.*

Unfortunately, Adam's need for a *contre* was again manifested soon enough. After about an hour, by which time they had left Melinda far behind but were still in Tuyunu territory, the Toyota's engine coughed several times and then died. The four-wheel drive drifted to a stop in the middle of some scrubland. Festus popped the hood and spent a minute tinkering with the engine. He tried the ignition again, but to no avail. A burst of Ome invective passed between Yusuf and Festus, with Festus angrily gesticulating back in the direction of Melinda.

"OK, what's going on?" Adam asked in an overly patient voice, which did little to mask his own growing frustration. The last thing he needed was to be fucked up in the boondocks.

Festus answered. "The damn Tuyunu. They gave us bad watered-down gasoline when I had the car filled up this morning. I knew that we were taking a chance but there was not much we could do about it."

Festus's morosity deepened. "It is now 5 p.m. I doubt that any repair can get here before dark, and you do not want to travel after the sun sets. I am afraid, Mr. Adam, that we will have to spend the night here."

The three men sat thinking. "Here" appeared to consist of an unyielding stretch of Kombonian bushland, only broken by a nearby signpost indicating that this location was Kilometer Ninety-two between Melinda and Kayemba City. As Adam scanned the horizon in despair, however, he saw a village shimmering through the heat in the distance and what appeared to be a crowd of people, led by running children, advancing toward them. *Oh shit, what are we in for now?*

Concerned about what would happen next, Adam unlimbered his frame and clambered out of the vehicle with Festus. Soon the group of about twenty children had reached them and an uneasy quiet enveloped the scene. Then one kid looked all the way up and pointed at Adam, who towered over them, and mimed dribbling a basketball around him. Getting into the spirit of the moment, Adam pretended to have been totally faked out by the basketball move, and the kids figuratively collapsed in collective laughter.

The tension of the moment was broken. As the adult villagers caught up with the children, Adam invited Yusuf to come out and meet them. He declined, saying that he preferred to stay in the vehicle. One of the adults gestured for them to accompany the group back to the village. Festus and Adam glanced at each other, both deciding that it might be best to comply. By the time they reached the outskirts of the village Adam asked Festus to find out where the village headman could be found. He needn't have expended that effort, because soon a tall, elderly man bedecked with ornamental clothing made his way through the crowd, introduced himself as the chief, and addressed them in a welcoming voice. Adam nudged Festus, "What the hell is he saying?"

"I don't know," he replied in a clipped tone. "I don't speak Tuyunu." Adam mentally slapped his forehead with the palm of his hand. *God—I always have to remember who doesn't like whom in this damn country.*

"Well, do you think anyone here speaks Ome?" Nervously, Festus suggested they not pursue that line of inquiry.

The ensuing silence was broken by a voice behind him saying "How about good old American English?" Shocked, Adam turned to see an attractive American woman of maybe twenty-five smiling at him.

"My God," he exclaimed. "Who are you and what are you doing here?"

Laughing, she stretched out her hand and responded, "Hi, I'm Lisa Johansson. I'm in the Peace Corps here—I'm the local English teacher." Looking around at the children who surrounded them she said, "Good afternoon, children."

"Good afternoon, Miss Johansson," rang out dozens of sing-song voices, in an attempt at unison. Adam looked around, and saw the village chief sharing in the common laughter. Fifteen minutes later they were seated in his hut. The chief was obviously very proud of having Lisa in his village. Adam was served bowls of a savory stew; he preferred not to contemplate its ingredients. Using broken English the elder complimented Lisa on her teaching work in the village, and with a flourish correctly pronounced the name of Lisa's hometown, Minnetonka, Minnesota. Upon Adam's prompting he also explained the types of crops grown by the villagers, and noted that a big change in recent years had been the introduction of cell phones. No one in his village was rich enough to own and maintain one, but a couple of enterprising villagers had pooled money to buy and rent them out for calls.

As dusk fell, Adam was accompanied by the villagers, including a large gaggle of children, back to his car. Feeling a tad impish, he started singing a line from the Mickey Mouse theme song along the way. Captivated by a tune that they had never heard before, the children joined in with glee. They quickly picked up that the game was to repeat the refrain, so off-key renditions of "M-I-C-K-E-Y, M-O-U-S-E" rang out from lusty, young Kombonian throats. Then, Adam turned even more mischievous, and started singing "Rule Britannia." No one understood the worlds or appreciated its irony of being sung in rural Kombonia, once a British colony, but that didn't matter. Many disappointed kids departed back to their village when the singing was over, but the experience invigorated Adam, who was a ham at heart.

Adam returned to the vehicle. Festus had bad news. "I have been able to speak with the automobile repair shop in Kayemba City. With the curfew in place, they will definitely not be able to come here until tomorrow morning."

Yusuf remained in the vehicle, with a sullen expression frozen on his face. "What's your problem now?" Adam asked.

Yusuf responded, "Spending an uncomfortable night out here was not part of our arrangement. Also, I do not trust these people."

Adam didn't have a lot of patience for this. "OK, so it isn't going to be comfortable. The car broke down. Live with it. These are good folks here. Make do. Aren't you Kombonian? This is part of your country too. You should be out talking to these people, learning about them as human beings. You'll get a beautiful night out under the stars. Why stay stuck up in this car or, for that matter, in your damn capital all the time. Get out and mix it up with people a bit."

Yusuf's response was a sullen, "That is not the way we do things," followed by silence.

Is this a cultural thing I am not getting, or is the guy, deep down, an asshole?

After a restless night, the next morning saw the arrival of the repair vehicle with a couple of mechanics. Adam, Yusuf, and Festus, all bleary-eyed, swapped vehicles with them and made their way back to Kayemba City, thankfully with no further ado.

Chapter 12

Aftermath and Next Steps

The next day, after a long shower and good night's sleep, Adam eagerly sought Marie out. Over drinks and dinner, they alternated between personal conversation and talk of Kombonian politics. Adam also got Marie to speak more of her time in Kombonia after her university studies.

"I wanted to do something important for my country," she said, in explaining why she decided to follow the path of journalism. "It isn't easy to do that here, but people need to have information about what this government is doing, how it is keeping ordinary people down, and how its only plan is really how to keep itself in power."

They talked for a while about the state of the press. Marie opined that, "On the surface, the Kombonian press appears to be quite free, particularly in comparison with other countries in the region. Several newspapers are published daily, and even the government-run newspaper sometimes criticizes the government, but never on an important subject. It is true that political debate can be lively on the radio, especially for some of the call-in shows, but television remains bland and fairly uncritical of government."

"That doesn't sound too bad," Adam suggested.

"You have to look underneath the surface. The government has cut the internet off a couple of times when they were nervous about what was going on and afraid that more opposition might get stirred up online. And the government takes the press to the pro-government courts frequently, often on false charges of, for example, defamation. This intimidation tactic has the unfortunate effect of resulting in some self-censorship by the press. In addition, some journalists lack the proper investigative skills to be effective and accurate reporters. The government starves the independent press of resources. As you will notice, all the government advertising goes to the pro-government newspapers. Some opposition journalists are refused press credentials. The situation is far from healthy here."

Adam asked Marie about the role of traditional leaders. She agreed with much of what the younger party leader had said at the beginning of the seminar, but noted that the situation was different in Pohaneland. "There, they have a split between traditional leaders who have been bought out by the government, which provides them with subsidies and protection, and those who support the RMK. It is a very serious problem. Gas has been poured on the fire by the government's refusal to engage in any meaningful dialogue. The people have had no choice but to become more radicalized there. They do not see a future for themselves in this country where they are treated as second- or third-rate citizens."

Toward the end of the meal, Adam felt the vibe was right to steer the conversation to a more personal level. "You seem so busy and committed to work, I wonder if you have any time for other things in life."

He was correct. Marie's eyes sparkled alluringly, which only further fueled Adam's already charged libido. "Why don't you come back to my apartment, and I'll let you know."

Adam didn't need a second invitation, and soon found himself in her apartment, in an upscale section of the city. "Wow, this is a nice place." *How could she afford this on a journalist's income?*

"Why don't we stop talking," she murmured.

Adam moved in to kiss her, and the spark of ardor was lit. They eagerly disrobed and, to his delight, he soon discovered that Marie had experience in subjects other than politics. They made love with an animalistic hunger and urgency that left them totally spent.

When they were finished, Adam got up. As he moved toward the bathroom Marie said impetuously, but languidly, "You know, I think you should be in charge of ensuring my sexual happiness."

With a gallant, albeit naked flourish, Adam bowed deeply and replied, "Madame, it would be an honor to be charged with such a responsibility."

***

In the aftermath of the successful seminar and his encounter with Marie, Adam had a bit more of a spring in his step. This was buttressed by an idea he was starting to chew on, one that he hoped might have the potential to significantly help the elections be legitimate.

Adam met with Yusuf a week later in the KADD offices to brainstorm how they could most effectively play a role in the upcoming elections. Adam suggested, "Look—elections are eight months away. Time is passing. You know that our money from USAID includes some sub-grant funding for KADD. How about if we do some free association thinking about the various things that you guys could do? I know that you and Duwango have been thinking about this, as you should be. Let's not worry too much at this point about how much these ideas might cost and just be creative."

Yusuf let out a slight chuckle. "Well, my friend, the list could be a long one, but we do have several thoughts of areas where we could be active. We could sponsor debates between the leading presidential candidates. We could monitor the media coverage of the campaign. We could undertake voter education programs."

"OK. All these ideas sound good, and I think they are worthy of more thought. But given how important this election is going to be, let's really think outside the box—what else could really have an impact?"

Yusuf resisted to go down this path a bit at first. "I agree, of course, that this election is of vital importance. To my mind, that makes it especially important we do not undertake any activities that might be too risky. Let us focus on what we can realistically do that will have an impact."

Adam took a deep breath, and then demurred. "Look, my man. Don't sell yourselves short. You can do this thing. What you are suggesting in terms of activities are all good. But will they really move the needle? We all know how entrenched the KRP is, how likely they are to mess with the election to ensure their own victory, no matter the popular will. You have got to do more. I don't suppose you are familiar with American football, but there is a play in it called a 'Hail Mary pass.' This is where one team takes a big chance to win the game. With your organization and our help, I bet that KADD could throw a Hail Mary and play a big role to help to anchor democracy here." Adam then pulled out his ace card. "And I also bet that your boss Duwango would be in favor of this."

Yusuf conceded that Duwango would want to go big. "Well then, what do you have in mind?"

Adam decided the time had come to toss out as a test balloon his idea. Adam knew that one of CDP's major focus issues was to support the development of nonpartisan election observation; it had proven critical in many elections around the world, ranging from Chile to Bulgaria to the Philippines. But he also knew it was a major task that required considerable organizational skills, and was not to be undertaken lightly.

"Well…what about organizing some sort of civil society non-partisan election observation mission? We all are concerned that the KRP and the government could interfere in the election. They could mess with voter registration, the freedom of the opposition to campaign, and with the actual counting of the votes; many Kombonians deeply believe that the government would never permit a free and fair election to occur."

Yusuf's reply was measured. "That idea is interesting. Let us think about it for a couple of days. I will consult with Duwango about this idea and then maybe we could talk about it some more."

At the beginning of the next week, Adam reconvened with Yusuf and Duwango in the latter's office. Adam had learned early about Duwango's sense of self-importance and protocol; he had been offended when Adam once suggested that they meet at the CDP venue. Adam began the meeting by noting the range of possible alternatives for KADD election-related activities, and suggested that it would be useful to reflect more on what specifically should be done, and what the timetable could be.

Duwango spoke next. "We foresee a major role for KADD in the elections. We agree that there should be a large-scale election observation effort. Other countries in the region have done this, to good effect." He narrowed his focus to Adam and gazed at him unblinkingly. "There are about 12,000 polling places in

Kombonia. We would need at least two observers at each polling place. We estimate that we need 25,000 people, including staff."

Holy shit. This guy is asking for the moon. I feel like I am being dragged into a huge scale version of those negotiations I see in the Kayemba City market stalls. Adam felt a pit in his stomach at having to decide whether this was a good idea, and if so was it at all realistic to go to USAID with what would be a massive ask for additional funding. He glanced beseechingly at Yusuf, but the latter provided no help, maintaining his silence and poker-faced expression. Adam understood that he wouldn't speak freely in front of his superior in this case.

"Well Mr. Duwango, this is a very ambitious project that you propose. It leads to a lot of questions. Where would the people come from? How would they be trained? What kind of logistical support would they require? Would they have permission from the government to function?"

Irritated, Duwango interjected, "Why do we have to ask permission from the government to judge whether elections are fair? This is the same government that has suppressed our democratic rights for years! Who are they to say whether we can observe elections or not?" His tone softened slightly, "As to your other queries—I am sure that you and Yusuf can work all that out. And now you will excuse me, as I have another meeting."

Adam and Yusuf retreated to Yusuf's office. "What the hell!" Adam spat out. "Well, at least I guess he liked the idea. But does he really think that is how it is going to go—he just snaps his fingers and expects us to only ask, 'how high?'"

"Listen," Yusuf replied calmly. "Duwango knows you are the rich Americans. And you need to understand how things work here. People never get anywhere asking for just half a loaf. Indeed, nothing ever happens even if you ask for a whole loaf. You must ask for two loaves if you are prepared to settle for one, especially when you are dealing with the Germans, British, Scandinavians, and especially the Americans. But you and I, we can talk about what is actually possible."

Still steamed but somewhat mollified, Adam let out a long breath of air. "OK. Let's get back to the land of the real. Even if you could come up with 25,000 trained people between now and the elections, can you imagine how much that would cost?"

Yusuf surprised Adam with his response, although Adam should have known better by this point in their relationship. He swiveled around to face his computer and pulled up a file on screen. "Actually, we have been thinking about this. We estimate that with people, training, vehicles, communications equipment, logistical support, per diem payment for the observers, and our in-house cost the project would come to about $3.2 million."

Adam burst out laughing. "Oh boy, that is a good one! Where in God's name do you think I am going to come up with that amount of money? Our whole project is only $500,000."

Yusuf showed another expressionless face. "Maybe you could find some supplemental funding."

I. don't. think. so. "In case you haven't noticed, Kombonia is not exactly at the top of the US government's list of priorities these days, even with the increase in terrorist activities in the region. Look, we really have to have a more rational discussion about what is possible."

Now Yusuf permitted a disappointed expression to appear on his face. "I suppose if we had to, we could decrease the size of our observation mission. But it is a matter of pride to Duwango that we cover the entire country."

"Well, I am sorry if he incurs a bruised ego, but we have to figure something out here." A thought then occurred to Adam. "We could do a Quick Count."

"A what?"

"Look, before I came out here, I had a briefing from Patricia Morgan, the CDP elections expert. She told me about something called a parallel vote tabulation, or Quick Count. This has become a main feature in CDP's menu of election-related activities. The idea behind the Quick Count is surprisingly uncomplicated. You know that the counting of ballots in most polling places around the world is usually done, at least initially, by the polling place itself. These results are communicated to local, regional, and then national counting centers where they are aggregated.

"Given the vastness of many lesser-developed countries and the cost and logistical problems associated with reaching and reporting results from each of them, a Quick Count simplifies the process. A reduced number of polling places are chosen after being determined to be representative of the country as a whole."

Yusuf was intrigued. "Where has this been done?"

"If I remember correctly, the first time was by the Philippine civic group NAMFREL—the National Citizen Movement for Free Elections, I think, when the dictator Marcos tried to rig the presidential election way back in 1986. The information they generated helped fuel the movement that forced him to leave power after the elections. Since then it has been done in many places. The key is having a good local civic group to field the people—and much fewer are needed than for a full-scale observation. KADD could fit the bill splendidly."

Yusuf was still wrapping his mind around the concept. "So, let me guess a little bit more about how this Quick Count idea works.

It seems vital to me that the selection of polling places from which to aggregate the votes should be, as you say, representative of the country as a whole. So I am thinking that the criteria for choosing these polling places might include its location, the ethnicity of people voting there, whether it is urban or rural, and what region it is located. All this is to say you need to choose places which, in their totality, reflect the country as a whole."

Adam nodded, with a smile. "You got it, buddy."

Yusuf went straight to the point. "How many polling places do you need to cover?"

Glad I found time to read some of those voluminous CDP briefing materials. "I seem to recall that if a good representative sample of less than 10 percent of polling places—say 8 percent—could be drawn up, you could have a result with 97 percent certainty of matching legitimate final results."

Yusuf pulled out his cell phone calculator. "Let us see… 12,000 polling places here in Kombonia divided by eight percent means that you could have a very accurate result by covering only…. 960 polling places." Yusuf thought about this a bit. "You know, it seems to me that your Quick Count has another advantage, as shown by its name. As long as you get the voting results from the KADD people at those 960 polling places soon after the vote has been counted, and if you believe in the statistical accuracy of your results, then you will in all likelihood have the results quicker than the national election commission."

"Bingo, my Kombonian pal. And the election commission will know that. They will know that if someone tries to cheat, KADD will have the real numbers. It is a pretty powerful tool."

Yusuf smiled. "I definitely see the merit of this idea. Let me discuss it with Duwango."

Within a couple of days, Yusuf reported that, after initially complaining that a full observer effort would be more prestigious and highlight the KADD's importance, Duwango reluctantly accepted the logistical and financial arguments in favor of undertaking a Quick Count. Things moved rapidly at this point. Two weeks later, Adam had approval to move ahead with fleshing out the concept from Mulcahy at CDP and Barry Johnson at USAID.

The next step was to arrange a short visit from Patricia Morgan in Washington to work with Yusuf and his colleagues on the nuts and bolts of undertaking a Quick Count in the Kombonian context. Morgan, a long-time veteran of elections, had been one of the first people at CDP to make contact and engage with Hungarian reformers after the Berlin Wall crumbled and as that country moved toward the Eastern Bloc's first democratic elections in the late 1980s. Since then she had traveled the world helping to organize Quick Counts and advising host country NGOs on the ins and outs of conducting domestic observation missions, in addition to leading international election observation missions. She had a wealth of stories to tell, including a number of harrowing close calls with ruling party government officials in several countries. They usually would criticize CDP's election observation work on the grounds that it ignored their national sovereignty and represented interference in their country's internal affairs. In reality they usually were not enamored by CDP's leadership in providing greater transparency regarding elections, which had previously escaped scrutiny and thus had been easier to manipulate.

After Morgan and Adam had settled themselves with Yusuf and three of his colleagues in the cluttered KADD conference room, Morgan began to outline how the Quick Count worked. It became clear early on that while the basic concept was simple, its success required the proper functioning of moving parts.

"First," she began, "you need to have a plan, and an understanding of what is necessary to ensure a credible Quick Count. You must have a disciplined organizational structure. It is crucial to know what it will cost so that you will have the available funds ahead of time. You must also have criteria for what you are looking for in terms of volunteers; how many you will need, and how you will recruit them.

"Then these people will need to be trained. How will that happen? Let's say you need 1,500 volunteers. Can you train them all at the same time? Probably not. And if not, how will they be trained? I will tell you that we have had good success in many countries with a train-the-trainers cascade method, in which we train an initial core of trainers who then spread out across the country to multiply the training. But it isn't simple.

"So, the question I have for you is can you recruit the needed number of volunteers? How would you do this? I am not sure about the situation here in Kombonia, but churches have helped form the backbone of nonpartisan election monitoring organizations in other African countries like Zambia, Malawi and Nigeria."

At this point Yusuf spoke up. "I think it will be possible to find the people. We already have several hundred members of KADD, and they all have their own networks and friends who could be contacted. In addition, you may know that we have the Catholic bishop of the Kayemba City diocese on our Board, as well as the iman of our largest mosque."

Morgan was curious. "That's encouraging that you have the iman on board. What role does Islam play here in Kombonia?"

Yusuf was happy to answer. "Islam is more flexible and less doctrinaire in its interpretation here than in some other countries.

A significant minority of the population is Moslem. This moderating role of the Islamic community puts the lie to the argument that Islam and democracy are fundamentally incompatible. In that sense we are a bit like Indonesia. As far as this relates to KADD and civil society groups, fundamentalist Islam seeks to impose a rigid code of conduct on its adherents that leaves no space for the existence of independent institutions like KADD. In Kombonia, by contrast, Islam and Christianity have—so far—not clashed, and leaders of the Moslem community should be willing to work with us on the observation effort."

"That's excellent," Morgan responded. "But you can never have too many people. Are there any other ways that you could recruit volunteers?"

Ezekiel Nbangwo, a university student and KADD staffer, asked Yusuf's permission to speak. "You know we have a few people who are quite popular amongst many of the youth from all over Kombonia. Their popularity transcends ethnicity. I am thinking, for example, of Charlotte Kutemebi, the singer, and Mohammadu Sherif, the most famous member of our national football team, the Gazelles. I am wondering if they could be helpful in some way."

Morgan responded with enthusiasm, "No doubt. We've had some very successful examples of famous people—role models, if you will—undertaking public service campaigns to educate people about elections, including what Quick Counts are and how they can be involved."

A few days later the team held another meeting during which a number of critical decisions were made. First, Adam announced that he and Yusuf had developed a notional budget for the Quick Count of $275,000. While that money was not currently available within the CDP country budget, USAID's Johnson had indicated to Adam that he thought that USAID could provide supplemental funding to cover this expense.

Second, Yusuf briefed the team on plans that KADD was developing to publicize and recruit for the Quick Count. This led Adam to pose the sensitive question, "Do we need to inform the authorities about this initiative?"

Morgan responded, "I think it would be pretty unrealistic and not in the spirit of transparency if you were to try to do this on the sly. After all, one of the biggest advantages of a Quick Count is that people—including the authorities—know if it is happening ahead of time. It can serve as a deterrent to cheating."

This led to a discussion about how the authorities should be informed. "Perhaps we should just send a letter to the election commission," Yusuf opined.

"But at some point, you want the public to know about this as well. Perhaps you should just issue a press release," Adam suggested.

Yusuf had a different thought. "We need to follow protocol on this. I think it is best to first inform the election commission, and then subsequently make the press release. I am thinking that I should perhaps informally advise an election commissioner I know about this idea, so that it does not come as a complete surprise to them."

Adam probed Yusuf. "Wouldn't that just give them time to oppose the concept? Is that really a good idea?"

"I think so. It is the way things are done here." Adam couldn't find a response to this, so the matter was decided.

Yusuf then suggested that they move on to the crucial issue of how to create a sample of the estimated 900 polling places selected for the Quick Count. The results from these places would need to be collected and transmitted. Morgan asked everyone present to draw up a list of the four-to-five most important social, political, economic, cultural, and demographic attributes of Kombonia that would need to be considered in determining a representative sample of polling places. The group took fifteen minutes to individually draw up the lists. Most of the items identified were not surprising. They included:

- ethnicity/language spoken;
- previous political preference;
- region of the country;
- rural or urban location;
- level of literacy/education;
- gender; and
- occupation.

Many of the Kombonian participants quickly began to notice some connections between categories. For instance, rural Kombonians were rather naturally expected to have lower education levels than their urban brethren. Regions and ethnicity were also closely correlated.

Once the group reached a consensus on these themes, the discussion turned to selection of locations that could, in aggregate, reflect these considerations. Most of that conversation took place amongst the KADD participants who, of course, had the deepest knowledge of the country. After about an hour they had identified thirty localities that they thought would be a good initial location list, although much work remained to specifically identify the actual polling places. The project was launched and underway.

At about the same time, the president's chief of staff, Aziz, had a short phone conversation with the new head of intelligence, who told him, "We have confirmation what we long suspected—the journalist, Mfalla, is a member of the PMLP leadership cell. She is behind the murder of several policemen and KRP supporters. We have enough proof to arrest and make an example of her. We think that the president should know about this and approve the arrest."

Aziz put his phone on speaker, leaned back in his chair, and made a temple of his fingers. "Don't we know from surveillance that Mfalla is in a relationship with that American, Adam Edwards?"

"Yes sir, that is true."

"So, hold off on doing anything with Mfalla for the moment. I think this Edwards perhaps needs some advice on how to do his job."

Adam was intrigued and a bit flattered when he got a call the next day from Aziz inviting him to a lunch meeting. He quickly accepted, and a couple of days later found himself breaking bread with Aziz in a secluded patio corner of one of Kayemba City's most exclusive restaurants, Chez Françoise, run by a late middle-aged, chain-smoking, French expatriate woman. She spent most of her time at an isolated table, dourly surveying the other tables and sipping an omnipresent Pernod.

"How are you finding your time here so far in Kombonia, Mr. Edwards?"

"Oh, please call me Adam. Your country is beautiful, the people are warm and hospitable, and I love the music here. So, what is not to like?"

"Well, I am so very glad to hear that. And surely you must know that we are engaged in an important democratization process. We have elections coming up and it is very important that the international community understands how truly democratic they are. It is my understanding that you and your CDP organization are planning to be helpful in some way?"

Adam wanted to be as forthcoming as possible, but he and KADD had not yet shared the Quick Count idea with the government, given the sensitivity of the activity. "We sure are. We have been thinking about some sort of observation effort to shine light on the electoral process and help promote transparency."

"That's good, that's good," Aziz replied with a note of manufactured joviality. "We need the outside world to understand that everything went well in this election."

Do I smell a skunk here? Adam took a bite of his basque chicken before answering. "Well of course, Phillip, if I may call you by your first name, we are not in a position to make a determination about how free and fair the election is until it takes place."

"I know that. But it is important that you be, shall we say, well disposed to the idea that the elections are legitimate."

What the hell is this guy getting at—is he trying to put the squeeze on me??

Aziz continued. "By the way, it seems that you have developed an appreciation for more than just the journalist Marie Mfalla's writing skills."

What is happening here?

Aziz continued, leaning over his plate and fixing his eyes on Adam. "It is known to our intelligence services that she consorts with the terrorists. Some people want to arrest her, and are even asking questions about you. But you are fortunate because I could make sure that bad things do not happen." Leaning back, he said matter-of-factly, "I will just need your cooperation regarding the elections."

With that, Aziz snapped his fingers at the waiter. "I enjoyed our lunch. Don't worry about the bill. I must go now, but please enjoy your coffee."

What the fuck?

Chapter 13

Candidate Declarations

On a typically humid afternoon in late July, an atmosphere of relative normalcy enveloped Kayemba City. The streets were full and cacophonous with vehicles and animals of all sorts. In his office, President Mushi instructed his secretary to close the windows, turn up the air conditioning, and hold all calls. He prized peace and quiet when he was ready to make a major decision, of which the biggest of his life confronted him. Was he going to seek election in a poll that, unlike others in the past, offered the possibility of him losing? Mushi was under no illusion that he would be a shoo-in to be elected. There were too many unknowns and variables in play.

He did not see himself as a president for life. Mushi was all too aware that many of his counterparts in the region had confused their existence as presidents with what was best for the nation. To be sure, Mushi thought he was the best qualified, knowledgeable, and wisest option to lead Kombonia. He could not discount the possibility of some faction in the military revolting against him, and staging a coup. He had thought often of so many of his predecessors, not just in Africa, who had died at the hands of their own soldiers. Perhaps paradoxically, that prospect, if anything, strengthened his resolve to stay in power. Mushi felt that he owed it to Kombonia to see the election through, and do what he could to anchor the country's politics in a constitutional process. He wanted military coups to be a thing of the past. He believed in the African Union's principle of not recognizing governments that had come to power by a military coup. And, hopefully, of course, he would be reelected.

He knew that he wasn't the only option, however, and accepted that reality. In fact, although he would never admit it to anyone, he thought that Ruwoyo would probably be a good president, as long as he respected the democratic rules of the game. But countervailing governance institutions, such as the parliament, would have to function effectively in order to serve as a check. Mushi knew that the old adage, that power abhors a vacuum, was all too true. Mushi wondered if he should be doing more to respect the parliament's role and acknowledge its legitimate right to oversee the executive branch. After all, the parliament was in the hands of the KRP. But who knows what would could happen if MPs thought they could challenge the government at every turn? Might that not jeopardize his carefully scripted democratization plans? It is awfully difficult to act in the country's long-term interests when they clash with shorter-term realities, he mused.

The reality was that Mushi had no desire to leave the presidency, partly because he had grown used to exercising power, and partly because there were forces weighing upon him to stay. He had to be concerned about the welfare of his extended family. Beyond that, he had responsibility to his clan, whose welfare he had pledged to safeguard, as his ethnic leader forebearers had done for centuries. And finally, of course, he was aware of the various senior leaders in the KRP and the military who had attached their stars to him. Mushi had always kept an emotional distance from even his closest advisers. In fact, he had never had an introspective, open conversation with any of them about his own personal future. He suspected—no, was certain—that an announcement by him that he was not going to run for president again would set off all sorts of palace intrigues and destabilize his government. He did not rule out a scenario where he could be coerced by those near him to run again. He was not a man given to drama, but Mushi reflected that if he refused their entreaties, there was a chance he could be overthrown or even murdered by some in his entourage.

Mushi sipped a cup of tea as he pondered his situation further. The country was in revolt, the economy was contracting, and the region was suffering from Islamic fundamentalist terrorism. He thought he could master these problems should he win the election, and be seen by history as somewhat akin to Jerry Rawlings in Ghana. Rawlings was a former air force officer who seized control in a military coup but who then oversaw the development of a vibrant democracy. And, even if he were to lose, he saw a legacy for himself similar to that of Kenneth Kaunda in Zambia; he would be lauded as the first president of Kombonia ever to leave power voluntarily. His decision was made—he would run again for president.

So, in the second week of April, Kombonian flags lined the streets from the presidential palace to the Chinese-built convention center in the heart of Kayemba City. The KRP was to have its annual congress. A festive atmosphere, paid for by the party, enveloped the surroundings of the center, with dancers, music, and supporters milling about. Finally, after a number of speeches by lesser luminaries the presidential motorcade arrived, first featuring a line of what were called "spider riders"—the uniformed SPB guards on motorcycles with sirens blaring—followed by vehicles with various staff members, and then the presidential limousine. Mushi stepped out of his armor-plated vehicle, waved to an in-house KRP crowd and ululating traditional dancers, entered the hall, and mounted the podium. To a hushed crowd he made his long-awaited and anticipated speech. "I have heard the expression of the people's will. You are asking me to run for reelection. My response to you is that I have always respected the will of the people, and I will continue to do so. My decision to run is an affirmation of my commitment to democracy. I am hereby a candidate for reelection to the presidency of the Republic of Kombonia!" Huge applause filled the convention center—although a cynic might have suggested that its tone was somewhat more dutiful than rapturous.

No such hesitancy was apparent in the state-owned press, which trumpeted Mushi's announcement in banner headlines the next day. The independent media, however, had a different response. Business-oriented news outlets adopted a cautious wait-and-see perspective, hoping that no matter the result of the elections, social peace and a lessening of tensions in society would result.

The *Clarion* newspaper noted that opposition parties had a severe disadvantage in terms of material preparations, infrastructure, and resources. In a headline entitled "Mushi Seeks to Extend Autocratic Rule," the paper criticized the president for not taking the opportunity to help entrench democracy and ensure a transfer of power by simply declining to run. The paper went on to query, "Why do so many presidents in Africa—and elsewhere—feel as if, once in power, they have a divine right to rule for life? We thought that this period was thankfully ending with the wave of democracy that washed over the continent in the 1990s and 2000s, but we have been deceived. There seems to be something about the office of the presidency that turns ordinary humans into conceited egotists. The only difference between the current crop of dictators and their predecessors is that they have now developed more sophisticated schemes to stay in power—always cloaked in some other rationale that hides their true intent. This must stop now!"

Adam was called one day by the leader of the Kombonian Peace and Prosperity Movement, a small party that drew its support from some of the poorer areas of Kayemba City. "I wish to inform you that I plan to announce my candidacy for the presidency early next week," he intoned.

"Well, that is excellent news. I wish you and your party the best of luck."

"Yes, well, there are some problems that you could perhaps help us to resolve."

"Maybe you could let me know what they are and how I can be of assistance." *What does this guy want out of me?*

"It sems as if the ruling party is afraid of us. That is the only reason I can find for why there are so many onerous and repressive rules and laws if one wants to run for public office."

"Which ones in particular do you find most onerous?"

"For example, you may know that election rules state that any candidate has to submit a deposit equivalent to $30,000 USD. The deposit will only be returned if the candidate secures over five percent of the vote. Another rule requires candidates to produce 250 signatures from supporters in eight of our twelve provinces."

Adam decided to play devil's advocate. "Well, don't they have a point there?"

Suppressed anger. "The government has justified these rules

by stating that they discourage those whom they consider to be a nuisance or minor candidates and whom, they claim, have no realistic chance of winning. But what gives the government the right to determine in advance who is popular and who isn't? Do they think they are omniscient gods? As I say, they are scared that we would show how popular we really are if the elections were truly to be free. They want to stifle the growth of opposition leadership and new alternatives to the ruling party."

Adam subsequently had a conversation with Yusuf about this. The latter saw both sides of the problem. "Well, it is true that without any way to reduce the number of candidates, you could have thousands of them. Just about every Kombonian wants to be president—but that would create massive confusion. How would you know for whom to vote? Just imagine how long the ballot paper would have to be, and what it would take to find your chosen candidate on it. You cannot have so many candidates that the whole exercise turns into a joke."

Adam concurred. "And look at Ruwoyo and Obewame. While they have been critical of these rules, neither has strongly objected since they were certain of being able to meet the requirements. I'd bet that they are reasoning the rules' effect is to channel more support behind their candidacies."

"Yes, that is true. But the opposition parties do have some legitimate grounds for complaint. There are many other ways that they see the government and ruling party tilting the playing field against them. There is the fact that voter registration has taken place during the harvest season—many peasants in more fertile southern parts of Kombonia, which we know is the heart of opposition to the KRP—couldn't spare the time to walk the one or two days needed to reach a voter registration center. The reality is also that the government has a monopoly on newsprint, and that supplies are sometimes mysteriously limited for opposition newspapers.

"Similarly, the opposition has opposed a recently enacted law increasing criminal penalties for any social media posts deemed to be a 'menace to public order.' The minister of information claimed that this was a needed step to ensure what they called 'social harmony and calm' in the run-up to the elections. The opposition, however, has loudly proclaimed that this was an attempt to muzzle legitimate freedom of expression."

Yusuf was clearly bothered by one other point. "You know, we have seen time and time again in Kombonia that an autocratic government wants to use the cloak of legality to mask its true intentions. They say they do something for an apparently acceptable and logical reason, but its underlying purpose and effect is to limit the ability of the opposition to win an election.

"And, you know, this happens in your country too. For example, in the state of Georgia the Republicans enacted voter legislation that makes it illegal to provide food or water to people waiting in line to vote—Republicans claimed that this could be interpreted as an attempt to inappropriately influence voters, but it was obvious that this was part of a package of measures designed to suppress the opposition votes because longer lines happen in the more populous areas, which generally vote Democratic. We know that this was even memorialized in one of your comedy series on television. I do not recall its name, but I think its star was named Larry David.

"The government here can do this in a more subtle fashion. It has, for example, enacted a law requiring the parents of presidential candidates to have been born in the country. They say that this is to ensure that the candidates have the interests of the country at heart. And to justify this, they cited a similar provision in your constitution stipulating that to be eligible, prospective candidates must have been born in the US. However, we all know that the reality is that many of the Ome people have grandparents who migrated here from other countries in the region; this means that some otherwise qualified candidates, who might not support the ruling party, cannot run for the presidency."

In addition to all this, Adam had not slept well since his unsettling encounter with Aziz. In fact, he hardly slept at all, tossing, and turning with a queasy feeling in the pit of his stomach. *Oh Jesus, how do I get out of this? What if I have to tell Mulcahy?? This is so embarrassing.* The stress was building on him, compounded by his inability to tell anyone or take any sort of proactive steps. He thought of just bluffing through the whole thing, pretending it hadn't happened; but then visions of a knock at the door, of him being arrested on some BS charges of being an accomplice to a terrorist thundered through his brain in technicolor, leaving him exhausted. Finally, after yet another sleepless night, he decided he had to confront Marie, as risky as that might be, and even though he did not have a clear game plan. He called her and, attempting to sound normal, invited her to a drink that evening, saying he had a surprise for her. She replied that she loved surprises, and they agreed to meet at 8 p.m. in a quiet bar.

"I have heard something that is, frankly, very troubling. So, let me ask you a question. What do you think of the PMLP?"

"The people of Pohaneland have some very legitimate complaints. That is why the RMK, and yes, even the PMLP exist."

"So, let me ask the question in a more direct fashion. Do you have anything to do with the PMLP?"

Adam had previously seen Marie's demeanor change and become tenser when the subject of Pohaneland had come up. Now her voice hissed, and her eyes narrowed into slits. "What do you mean?"

"Marie, you are the opposite of stupid. You know exactly what I mean."

"What information do you think you have, and how did you get it?"

Jesus, this is like pulling teeth. I am glad no one is sitting near us.

"OK. Here is how we are going to do this. First, I will tell you what I have heard. You will then answer my question. And then I will answer the second part of your question. See? You win this negotiation—you'll be getting two things and I only get one.

"What I have heard is that you are a terrorist—that you are involved with the PMLP."

Marie directed a steely-eyed gaze at Adam. The proverbial pin then dropped. "That is partly true. I am a member of the PMLP's executive committee. We are not terrorists. We are fighting for the freedom of Pohaneland. Your turn."

Oh shit oh shit oh shit oh shit. And that guy by the moped has been watching us. I wonder if we are under surveillance. Stay focused here.

Adam took a gulp of his beer. "Aziz told me."

"Well then, let me tell you something. I am proud to be fighting for the freedom of the Pohane. I am risking my life to enable the Pohane to live in dignity. It is the government that is the terrorist here. It is they who have killed far, far more people than us. They have kept our people under their boot. They have destroyed thousands of lives and treated us as subhumans!"

"If we are to talk here you have to keep your voice down and make it look like we are having a normal conversation. I truly understand that the Pohane have been mistreated. But that doesn't give you the right to break laws and kill people. What are you achieving by this? Why are you, Marie Mfalla, doing this?"

Marie leaned into Adam and seethed. "I want there to be a coup. It will show the weakness of the KRP. You know, the military doesn't like the way things are going and are finally taking things in hand."

"I don't get it…don't you think a military government could be worse and more repressive than the KRP?"

"Oh, Adam, you have so much to learn! This means that the people's movement against this dictatorship is being heard, and the rats are getting scared. If the military takes over, two things can happen. Either they can come to their senses—and we do have some sympathizers amongst them—and enter into a dialogue with the people of Kombonia to let us make a democracy here. Or, they can be worse than Mushi, in which case the situation will be crystal clear. The people will be facing a corrupt, oppressive, and thieving military.

"Now, as to why I am doing this: I have had a life of privilege but that didn't keep me from seeing what has happened to the Pohane. I may be only half Pohane but I feel as if I am fully Pohane. I have had relatives who have suffered at the hands of the government. It would take hours to tell you all about that, and you would be sick to your stomach.

"Regarding your concern about operating within the laws of the oppressor—well, all I can say is—you stupid little American. Why don't you remember the history of your own country? You don't have a problem with George Washington leading a rebellion against an oppressive government. And speaking of history, it is full of other examples of brave leaders risking their lives to throw out the oppressor. Many of them were initially called a terrorist. Haven't you heard for example about Menachem Begin in Israel and the Stern Gang? What about Nelson Mandela and the Rivonia Trial?"

"And you for your part have clearly not learned about Martin Luther King Jr. and the power of nonviolence. But I am not going to get into a history argument with you. Don't you get that you have threatened my work here?? Now I am under suspicion. You know what? You aren't the person I thought you were. In fact, I am not going to talk to you again. Goodbye." Adam stood up and walked away.

Marie Mfalla's last words ever addressed to Adam were like knives flung into his back. "You fool—who do you think suckered you into the RMK rally?"

The man on the moped was paying particular attention to cleaning his nails as Adam strode out of the restaurant past him.

Feeling depressed and lonely, Adam texted Sarah on an impulse to ask if she might be free the following Saturday and interested in visiting a national park that was home to herds of giraffes, about a ninety minutes' drive northwest of Kayemba City. His heart did a little flip when Sarah accepted.

On the appointed Saturday morning, Adam loaded up his four-wheel drive with the requisite extra petrol supply, a first aid bag, bottles of water, and juice and snacks.

"My goodness, you have learned how to travel here in Kombonia," Sarah laughed as she hopped in the vehicle.

"Well guess what—my time in Kombonia has been nothing

if not a learning experience." Adam was relaxed, enjoying the easy banter, and the presence of Sarah.

After exiting the outskirts of the city, Adam gunned the engine as they drove across the bush, the wind whipping their hair. "Boy, I'll tell you, it is times like these that I feel truly alive."

"So, I'll do you one better. My ex-boss, the former Peace Corps director here, served as a Peace Corps volunteer in rural Niger. He was the object of curiosity by all of the villagers and felt that he had none of the privacy that to us, as Americans, is so important. So, guess what he did. He bought a horse and would take it for long rides in the bush. He said that feeling of freedom, of being loose and alone in an exotic land made him feel like Lawrence of Arabia."

"Sounds romantic."

Sarah laughed. "Well, it didn't end up quite so well. Turns out that as the guy's Peace Corps service was ending, and before he returned to the States, he had to decide what to do with the horse. He didn't want to sell it—it was an emotional link with his time in Niger—so he entrusted it in the care of the village elder. It turns out that the elder died a few years later and there was a big hullabaloo over who would inherit care of the horse. I guess the inheritance laws were a bit fuzzy on what was to happen…my former boss still doesn't know how that ended."

Eventually, they got to the park and paid their entrance fee. They picked up Isaac, a guide who promised to lead them to the giraffes, and headed off into the scrubland. After about ten min-utes, they sure enough saw their first herd loping along gracefully. Adam let out a whoop. "Hot damn! This is great—look at those guys! Wow—what an experience!"

Isaac smiled politely, and Sarah's reaction was also different.

Chuckling, she said, "I have to share a confidence with you. This is only about the tenth time I have come here."

"Ouch—I am so so sorry. I should have thought of that. Why would you have agreed to come if you had already been here so many times?"

Sarah wiped a wisp of hair off of her forehead and looked off into the distance. "Let's just say that there are other animals around here that I find interesting."

Once back in Kayemba City, as he dropped Sarah off at her house, Adam remarked, "You know, I have been meaning to ask what you meant by that remark in the park about other animals."

Sarah looked him in the eyes, and then gently brushed her lips against his.

Chapter 14

Coup Attempt

Parliament House is a large, whitewashed building set on a dusty circle near the center of the city. It was built by the British in the 1920s as the seat of the Legislative Council, the body made up of colonials and at first a few, then over the years an increasing number, of the local elites. The building itself stands as testimony to the checkered history between the presidency and parliament in Kombonia. A smattering of pockmarks litter its walls, the result of gunfire during a failed rebellion by an army unit a quarter century ago. The closer one approaches to the building, the more its decrepitude, the result of years of little or no upkeep, becomes apparent.

In contrast to the general sense of unease layering Kayemba City, the overwhelming impression that Adam felt as he entered the building was one of quiescence, of placidity, even though the parliament was in session. A couple of peacocks grazed on the dusty lawn, no one was entering or exiting the building, and it seemed as if the parliament was content to let the world pass it by. *Huh; not exactly the feeling one would get if this place were hurtling toward political crisis and civil strife, but neither is it the hotbed of expected activity were Kombonia a democracy.*

Entering the front hall, he asked a somnolent guard for directions to the speaker's office. He was shown the way along chalky halls to a staircase that had more than its fair share of bat droppings. As part of his effort to make contacts with a wide range of key political figures, he had received an introduction to Lindsay Fobedu, the speaker, who was a stalwart of the ruling party. It was also rumored that he was more open to the possibility of change than others around President Mushi. Adam was both nervous and excited about meeting him, even though Fobedu had a reputation for brusqueness.

After opening pleasantries and the obligatory offer of coffee or tea, Adam asked the speaker about his view of the democratization process in Kombonia. His answer struck Adam as seemingly well rehearsed.

"We are just starting out with democracy here. We will certainly make mistakes and stumble along the path, but I am convinced that the foundations for a firm multiparty democracy are being laid. You have to understand that this is not an easy task for us—there is no textbook written on how to institute a democracy. Why should we expect people to immediately embrace democratic institutions? There will be growing pains. We have to accept that progress will not be linear. At least the various groupings active in the country's political life have a common view, that change is needed. The challenge is that we must also learn how to deal with each other in a mutually respectful fashion. We welcome your assistance, and are sure that you and your institute will be able to help us."

Adam decided to be straightforward. "Why, Mr. Speaker, should the KRP leadership be interested in change? After all, you are in charge of the country now. Change might mean that you lose power."

If Fobedu was taken aback by the directness of the question, he did not show it. In fact, he let out a small laugh, and then took a sip of his coffee.

"Well, my friend, there are many different answers to that question. And I too will speak frankly. First, some of my colleagues do tend to see things the way that you have expressed them in your question. But that is not surprising. We are a democratic political party and differences of opinion should be expected. I would say, however, that most recognize the need to reform the system, and that by being in the forefront of this change, the Kombonian people will give the KRP credit for leading the forces of change to an even more democratic system. As I tell my colleagues, politics fits into Darwin's theory of evolution—you must adapt in order to survive." Left unsaid was whether Fodedu meant that figuratively or literally. "And," he added with a wry smile, "certainly the donor countries would not object to greater democracy here."

Given the honest tenor of the conversation, Adam decided to risk an even more provocative question. "Are there elements within the existing power structure that would not accept a transfer of power, in case the KRP were to lose the upcoming election?"

Again, Fobedu paused for more coffee.

"Oh, do you mean like your President Trump? Well first, let me tell you that it is very unlikely that the KRP will lose the upcoming election. President Mushi has this country on the right path and the Kombonians have shown, and will in the future manifest, their appreciation for his rule. But let us consider the hypothetical that you have presented. I could simply say no, that everyone would be on board with handing the keys of the presidential palace over to someone else. But the real answer is not so simple. First, what if the election process does not run smoothly? You know that there are fools out there shooting guns at night and trying to upset things. The terrorists of the PFLP want to polarize the situation so much that people will be afraid to vote. But if they go out and throw their bombs before the election and create instability, they will then claim that it is because of us! What they really want is to have the situation in this country so unsettled that they can take it over by undemocratic means. They don't care about democracy. So, I ask you: How democratic would an election be if people are intimidated from going to the polls? If they are shot for participating in democratic elections?"

Not having an answer to that question, Adam posed another. "Is that the only challenge to elections here?"

"No, of course not. It is true that there are some in the military —not all, by any means—who wish that time could stop and the status quo could continue on indefinitely. But there aren't many. You don't need to worry about them."

Upon leaving the building, Adam again felt enveloped by a feeling of unease in the streets. In the afternoon some scattered demonstrations were quickly broken up by truncheon-wielding members of the security forces. Streets quickly became deserted once the business day ended. A number of the street vendors who normally and good-naturedly solicited Adam's business during his commute to and from the CDP office were absent.

That evening, Adam attended a cocktail party offered by Ambassador Anderson in honor of a visiting artist from the US. What, in regular times, would have been a festive occasion was subdued. Adam found himself in a group with Harlan Stuart,

Sarah, and Ralph Jeffries, the embassy deputy chief of mission whose party Adam had attended early after his arrival in-country. It was the first time he had seen Sarah since their giraffe expedition, and their eyes briefly met.

Adam felt an electric volt surge through him. *Be professional.* "What do you think is going to happen next here?" Adam queried the group.

Roberts was the first to reply. "Well, it's clear to me that Mushi will be able to pull off the election. I can't see how he wouldn't get reelected. As long as the opposition accepts the results, and probably even if they don't, things will move on."

"And what if they don't?" offered up the DCM.

Stuart's normally serious demeanor lengthened. "In that case I think there will be violence. Some people will lose their lives."

"And what are the odds that that would result in some kind of civil war?" asked Adam.

"I don't think they are very high. I think Mushi has it under control. And, as you know, Abdallah, the Interior Minister, is a hardass. He'll crack down on any mischief makers pretty quickly."

Adam glanced at Sarah and noticed that while her face remained mostly expressionless, one eyebrow could not help but arch. A few minutes later he sidled up to her at the bar. In a low voice Adam said, "I'd like to talk about pleasure with you but I guess we should discourse about business here."

Sarah suppressed a smile. "Well, I'll take a raincheck on the former. What do you want to ask about the latter?"

"I have a slight suspicion that you did not find Stuart's analysis particularly trenchant. Pray tell."

Sarah motioned for Adam to accompany her to a quiet end of the patio of Ambassador Anderson's spacious residence, and took a sip of her South African white wine. "That guy is full of shit. This place is a powder keg and it could blow anytime soon—it just needs a spark."

"What could that be?"

"I don't know. I may have lived here for four years, but I am still far from being an expert about this place. It could be a seemingly small mistake someone makes; it could be that someone's ambition outweighs his judgement; it could be that some of these poor Pohane finally get so sick and tired of being Kombonia's version of India's Untouchables that they explode. It could be some corrupt business deal gone wrong. It could be one or a combination of these things. All I know is that the kindling is set and dry—it is ready to go."

"Let me ask you a crazy question. Do you think it would be better if there weren't elections?"

"Oh my God, no. Everything is tense here precisely because there have never been meaningful elections. This place is a pressure cooker—there has been no real outlet for people to express themselves and feel like the government is really responsive to their needs. At some point, things are going to blow if all of the actors here—but especially the KRP—don't find a release valve. The government here could be doing the best things in the world— which they are not but just for argument's sake let's say they are—if a significant part of the population feels that they are corrupt and out primarily for themselves, any good work the government may have done will go up in smoke. And I mean that literally as well as figuratively."

"So what needs to be done?"

"We, and that includes you and CDP, have to stay the course and help the people figure out how to redirect the pressure in this cooker toward legitimate elections that will result in a government that is seen as both reflecting the will of the people and being responsive to their needs. I know that sounds like BS but it is the truth. This country needs that badly."

This woman has got it together on so many different levels. "I hear you and like what you are saying. Let me ask you another question. I'm thinking that maybe some of those release valves you are talking about might include, in addition to elections, the development of institutional checks and balances between the executive and legislative branches, and also decentralization of more power down to the people?"

"That sounds about right, if a bit academic-y. These are great ideas, in theory. The challenge is how to translate them from theory to reality in the Kombonian context. It is a pretty tall order and there is, as they say, 'many a slip from cup to lip.' But I think you are on the right track."

She hesitated pensively for a moment, running her hand through her long brown hair. Then she let out a long sigh. "Good luck on translating all this into action. And I do respect what you and CDP, along with KADD, are trying to do here. But I must confess that I haven't really thought it all through in detail; it isn't my field. What I can tell you is that being involved in the Peace Corps here, and being in touch with Kombonians from all levels of society, I have a feeling deep down that things are heading to an explosion here."

As he looked at her and took in her words, Adam felt a stirring for her that combined physical and personal attraction, with a sense of intellectual connection. Startled, he realized, unbidden, that this combination was encompassing him like a cloak, and provoking in him a powerful feeling of excitement and awe at this woman. *Wow.*

These are super intense feelings I have never felt before in my life.

Coughing to cover his unsettled demeanor, Adam asked Sarah what impelled her to live the life that she had chosen. "Well, I guess it is because I love the challenge. I don't want to sit at home and expect life to come to me. I like to be out there trying to figure things out. There is absolutely no real training that can prepare somebody for this type of life...And I think that is pretty cool. Don't you?"

Be still my beating heart. "Yup, I would say that you have pretty much hit the nail on the head."

The following night Adam was awakened sometime after midnight by the sound of gunfire. Over his time in Kayemba City, he had gotten so accustomed to distant nocturnal gun bursts that he didn't pay much attention. Restless, but yearning to sleep, Adam even tried counting sheep to the gunfire, but it seemed to increase in intensity. When it hadn't quieted down after an hour, Adam turned on his computer but had no internet reception. The radio wasn't playing its regular programming; strangely it was featuring martial music. Unsure of what to do but unsettled simply lying in his bed, Adam finally decided to venture out and head to the office, but he didn't get far. As soon as he steered his Toyota onto July 25th Avenue, the main Kayemba City thoroughfare, he saw it was mostly empty. Except that, about six blocks away, two tanks and what appeared to be four armored personnel carriers lurked outside the building housing the KTRS, the Kombonian Television and Radio Services complex.

While he was absorbing this scene and choosing what to do,

the choice was made for him. With a roar, one of the tanks fired a shell, almost point-blank, into the building. The winking lights of return rifle fire from the building signified resistance. Screaming, "Oh my God!" Adam jammed his gears into reverse. As he sped away from the scene, an armed half-track pulled into his path. An enraged soldier jumped and rushed to Adam's vehicle, first slamming the butt of his rifle on its hood and then shattering the driver's side window, shouting, "Who are you! What are you doing?"

Adam immediately jerked his passport out of his pocket. "I am an American. What is going on? What are you doing? Why did you smash my window?" The soldier looked at him for several seconds, but for what seemed to be forever to Adam. *Jesus, he must be deciding what to do with me.*

Finally, he gave Adam another blood-freezing stare and then barked, "Go home. Get out of here!" Adam instantly decided that the broken window was a cheap price to pay for relative safety; he carefully drove home without further incident.

He immediately called Johnson at USAID. "We don't know much more than you," was his contact's tense and not very helpful reply to Adam's query about what was going on. "Looks like some kind of coup."

Not surprisingly Adam gave up trying to sleep. About an hour after he got back home, and as the first light of dawn began to illuminate Kayemba City, he succeeded in getting through on his cellphone to Yusuf. He had information that struck Adam as being measured and credible. "Here is what my sources are telling me. Mushi decided that he didn't trust Abdallah, but felt like he couldn't challenge him directly. So yesterday he apparently decided to retire Abdallah's ally General Buwinga, the head of the presidential guard, the SPB. Buwinga and Abdallah were both outraged by this and decided they would resist this order. They instructed the presidential guard to attack the state media offices and some other government sites around town; whether they were doing this as a show of force, or to actually overthrow Mushi, I don't know."

"So, what happened?"

"Well, this all took place during the night and may still be going on, for all I know. What I have heard is that before the SPB finished its attacks, Mushi got the regular army to intervene and go after the SPB. And apparently a lot of people also went out into the streets to resist and demonstrate against the SPB. That was a pretty courageous thing to do. There was a lot of fighting, but as of right now it seems like Mushi has come out on top. Be careful, though, as we have not yet confirmed this."

"Holy shit." Adam's mind was ablaze with a cacophony of thoughts. How frightening and embarrassing for Mushi that he couldn't trust his own personal security force. Marie's prediction of a military uprising had come true, although not in the way she had intended since it wasn't a reformist military revolt against Mushi. What this meant for the country, for democracy, for the CDP program—everything tumbled around in his brain like clothing in a dryer. He tried to sleep but before he finally drifted off for a couple of hours' restless dozing, his mind flashed back to two things Fobedu had said: "Progress will not be linear." *You can say that again!* And, referring to the military, "You don't need to worry about them." *Looks like Fobedu sure got that wrong.*

Later in the morning Adam ventured back to the scene of the fighting around the radio and television stations. What he saw reflected the carnage that had occurred. Corpses surrounded the burnt-out, but still smoldering, hulks of two tanks and two armored personnel carriers that had taken part in the attack, but which were then destroyed in a counterattack by the regular army units loyal to President Mushi. People wandered about the rubble with dazed looks on their faces.

Meanwhile, on the outskirts of the city, in a secluded area of an army training facility, two of the rebel soldiers were dragged, bloodied and blindfolded, across an exercise field to a rope-climbing structure anchored by two telephone pole–sized posts. A squad of eight soldiers tied their hands and waists to the posts. They then took up positions twenty-five feet away from the two men, and aimed their South African–made Vektor R4 assault rifles at them. The squad commander shouted, "Fire!" and the rifles barked. Restrained by the ropes around their waists and hands, the two men's torsos jerked backward upon the bullets' impact, and then crumpled forward, performing the obscene bow of the dead.

Chapter 15

The Run-up to the Election

I n the aftermath of the failed coup attempt, Kayemba City returned to apparent calm. General Buwinga and Minister Abdallah were arrested and charged with treason. In reality, however, the coup attempt had been a closer call than what was even publicly known. At noon the day after the coup, Oscar Mboye, Mushi's chief of intelligence, was ushered into President Mushi's office. He wasted no time getting to the point.

"Mr. President, you should know that the rebels were on their way to the presidential palace at 3:15 a.m. We know from interrogating them that their plan was to arrest and, if necessary, murder you. They were about fifteen minutes away from the palace when our forces intercepted and neutralized them."

Mushi's heart skipped a beat, but his gaze stayed calm. "What exactly happened?"

"Army units armed with bazookas and rocket-propelled grenades were able to destroy the lead vehicles, and then they moved in. They killed nine rebels and injured fifteen more. We also took a dozen prisoners. We only had a couple of wounded."

"All right. I want to go and visit the injured soldiers. And I expect a full intelligence report on what transpired by tomorrow morning."

Mboye hesitated. "There is one more thing, Mr. President. I regret to inform you that we have proof that Aziz was one of the plotters. He has also been arrested."

Mushi reeled from that news. Phillip Aziz has been one of his closest aides for years. And now he had tried to oust Mushi. That was almost more than he could bear. Mushi vowed to never speak with him again. And that the man would never see the outside of a prison cell.

Mushi then called Bowdoin Karanja, his press secretary, into his office.

"I need to issue a statement. It should say that the coup leaders were simply a group of disgruntled individuals with no broader support, and that the situation is returning to normal."

"Very good, Mr. President. Is that all?"

"No. The statement should also emphasize my commitment to democratic processes, and underscore the fact that the elections will proceed in December as according to the law and the constitution."

Uncharacteristically, Mushi then slammed his hand down on his desk and in an intense tone, slowly articulated his words. "We must find a way to guide the country through this crisis. We owe it to lay the foundations down now so that it can move forward in peace and stability, and, as difficult as it may be, develop a more democratic system."

Karanja absorbed this perspective for a moment and then asked, "Do you have thoughts on how specifically that can be achieved, sir, given the situation in which the country finds itself?"

"You know, Owemu used to say that single-party states were indeed democratic, that there was such a thing as a single-party democracy system, which embraced African traditions of emphasis on consensus and the community, rather than the individual. Well, experience has shown us that this isn't true. Without the checks and balances inherent in a multiparty system, democracy doesn't work. However, the transition to such a system—and not, to be honest, the imperfect example that we have had here—is a difficult one under the best of circumstances. The process is extremely fragile, as yesterday showed.

"But beyond the fears of my colleagues who have supported—and benefitted from—our KRP rule and are concerned that they might lose everything, there are those other interest groups and political parties competing for public support. Some may even wish to tear the country apart. We can't let that happen, but we still must channel the people's expression of opinion into the arena of political competition. Not violence. I am sick of it. We haven't seen the last of it yet, but we must end it. There is no exact blueprint for the democratization process. We must all feel our way and fairly make up the rules of the game as we go along. Doing so will be my legacy."

Not long thereafter, Adam and Yusuf had the opportunity to meet with the Kombonian Independent Election Commission. By law it was composed of seven members: two from the ruling party, two from the opposition (one from the KDPR, one from the RMK), and three retired judges. Its president was the former chief justice of the High Court of Kombonia, Wilfred Buwemu.

The day before the meeting Adam asked Yusuf, "So, in your opinion, how truly independent is the commission?"

"We all know that the government in theory can say that the

commission is balanced between the opposition and the ruling party and three, quote, 'impartial,' unquote, retired judges. The reality is that the Commission is pro-government—those judges are all, to a greater or lesser extent, part of the existing pro-KRP establishment."

"And how does the opposition feel about this?"

Yusuf quietly snorted. "You can imagine that they complain about this setup. The KDPR feels doubly aggrieved because they also think they should have more representation on the commission than the RMK because they are a larger party. But it is at least a good thing that the KDPR and even the RMK do not boycott the commission. Some of their more radical people say that by simply participating on it, they legitimize a system that is stacked against them. But the parties' leaderships understand that taking themselves out of the process would just make things even more polarized and worse for them. And to be fair, at times Justice Buwemu has actually shown a little bit of an independent mindset. A few years ago, for example, when he was the sitting chief justice he ruled in favor of a KDPR vice president who had been falsely charged with corruption."

At 11 a.m. the next day, they entered into the Election Commission's headquarters and were ushered into a waiting room replete with overstuffed leather chairs and sofas. The door to the conference room opened, and Adam and Yusuf were introduced to the Electoral Commission.

They then sat at an oblong conference table with all seven members looking expectantly at them. After some opening pleasantries, Justice Buwemu spread his hands out wide and intoned, "We are pleased to welcome our new friend from the Center for Democratic Progress as well as our old friends from KADD here to meet with us. How can we help you?"

Adam took the lead in replying. He did so carefully, having decided with Yusuf that it was premature to disclose to the Electoral Commission that they intended to undertake the Quick Count; a project which they would likely view as undercutting their authority. "Thank you so much for agreeing to meet with us. As you may know, CDP is pleased to be here in Kombonia to determine if there are ways we can assist in the electoral process. We are thinking about some sort of electoral observation mission. We may also look to help find ways for political parties to engage productively in the electoral process, along the lines of the seminar we undertook not long ago in Melinda."

The Chairman nodded his head. "Yes, we heard about that. It seems like, all things considered, that it was a success."

Adam winced, interpreting the comment as a subtle reference to his Politburo screwup. He decided to change the subject. "We also would like to have your perspective on what the key issues are regarding the administration of elections."

Buwemu said, "Let me explain a few things about our election system so that we all have the same perspective. As you know, the president is elected by a simple plurality of the vote if he receives at least 40 percent. And to be eligible to cast a ballot, as is the case in most democracies, all eligible voters must have previously registered with the Electoral Commission. This process has been proceeding well."

Yusuf interjected. "Mr. Chairman, forgive me, but you are of course aware that the recently terminated voter registration process has provoked considerable controversy. KADD estimates that up to 10 percent of the electorate's names are not on the lists published in the last registration period. Another key problem has been the distribution of national identity cards, which have been required documents for voting. Many unauthorized individuals with ties to the KRP have been distributing these cards. Also, voter registration began before provincial and local election commissions were installed; this created concerns as local election boards were supposed to oversee the process. There have been numerous examples of multiple cards being issued to a single individual. Underage individuals have been provided with the ID cards, while there are many cases of opposition party supporters being unable to secure their documents. We also have credible information that voter registration cards have been held by government authorities to be distributed on Election Day in some instances to ensure that people vote."

Buwemu had listened without expression to Yusuf's list of complaints. "We at the IEC understand that there are flaws in the identity card distribution process. I can't speak for them, but I would suggest that the ministry of the interior, which has responsibility for the election logistics, has recognized its mistakes in this regard. But let us keep things in proportion. Some of what you say may be true, but no election, no matter where in the world, is an exercise in perfection. In fact, expecting perfection can be, if I may say so, the enemy of the good.

"Now, some of the problems to which you allude can be corrected and should not be of a magnitude to impact the election results. To be frank, we see that some of the problems may be due to overzealousness of party cadre who do what they think is desired by the leadership."

Yusuf plowed on. "With respect, I would recommend that the authorities institute greater neutrality in state media and allowing media space. Regarding election management, even seemingly small things are critical, such as adequate lighting in polling places, especially for vote counting in the evenings. Resources also need to be identified so that political parties can have observers at polling places. Again, with respect, I would suggest that the Election Commission should more proactively engage and consult with the political parties, including the opposition."

The atmosphere in the room became tenser. Buwemu, somewhat defensively responded, "You know that the government and the IEC have undertaken some positive steps. In response to recommendations resulting from the last elections, the revised electoral code stipulates that only a single ballot is to be used. And in 2018, the IEC agreed that proxy voting, by which someone could cast a vote for another person, should be eliminated. It also agreed to reopen registration for those who have not received cards for a limited, but as yet unspecified, amount of time."

Yusuf was not to be deterred. "Yes, but we are concerned that the KRP continues to seek to quietly manipulate the pre-electoral environment. There have been attempts to sow divisions within opposition parties, an overly broad interpretation of laws forbidding opposition party meetings and demonstrations on the grounds of maintaining public order, and even the physical intimidation of opposition party supporters at times. The ministry of the interior has the power to forbid political party demonstrations on the grounds that they may 'disturb the public order.' The vagueness of this terminology gives the authorities considerable discretionary power."

Buwemu shifted in his chair uncomfortably. "We can dispute much of what you say. But even if we agreed with you, many of these issues are beyond the purview of the IEC. We simply do not have jurisdiction on some of these sensitive election administration issues, but we are committed to correct problems where we can."

As the meeting concluded, Adam said, "We greatly appreciate this meeting and the chance to have a substantive and open exchange with you on these election issues. I know that we all have the interests of Kombonia at heart, and that a legitimate election is the key to this country's future. We look forward to our future contacts."

Buwemu soberly acknowledged the remarks, nodded and shook Adam's hand. "We all share your thoughts in this regard. This election must be a success."

A day later, Adam had a chance encounter in a restaurant with Michael Kituyu, a senior KRP leader who had been at the Melinda seminar. They talked elections. Kituyu was firm in his views. "Ethnicity is not the problem. The problem is that the opposition is whipping up resentments in order to turn people against the government so that they could win the election and establish a dictatorship. And the civil society plays into their hands. In reality we all know that they do not like us and thus support the opposition, even if it is undemocratic at heart."

"But what about the specific criticism of the election preparations? What about, for example, the voter's list issue?"

"That is not a huge problem. Yes, there was some underage registration, but it is not at all certain that younger voters would necessarily support the ruling party. By the same token, there have been some foreigners registered, but it is not clear for whom they would vote. Everyone knows everyone in the rural areas; this is a natural way to control fraud. It is the responsibility of political parties to mobilize their supporters to register. The senior KRP leadership knows that insurgents recently killed in various incidents were PMLP militants, but they have not trumpeted that fact to avoid inflaming the situation; this is an example of us acting responsibly.

"We and President Mushi are generally well liked in the country; we are popular. That may not be quite so evident here in Kayemba City, but I can assure you that there is much support for us in other towns and rural areas."

Adam did not automatically accept this self-serving line. "But given the absence of credible polling in Kombonia, how do you know how much support you really have?"

Kituyu laughed. "Oh my goodness. All you have to do is come and travel with us on one of our campaign tours. In fact, you must have watched them on television—you can see the crowds and the enthusiastic support we get."

As part of getting the lay of the land regarding the elections, Adam asked for and was granted a meeting with Ambassador Anderson to discuss the perspectives and likely election-related roles of countries providing significant amounts of aid to Kombonia. Anderson pointed out the basic challenge they faced. "The reality is that donors are wrestling with a situation where they may end up either supporting a process which could result in an illegitimate election, or not being engaged, and thus risking the same result. The European Union will probably send an observer delegation because of the underlying importance of a stable Kombonia in the region."

"Is that really important? To be honest—and I am not saying that this is necessarily the situation here—I wonder if sometimes there is a tendency to overstate the 'strategic importance to the US' argument just to make the case for increased support to a country." *Hot damn. I'm getting more self-confident. I wouldn't have spoken like this to the ambassador even just a few weeks ago.*

Anderson took no offense. "No, you're right, you're right; I have seen that happen sometimes. But not in this instance. What with strategic minerals mined here, the regional terrorism, and the potential for humanitarian disaster if Kombonia were to go the way of a 'failed state'—no, there is more than enough reason for us to be very concerned that this country move toward stability, democracy, and sustained development."

"How about other actors such as the UN?" Adam asked.

"They are thinking of having a modest election monitoring effort by placing a couple of dozen observers in four regional hubs, but this has yet to be approved by the government. The African Union will undoubtedly send some observers, but to be frank, the history of such missions shows that they usually end up supporting the governments in power. Stated politely, political and diplomatic considerations may complicate the capacity and will of some of these groups to objectively assess the electoral process. Put more bluntly, the good ol' boys' network on the continent remains very strong.

"The European Union is looking at several different ways to promote the electoral process here. They have an approximately $600 million budget for Kombonia for the next seven years. Like us, they have considerable interest in promoting a legitimate system of governance in the country so their other interests here don't go up in smoke."

Anderson continued. "These include contributing about $5 million to a basket fund sponsored by the UN Development Programme for election activities. This is frankly not the most efficient way to proceed, especially since some of this money would go to the ministry of interior, but at least some conditions would be placed on the government's use of this money so that, at least in theory, this wouldn't all go to support Mushi."

"What about a European Union election observation mission?" Adam queried.

"The EU is also thinking about this. A small, technical level feasibility assessment team is coming soon. And they are also conducting what they politely call an 'intensified political dialogue' with the government, where they have very frank discussions about what is needed in order for the electoral process to move ahead. The EU ambassador has told me that the government has proven to be very stubborn and unwilling to accept advice, except when it is accompanied with the threat of cuts in funding."

Adam was once again amazed by how much he didn't know, about diplomacy in general and Kombonia specifically. "Tell me more about this basket fund. How does that work?"

"So, it is a fund into which the donor countries can contribute. The idea is that the money can be allocated and spent in a coordinated and efficient fashion. The downside is that it is another layer of bureaucracy to navigate through. And the government is interested in getting its hands on this money, while we want it to be spent to ensure good elections."

"What happens to this money if the election process gets hijacked by the government?"

"The donors are certainly faced with the potential problem of whether and at what point they would suspend election-related assistance, i.e., what constitutes the red line in this regard. It is a subject I am discussing at this very time with my fellow ambassadors."

The KADD headquarters was a beehive of activity as preparations continued for the Quick Count.

Adam, Yusuf, the KADD academic adviser, field organizer, and communications person all met to discuss the status of the effort. Adam started off. "So, again, let's do the math. We know that the IEC has identified 9,122 polling places for an electorate of about five million people. We know that a well-drawn sample of polling places can produce a low margin of error result from about only eight percent of the country's polling places. Let's make a conservative estimate that we need ten percent, which works out to 912 sites. We'll need teams of at least two people per polling place. So, we are looking at having to field almost 2,000 observers.

"Regarding the sample, we have to look at issues such as ethnicity, geographic location, income, gender, religion, age, education levels, and language. All of these may have, to a greater or lesser extent, a correlation with each other."

Yusuf responded. "Right. We will produce a list of proposed sites that reflect these variables. We should understand that not all the data you cite exists or, if it does, is of a high quality. But we will do the best we can."

"Good. We also need to identify who the Quick Count observers will be, and how the operation here in Kayemba City will be managed. And what training all these folks will need."

Yusuf agreed. "Everyone will need to have a working cell phone. We need to be simple. I suggest that we use SMS technology to transmit the vote results according to candidate, and a simple one-to-five scale indicating the extent of any sort of problems in the polling—logistical security, administrative, whatever. One means no problems, five means huge problems. We also need to use social media to educate people and alert them to the purpose of this effort."

Adam then raised the sensitive subject of the Quick Count itself. "When should we go public with this? We have to be very careful. We don't want to be seen as some sort of 'secret' operation that is not transparent. If we are to be believed, people must under-stand how we arrived at our judgements. I suggest that it would be appropriate for us to inform the IEC perhaps three weeks before the election, and to also issue a press release for the public after we have let the IEC know what we are planning."

Adam then asked Yusuf, "What do you think are the chances that they would try to stop us from doing this?"

"We should emphasize to Buwemu and the IEC that this effort could help augment public confidence in the official results if the results end up being similar."

Adam pushed. "Would we make our results public before we inform the IEC? The government wouldn't like that."

"I think we make that call at the time. It should depend on what has happened and how well it looks like the election is going. In general, though, I would say that we don't want it to look like we are giving the government a veto power over our operation. The whole point is for us to be independent, and to arrive at an impartial conclusion about what has happened."

Adam was nervous. "I guess we live in interesting times."

Yusuf took Adam aside later in the day. "Think of how much the lack of an independent judiciary is a chilling factor on partic-ipating in politics. The government can use this to harass people. Now, granted that Mushi has kept the KRP from acting too egre-giously in this regard, but the threat is always present. For example, anyone convicted of a felony is disqualified from presenting them-selves as a candidate for political office. In addition, the voter regis-tration problems pose a serious threat to the upcoming elections."

Chapter 16

Presidential Debate

A week later Duwango called Adam into his office. Yusuf was also present. Addressing his steely gaze at Adam, Duwango was typically curt and to the point. "I believe it would be an excellent idea for KADD to sponsor a debate between the presidential candidates. This would be the first time ever that an electoral debate would happen in Kombonia, and it would be good for the country. Of course, in terms of organizing this, we would benefit from CDP's experience in this regard."

Adam was nonplussed and shifted in his chair, which, he had noticed, was lower than Duwango's. "Isn't it a bit too late to undertake such a project? We only have two months before the election. There would have to be a lot of work to make this happen, and it would be complicated and time-consuming. And, if this wasn't a success, it could adversely affect our Quick Count—the preparations for which, I might add, we are fully preoccupied."

Duwango replied unflappably, "I think that it is feasible to do both. We could get this debate set up within a couple of weeks."

"I have to object, Mr. Duwango. Why should we do this? It could be a failure. And, again, it would draw our attention away from undertaking the Quick Count."

Yusuf opted in. "If I may, I agree with Mr. Duwango. There are a number of good things that could come from it. It could help to focus the candidates on specific issues that need to be addressed here. And it would inform voters and give them a chance to understand what the candidates really stand for. It could calm the political waters by channeling the candidates together to talk about things, rather than not having any direct interaction. We should not let the fear of failure deter us."

Adam snorted. "Goodness, Yusuf, if I may say so you usually aren't so positive about how things could work here in Kombonia."

Yusuf defused the jibe. "I simply think it would be in all the candidates' best interests and a step toward creating a more democratic culture here. It would help voters make an informed choice at the ballot box and orient the campaign focus toward public policy issues rather than personality, religion, or ethnic loyalties. You may have perhaps noticed that the latter issues have been dominating the campaign recently.

"And for Ruwoyo and Obewame, it could certainly give them an image of being on an equal level with Mushi. It could help normalize the idea that people can run against the president. As for Mushi, he can show how reasonable and democratically minded he is. And the international donors would love it."

Duwango let out an approving chuckle. "And I sincerely doubt that there will not be many other opportunities for the candidates to be together at the same time in the same place."

Adam's opposition was crumbling. "Listen, putting aside what we need to do to prepare for the Quick Count, this thing is going to be complicated. Here's just one big question we'd have to figure out: who gets invited?"

Yusuf was on a roll—Adam suspected that he and Duwango

had already discussed this idea, and were not going to let Adam derail it. "We think the number should be limited. From an organizational perspective, involving all candidates would make the staging more cumbersome and reduce the time each candidate gets to speak. Limiting the number of candidates would allow voters to hear more about the policies of the front runners, who are most likely to win."

Adam reluctantly agreed. *Looks like I never had a chance. Oh well, this is their country.* "Ok. Let me do some quick research to get advice and ideas about how to organize this."

The next day Adam emailed Mulcahy with a request for any useful information CDP could provide about presidential debates in emerging democracies, which he quickly received. Three days later, Adam met again with Yusuf and Duwango. "I've been in touch with my people back at CDP headquarters. They provided me with information about how presidential debates have been handled in other countries. To be honest, I had no idea there had been so many of them. In Africa alone there have been official debates in countries such as Ghana, Kenya, Nigeria, and Malawi. And around the world, in Jamaica, Peru, Trinidad and Tobago, East Timor, Haiti, Serbia, Colombia, and Paraguay."

Duwango responded with alacrity. "Excellent. We now need to reach out to political parties right away to express interest in holding debates and get their feedback."

Adam refused to be rushed. "Well, before we do that, there are some things that I think we need to nail down. Such as, what should the threshold criteria be for participation? I know that there are reasons why the number of candidates in the debate should be limited, but I wonder if it wouldn't be good to cast the net at least somewhat widely? This could show Kombonians that there is a range of perspectives and possible candidates."

Duwango replied, "My friend, I admire your instincts, but let me tell you something—despite the impediments the government has placed in the way of opposition candidacies, there are still a lot of people aspiring to be president. So we have to be realistic. Do we really want to have a dozen or more candidates on the stage? Look at how you Americans have done it, with the place so crowded with candidates that they hardly have time to give meaningful answers. No, I think we have to plan that there will only be a limited number of candidates on the stage."

"OK, I guess I can agree with that. Then how about if we use the same criteria we did for the seminar in Melinda? That makes it simple—just the candidates of parties with elected members of parliament were eligible. So that would mean Mushi, Ruwoyo, and Obewame."

"Good. We are in agreement."

"So, now let me share with you some of the debate-related organization aspects that I got from my people at CDP headquarters. We have to figure out what needs to be done. We've got to figure out a debate plan. We'll have to decide, in consultation with the candidates' teams, issues such as the date, location, time, rules, topics, and format. And how much say will we allow candidates to have over the selection of a moderator and panelists?"

Yusuf spoke for the first time. "I agree—we need to have some organizing ground rules. First, this is a KADD-sponsored event. Obviously we have to be impartial, focused, and effective in producing this event. We must keep it simple. I think we should recognize that there may be mistakes along the way, but so long as the candidates' views get expressed, even if things don't go exactly as planned, the debate will still mark an important step ahead."

"So who should be the moderator? He'd need to be someone neutral and respected. Perhaps either the Catholic or Moslem religious leaders—Archbishop Semfala or Imam Abdel Nassar?" Adam queried.

Duwango quickly responded. "I don't think the imam or archbishop would be acceptable individually—they would be seen as representing their faith, which is connected to the politics of the country. But we could have them as co-moderators."

Adam demurred, "I think that would get awkward. Can we think of one person who enjoys widespread respect across the nation?"

Yusuf snapped his fingers. "How about Pascal Ngumbi, our national football hero? He is smart and articulate. He has remained above politics but cares a lot about Kombonia and knows what is going on. And he is used to dealing with the media."

Duwango nodded his head in agreement. Respecting Yusuf's judgement as he did, Adam certainly had no cause to object.

"Regarding the questioners," Yusuf continued, "I think we should just accept that the media reflects the reality of our political environment. I suggest that we have two questioners, one coming from state media and one from the independent side. But we would have to impress upon them that they are to be as evenhanded as possible in their approach."

Adam picked up the thread. "Let's say that the debate is to last ninety minutes. That should be long enough to be meaningful, but not too long. We could have five minutes for introductions and five for opening statements, then twenty-five minutes each for segments on substantive themes." Adam wanted to continue suggesting specific topics but he held back, sensing both that Duwango and Yusuf were buying into the flow of the planning process, and that he shouldn't try to dominate the planning too much. "I think you guys should make that decision."

Yusuf made a typically insightful comment. "Clearly, the question of ethnicity and how we can all live together is the core issue. The problem is that we Kombonians feel uncomfortable discussing this openly. Much is suppressed, like in Rwanda about the genocide, or in Ethiopia given its history of conquest and ethnic domination."

Duwango nodded and added a suggestion. "Let's have a topic called 'security.' That can include foreign relations and the protection of our borders, but it can also relate to internal security, which leads into the problem of peaceful coexistence here. And of democracy."

Yusuf agreed. "That is good. We should also have a segment on the economy, which could also cover a wide range of issues. And I would propose another one on social development. How are the candidates proposing to more fully support women's rights, for example? What about plans to improve health, education, and agriculture? And the environment? All these candidates promise to make things better, but in vague and general terms. Let's get them to provide some specifics."

Duwango concurred, but added a warning. "These are important, but let's not fool ourselves. This debate, and this election, is about whether Kombonia will end dictatorial rule and move forward, or whether it will become a failed state."

Adam jumped back in. "And, to get back to the debate format, candidates could be allowed up to two minutes to answer a question in these issue-specific segments. And rebuttals could last up to one minute. These would be followed by five minutes for closing statements." Neither of the Kombonians had any objections. "Now for a big question: where should it be?"

Duwango answered. "I think that is easy. The university would be an excellent venue; it is viewed by Kombonians as a somewhat neutral institution. Its conference center could hold a large crowd. And I am certain that the vice chancellor of the university would approve of this."

Similarly, gaining Ngumbi's acceptance as moderator proved to be simple. Yusuf played football in a weekend league with Ngumbi's brother, and used that connection to arrange a meeting with Ngumbi at his nicely appointed residence. Ngumbi reacted positively, but cautiously, to the invitation. "I'd be honored to do this. But I have never acted in this capacity before. What would it entail?"

Other than the emailed information he had received from CDP, Adam's debating knowledge was limited. His experience at the parry-and-thrust of debating, after all, had mostly been of the late-night, beer-fueled kind. But he felt confident and responded authoritatively. "There are really only a couple of key things to keep in mind. First, know the debate rules—you'll be in charge of enforcing them. Second, third, fourth and fifth: act, and appear to be acting, in an impartial manner."

"What role will I have in developing the questions?" Adam and Yusuf glanced at each other. They had discussed this point with Duwango, who had wanted to decide the questions in conjunction with Yusuf. The latter, with Adam's support, had talked him out of it, arguing that the moderator and questioners would want to, and should, be vested in the effort. The result was a compromise.

"You and the two journalists will have the responsibility of developing a draft list of questions. We will review them with you and together we'll make the final decision." Ngumbi nodded his agreement.

A thornier issue turned out to be approaching the candidates' campaigns and negotiating the terms of their involvement. For example, Yusuf had a meeting with Rafael Kibimwe, the RMK presidential campaign manager. After checking with Obewame, his response was ambivalent. "Well, of course it would be good for the people of Kombonia to have this kind of forum, from which they could understand how our leadership would benefit them. But it is not that simple a question. How would we know that we would be treated equally and respectfully? Who would be conducting the debate? What would be its format? How could we be sure that this process wouldn't be biased in favor of the other candidates?"

Yusuf reviewed the format of the debate and the steps that KADD was taking to address these concerns. "Alright—we will think about this and get back to you," was the reply.

Adam met with Ruwoyo himself, after having sent a message indicating the subject of the meeting request. Adam interpreted the quick and positive response from Ruwoyo as a good sign. Unlike his previous dinner meeting with the KDPR leader, the only other people in the room this time were Ruwoyo and two campaign advisers. Ruwoyo did have a number of questions that, like the RMK, reflected a lack of trust in the political environment, but he seemed open to the idea.

Seeking to close the deal, Adam said, "Let me emphasize some ways that the debate would be in your interest, if I may. A debate would provide you with a unique opportunity to speak directly to the voters without any filtering by the media. This would help level the election playing field where, let's be frank, the ruling party dominates access to the media. You would also receive a huge amount of free media coverage. You could connect with independent and undecided voters, who are less likely to watch or attend a campaign rally than your party faithful. It would also help to advertise your candidacy to Kombonians abroad, and to the international community."

Adam and Yusuf then met with Goodwill Monanga, President Mushi's campaign manager. The meeting took place at the campaign headquarters in a large villa in an upscale part of Kayemba City. The building was a beehive of activity, with a constant movement of people in and out. A seating area under the cicada trees contained dirty white plastic chairs, which were mostly occupied. "What is everyone doing or waiting for?" Adam queried Yusuf.

The latter let out a quiet snort and replied, "These are party precinct workers waiting for payouts to distribute to voters to, shall we say, encourage them to support the present."

After a half-hour wait, they were ushered into the ubiquitously freezing office of the campaign manager. Its atmosphere was somber, with drawn window curtains. Monanga, a former deputy secretary-general of the KRP, was a heavy-set man of indeterminate age. He mirrored the room's *feng shui* as he peered suspiciously over his glasses at his visitors and asked how he could be of assistance. Yusuf explained the purpose of the visit, which had already been alluded to in an email requesting a visit: to invite the president to take part in a campaign debate.

Monanga paused briefly. "This is a very interesting idea in principle, but I must tell you that we believe such a debate could be disrespectful to the office of the presidency. How do we know the opposition would not attempt to turn this into some kind of circus?"

Yusuf responded. "We would establish clear rules of procedure and be prepared to enforce them fully. This will be a disciplined event, I can assure you, sir. And it would be good for the country, and for the president, to be seen by the Kombonian people as engaging with the other candidates. I am sure you would agree that now is not the time to be perceived as hiding from the electorate."

Monanga skillfully parried this thrust. "I agree with you fully. It is important for the president to be amongst the people. And in fact this debate of yours would take time away from his campaign rallies. As you know the theme of the president's campaign is 'With You One-to-One.' He is placing the emphasis on meeting voters individually to the maximum extent possible."

"This will be one evening away from all that. And just think of how many people will see this."

Monanga changed tack. "Why don't you want to have other candidates besides Ruwango and Obewame? Are you favoring them for some reason? There are many others out there. After all, we want a pluralist democracy where all voices can be heard."

"We have thought about that but believe a larger debate could become unmanageable. The threshold of representation in parliament is a clear-cut and, it seems to us, justifiable one."

"Well, I do not have the authority to agree to this debate. You will have to wait to hear back from us."

Yusuf cast one more lure. "We certainly hope that your response will be positive. This debate will take place with or without the president. I am sure that he would not want to disappoint the people of Kombonia."

As they left the building, Adam whispered to Yusuf, "That's bullshit about other candidates. Mushi just wants the opposition vote to be split further."

"I agree. I also think that Monanga's lack of enthusiasm for this is because he really does believe the president is ahead in the race. He doesn't want to risk his lead by giving his main opponents credibility by sharing the stage with them."

"Did you really mean it about staging the debate, even without Mushi?"

A hint of a grin flickered across Yusuf's mouth. "I think you Americans have an expression—'if you build it they will come.'"

Adam demurred. "I bet you a goat this debate won't happen."

It didn't take long for Adam to be proven wrong. The next day Monanga reported to Mushi on the conversation. Mushi overruled his campaign manager's advice not to participate. "I actually think that our friends from KADD make some good points. I am not afraid of debating anyone, including Ruwoyo and Obewame. I can show the people that I am the only candidate with the experience and perspective to guide this country into the future. Tell them that I accept, and negotiate the details."

On October 10, Yusuf called Adam. "I have excellent news. I look forward to receiving a goat from you. Mushi, Ruwoyo, and Obewame have all agreed to participate in the debate! They want more information and have asked some follow-on questions about security and the debate format, so there is still a lot more to figure out from the logistical perspective, but it looks like this is going to happen!"

In the late morning of October 30, the day of the debate, Adam and Yusuf were going over some last-minute planning details when Justus, the KADD messenger and airport expeditor, rushed into the room. "I've just come from the airport and passed by the University of Kombonia's conference center—there is a huge crowd there. I stopped to ask some of them what was going on, and they said that they were waiting for this debate! It looks like this is going to be a huge event."

Later that afternoon, the KADD team went to the conference center. Indeed, they guessed that there were perhaps 10,000 people milling about, even though the venue only seated about half that number, and tickets had already been distributed. Adam had an inspiration. "Yusuf—what if we were to rig up at least one loudspeaker so that these folks could hear the debate."

Yusuf shook his head in amazement at the size of the crowd. "My goodness. All of these people here—they want to get in even though the event is being broadcast over radio and on TV. I do think that a loudspeaker would be a good idea although it seems like many of them are carrying radios. And they seem to be excited and good humored—it looks like many of them are opposition supporters. I hope that things don't get ugly with the security forces. Or that the PMLP or other provocateurs don't use violence."

There was a huge crowd pressing on the doors to the center. "Where is Obewame?" Yusuf asked no one in particular. "He was supposed to be here an hour ago. Mushi and Ruwoyo are already here." Finally, a convoy of vehicles pulled up and the RMK candidate emerged amongst a scrum of bodyguards. Without pausing to make any comments, he strutted into the convention center, looking to Adam like a prize fighter entering the ring.

A half hour before the debate was supposed to start, Justus

arrived with a loudspeaker set; he and a helper placed it outside and after consultation with a police colonel in charge of security, Yusuf made an announcement to the crowd that they would be able to listen to the debate.

Inside, with ten minutes to go, the moderator Ngumbi sat at a desk in the middle of the stage, flanked by the two journalists. Mushi sat to their left in an arc, while Ruwoyo and Obewame sat at desks to the left.

There was a last-minute technical problem when the lights went out five minutes before the debate was scheduled to start. This resulted in gasps of concern from the audience, many quickly assumed it was an attempt by one group or another to keep the debate from proceeding. After a long minute a back-up generator kicked in, and power was restored to the collective relief of participants and organizers alike.

Ngumbi silenced the crowd. "Good evening from the University of Kombonia. I'm Pascal Ngumbi, your host for our nation's first ever presidential campaign debate." Cheers flooded the arena. Ngumbi continued, "This event is sponsored by the Kombonian Association for Democracy and Development. "The debate will address real issues. We hope that the dialogue this evening will promote political tolerance, politics without bitterness, constructive dialogue, and politics in service to the people.

"Tonight's debate will cover a wide range of topics, including domestic and foreign policy matters. It will be roughly divided into five-minute segments. Each candidate will have ninety seconds to respond to a direct question and then an additional two minutes for rebuttal and follow-up. The order has been determined by a coin toss. The specific subjects and questions were chosen by KADD and have not been shared or cleared with anyone on the campaigns or on the commission." Ngumbi then held up colored placards in the Kombonian national colors (green, yellow, and red) to let candidates and the audience know when time limits had been reached.

"So, let us now welcome the candidates: the honorable Simon Mushi, President of the Republic of Kombonia and the standard bearer of the Kombonian Revolutionary Party; Mr. Ignace Ruwoyo, the President of the Kombonian Democratic Popular Rally, and Mr. Felix Obewame, President of the Renewal Movement of Kombonia. Gentlemen, I invite you to greet each other."

With only a momentary hesitation, the three candidates left their lecterns to engage in handshakes in front of the stage. They then held their hands up together. For the second time, rapturous applause erupted.

The candidates made their opening statements, with Mushi emphasizing his policy of a democratic opening with continuity and stability. Ruwoyo sought to present himself in a statesman-like manner, ready to govern, and Obewame launched into an attack on both of the other candidates. He garnered applause from some of the audience, which was quickly discouraged by the moderator, when he argued that Mushi was an autocrat and that Ruwoyo was a "carbon copy of Mushi in waiting."

They then moved into the first round of questioning. Ngumbi asked each candidate to explain what they would do to eliminate the politically inspired violence in the country. Mushi spoke first. "I understand the need for continued change. Too many people in this country still do not have what they need to live good and prosperous lives. Too many people have been left by the wayside in the development of this country. Too many people remain on the outside, looking in. I understand that.

"But the way to progress is not by radical change, by resorting to ethnic-based violence, by seeking to tear down all that we have achieved. The way forward is through thoughtful, measured change. We must tamp down the passions that abound in this country. The way to do so is to make sure that all legitimate political movements have the opportunity to meaningfully compete, and to let the people of Kombonia decide who should be their government. I pledge to make this happen." Mushi sat down to scattered cheers.

It was Ruwoyo's turn next. "Well, you have just heard some nice words. But they conveniently hide the fact that the status quo favors a certain portion of people in this country. Continuity in power will not change that. If elected, I promise to not only allow other voices to be heard, I will represent them!"

Ruwoyo continued, to rising applause despite Ngumbi's efforts to quell the audience. "President Mushi is right—Kombonia needs a change! Kombonia needs a change!! It desperately needs a change, but that won't happen if he stays in power. Let us start a new day, beginning now!"

Obewame was beginning to sweat heavily under the onstage klieg lighting. He mopped his brow. But now it was his turn to let loose. "Let me tell you the truth. I do not know what my opponents are thinking. They both talk about change, but it is not for real. Do you remember the story about the *Titanic*? Well President Mushi in reality wants to keep the deck chairs arranged the way they currently are. Mr. Ruwoyo wants to rearrange them. But both of these views ignore the reality—the ship is sinking!!!" The audience erupted.

Ngumbi stepped in. "Mr. Obewame, I must ask you to stop violating the agreed upon rules of the debate. Please do not make any more personal attacks against your opponents and respect the time limits."

Obewame's response was thunderous. "I am not making personal attacks! I am simply speaking the truth!"

Adam, offstage, murmured to Yusuf, "Holy shit—this is what I hate about populism; it gets people stirred up without thinking of the consequences."

Yusuf stared back at him for a second, and then whispered forcefully, "You still don't understand. These people have been suppressed for centuries. They have a legitimate reason to be angry. The question is whether Obewame can be a wise and forceful enough leader to channel this anger in a productive way, especially if he loses."

Toward the end of the debate, Mushi was asked, "Will you concede defeat if you lose?"

"Throughout Africa, presidents have lost elections and conceded defeat. If this can happen in Ghana and Kenya, why not here in Kombonia?"

Ruwoyo opened up a line of attack. "The electronic media is biased in favor of the ruling party. This fact is underscored by media monitoring undertaken by my party, which shows that coverage of the ruling party exceeded that of the opposition by a four-to-one margin. There are also complaints that local officials in several districts have cancelled opposition rallies on the basis that they constituted 'a threat' to public security. Three minor opposition candidates were refused permission to run on the grounds that they did not meet the constitutional requirement of parents having been born in Kombonia. There were also complaints lodged by the opposition that government workers solicited support, during working hours, on behalf of the president. Similar complaints stated that government vehicles have been used to deliver KRP campaign materials."

Mushi delivered his own critiques of the opposition. "The opposition likes to proclaim its attachment to democracy. But how truly democratic are they? Are you aware that we have received threats advising us against campaigning in opposition strongholds?"

Ngumbi then invited the candidates to make their closing statements. Ruwoyo went first, and made a completely unexpected offer. "I would like to propose that, for the remaining time before the election, our three campaigns adopt a joint code of conduct. This could include commitments to denounce all and any campaign violence, a pledge to accept the results of the election, and a promise to not undertake any dirty tricks. By doing so, the three of us could show the people that it is possible to compete against each other, but not as enemies; that violence has no place in an election; that we can allow our leaders to be chosen by the will of the people."

For a moment the audience was quiet, stunned. It then erupted in a spontaneous round of cheers and applause. Adam was shocked and amazed—it was as if the Kombonian people had been waiting—even yearning—for exactly such a moment.

Mushi knew that he had been tactically outflanked. But he also agreed with the idea, and thus responded quickly. "In the spirit of compromise and conciliation, I can assure you that my campaign would be prepared to accept and abide by such a code in principle. It is our strong desire that this campaign be seen by future Kombonians as reflective of the deepening democratic culture, and as a stepping stone toward peace and prosperity within the Kombonian nation." Seeking to regain the momentum, he then added, "There is no time to lose. My campaign manager would be prepared to negotiate the details of the code of conduct tomorrow."

Obewame was displeased by this turn of events. He too was taken by surprise, and by instinct was opposed to an initiative that could blunt his strident message. But he clearly couldn't simply dismiss it, given its apparent widespread popularity. He ad-libbed, saying, "It is all good to propose wonderful-sounding agreements. But we have learned through bitter experience that the devil is in the details. And we must be certain that such an offer is being made in good faith. There is not much time left before the election. So we shall see."

And with that, the debate was suddenly over. A wave of applause engulfed the candidates as they moved offstage. The KADD team gathered together in an almost giddy spirit of success. Later, as Adam was leaving the conference center, he saw Sarah lingering by a pillar. She was smiling at him.

"Hey—were you just waiting for me?"

"Maybe I was. Maybe I just wanted to tell you how proud I am of you, and the work you have done to make this debate a success. I know how much of a role you have played behind-the-scenes."

Adam was touched and excited by her expression of thoughtfulness and caring, even as he thought that she was giving him a bit too much credit. He covered up his emotions by hamming it up. Taking an exaggerated bow and sweeping an imaginary *Three Musketeers* hat off his head, he dipped forward, saying, "Adam Edwards at your service, m'lady. I was just doing my part. May I invite you out for a celebratory drink?"

"I'd be delighted."

Sarah wasn't the only one noting Adam's role. Mushi told an aide, "I don't think that KADD could have made this debate happen without that American's help. He seems to be intelligent, despite his previous mistakes. I think we need to keep him in view; he might prove useful to us—and perhaps Kombonia—in the weeks to come.

Chapter 17

At the Precipice

Three weeks before the election, in the midst of hectic eighteen-hour days spent working with KADD to oversee the Quick Count, Adam was shocked to see a headline in the *Clarion* stating, "PMLP Says No to Elections!" *What the hell? Wouldn't they, of all people, want to see this government defeated in the election?* The article went on to quote from a communique issued by the PMLP:

The entire system of Tuyunu dominance is rotten to the core. The KRP will do all in its power to steal this election. And the cadres of the KDPR have the same mentality as the KRP; the only difference is which elite sector of society would be favored. The injustices of this entire system must be vanquished! Make no mistake about it: we need a revolution to defeat the divide-and-rule mindset of our leaders! No one will be free until the Pohane have their rightful place at the table. This current election will not solve the problems of the Pohane people, nor of the Kombonian nation as a whole! We call upon all Kombonians to unite to throw off the oppressors. Join us in the struggle! Freedom or death!!

In a gesture of cooperation, and a recognition of the efficiencies involved, Yusuf had succeeded in negotiating an agreement with the IEC to hold joint training sessions around the country for IEC election poll workers and designated KADD Quick Count observers. These sessions were designed to provide information on Election Day procedures such as voter identification, provision of ballots, voting process, vote count, and resolution of disputes. The Saturday following the PMLP announcement, in the outskirts of Kayemba City, the KADD and Electoral Commission were holding a training session for about one hundred poll workers and observers.

The venue was a dusty schoolyard; Yusuf was present to see how things were going. It was about 3 p.m. A mid-level IEC official was explaining how the process worked. Suddenly, with no warning, three pick-up trucks careened into the parking area. About a dozen heavily armed fighters wearing face masks jumped out and began shouting, ordering everyone to lie down on the ground with their hands stretched out in front of them. Initial screams and shouts from the poll workers quickly tailed off as the shock of the moment settled in, and they complied with the terrorists' demands.

After a few minutes, one fighter detached himself from the pack and strode to the front of the yard. Facing the prostrate audience, he announced, "You are all the guests of the PMLP! Do as we instruct and no harm will come to you. You are to slowly take out your cell phones and give them to us. After that, stay as you are."

Some of the fighters then began moving amongst the workers, collecting the phones. Yusuf, toward the back of the group, was able to surreptitiously send an SMS to Duwango, who knew where he was, before surrendering his phone. It simply said "HELP."

After the phones had been collected, a bizarre calm briefly settled over the school grounds. The sounds of rapid breathing came from some of the people as they began to absorb the horror of their newly acquired hostage status. Little was said; the fighters paced around, a few began to look at their watches. After a few minutes, Yusuf saw, out of the corner of his semi-closed eyes, the apparent leader take another fighter off to one side and have what seemed to be an increasingly animated conversation.

As the minutes dragged by, Yusuf began to feel the heat of the sun increase and accumulated sweat drip off his body. The dust near his forehead began to be muddied by his sweat. He wondered if this was to be the end of his life. Would he and his compatriots end up as machine-gunned carcasses here; proverbial, wasted by-products of the PMLP's wrath? Was that what this was coming to? What purpose would that serve?

After about fifteen minutes, the leader received a phone call. It led to a shouting match after which he ended the call in disgust. He then ordered a half dozen of the fighters to form a perimeter outside of the school. This was a prescient move as Yusuf, still prone on the ground, could hear and feel approaching vehicles. Soon thereafter, there was some indistinct shouting, and then machine-gun fire tore through the air. Cursing, the remaining fighters ran out of the yard toward the firing.

Yusuf gathered a group of poll workers and urged them to quietly get up and head to the side of the school where there didn't seem to be any shooting going on. They crowded into a couple of classrooms and began to animatedly discuss, in hushed tones, what to do. Some wanted to make a run for freedom via the surrounding buildings; others thought it best to remain where they were.

The debate ended when the firing suddenly stopped. A few moments later, they then heard a voice telling them to exit the classrooms with their hands up. Yusuf swallowed deeply as he emerged, not knowing whether his kidnappers or rescuers would be present. He reappeared into the sunlight to see two groups of uniformed army soldiers with their rifles drawn—one was escorting former hostages away, the other searching other buildings. A wave of thankfulness washed over him; he felt the unfamiliar feeling of relief at the sight of the Kombonian military as they acted as rescuers, rather than oppressors.

After a few minutes of interrogation—the military wanted to be sure there were no fighters amongst them—Yusuf was allowed to leave the premises. He saw a half dozen of the fighters; it was now their turn to be lying face down in the dirt. He also walked past the torn bodies of four of the terrorists who had been killed in the army's assault. He recognized one of them, eyes gaping sightlessly at the sky, as the journalist Marie Mfalla.

That evening Yusuf, who had been quietly aware of Adam's dalliance with Marie, called Adam, who had heard about the attack from several people, but had not gotten many of the details. Yusuf quietly explained the sequence of events, and then told Adam, "There is something else I need to say to you. I hope you are sitting down."

"Yes, of course. What is it?"

"One of the terrorists killed was Marie Mfalla."

Adam felt like he was going to be sick. He rocked back is his chair and gasped for breath. "Oh my God, oh my God." He found himself immediately besieged by a cacophony of thoughts. *What the fuck? What was she doing there? Why did she have to do this? What a messed-up woman. But what a waste. What does this mean for me? How many people knew I was seeing her?*

"Yusuf—I can't—I can't talk right now. Let's speak tomorrow. Good night, my friend."

Adam visited his duty-free scotch bottle and continued to absorb the news. Two fingers of twelve-year-old Laphroaig seemed to help. *What the hell— I need a smidge more. This stuff hasn't fully done its job yet.* Adam held his head in his hands and could taste the acid from his stomach. The opening line of Warren Zevon's classic song, "Lawyers, Guns and Money," about the ne'er-do-well who found out that his one-night stand girlfriend was a spy for the Russians, ran through his head.

———

The next morning Adam's cell phone rang—it was Barry Johnson from USAID. "I am sure that you know about the attack at the school yesterday. I have some more information that you may want to know."

Oh my God, do I really want to know more? "Yes—please tell me what the hell this was all about."

"A couple of the captured terrorists have talked. They were going to take the people hostage and spirit them away, sort of like Boko Haram in Nigeria. They thought that they would be able to negotiate them for independence for Pohaneland or, at a minimum, a large ransom."

"How the hell did they think they were going to get away with that?"

"Well, it seems like they were supposed to have a bunch of trucks with additional fighters to take the hostages away, but—get this— some of them got caught in traffic and a couple of others broke down. So they were sitting ducks for the military, who had been, by the way, alerted by Duwango that something was happening at the school."

———

In part to take his mind off the horrors of the school incident and the death of Marie, Adam threw himself into preparations for the Quick Count. As part of these preparations, he had a Zoom call with Patricia Morgan back at the CDP headquarters. During the call, Morgan asked a lengthy and rapid-fire series of questions about the logistics of the effort. This caused Adam to semiseriously complain, "This reminds me of an oral exam I had in college where my professor grilled me on the finer points of macroeconomic theory for an hour."

"Yes, well, if you don't get this right, there is more at stake than the election in Kombonia. A failure could negatively impact the credibility of CDP's other Quick Counts. We have six at various stages of preparation around the world. I know that the ruling parties in most of these places would love to be able to point to a screwed-up Quick Count in Kombonia as evidence as to why they shouldn't be trusted in their countries. So, the equities at play here are more than in just your backyard."

Adam was chastened a bit. "OK, I understand. What else should we talk about?"

"We haven't gotten to the details that regard ensuring the quality of the sample of polling places that have been selected. How certain are you that it reflects a representative balance of the factors in the country we previously discussed when I was with you?"

"Pat, I assure you, we have spent a lot of time on this. With Yusuf and a statistician from the university we double-checked that the choice of polling places represented as accurate a representative sample of the country as possible. This job is simplified to an extent because many of these factors have a correlation with each other. For example, the poorer provinces of the country tend to be more in the West, largely populated by Pohane who tend to be Christian with a higher birth rate. We have found other correlations that have also made it easier for us to draw up a sample—nine percent of the country's polling places—which we are confident will provide an accurate picture. I am frankly more concerned about whether the logistics of this whole operation will work. We have a couple of thousand volunteers involved in all the various stages of this operation. Just ensuring one key aspect of the Quick Count— the accurate transmission of information across this huge country with its poor communications infrastructure—is a huge challenge. One thing I lose sleep over is whether the government will interfere with the internet or cell phone communications."

"I understand, but just remember—it seems like Mushi wants this election to pass the minimum smell test of being democratic. Even if he wants to tilt the playing field, I doubt that he would do something so obvious, so overt, as to sever communications. That would probably end up being a two-edged sword; after all, besides giving himself a big PR black eye, it could mess up his people's communications, too."

"Well, OK. You are making me feel better. I hope you aren't going on vacation over the next few weeks—something tells me we will be in touch along the way."

"That's what I am here for. You and your KADD people are going to do great."

God willing. This business of continuously portraying a greater level of confidence than I feel is exhausting.

Especially given the rapidly approaching election date, it was tempting to try and cut corners, to do things as quickly as possible. Adam steeled himself not to act in this way though, as he knew that the fragile credibility of the untested Quick Count would be put to the test. In the wake of his conversation with Patricia he paid particular attention to ensuring that the adequate number of polling place and tabulation center (where vote totals from polling places were to be aggregated at the provincial and national levels) observers were found and trained.

He and his KADD collaborators ran a simulated Quick Count exercise in which one hundred KADD polling place observers were dispersed to various parts of the country with hypothetical vote totals, which they then reported by cell phones to the KADD provincial Quick Count tallying centers and then the country-wide headquarters in Kayemba City. Adam waited nervously in the crowded KADD offices for the final numbers to be tallied. As nighttime fell, Yusuf turned to him, and with a wide face reported, "The operation was a success—the numbers have come in without a significant delay, and they almost exactly match our aggregate target number. We only had a couple of minor problems where an observer transposed the assigned numbers when reporting them to the provincial office, but other than that, all worked smoothly."

Yusuf then allowed a smile to visit the corners of his mouth. "You know, for the first time I am thinking that this whole thing might actually work."

Adam gently demurred. "I'd like to join you in your enthusiasm, but there are so many damn things that can go wrong. What we just did does seem like a success—but the actual Quick Count will be ten times this scale. And all sorts of things could go wrong that we couldn't account for in this test. The observers might have problems accessing the polling places. What happens if violence occurs, or if polling places get overwhelmed by the numbers of people voting? Or if voting materials don't arrive in time? Or if the observers' cell phones don't work and they can't communicate the polling place numbers? Or if the government shuts down the internet because they don't like the way the election seems to be going? Or if we have technical glitches somewhere along the line and the whole process screws up?"

Yusuf regarded Adam dourly. "Excuse me, my American friend, but you are supposed to be the optimist here. If we all had your attitude, nothing meaningful would ever get done. You, and we, are doing the right thing here. We are preparing as best as we can for contingencies—we should sleep well with that in mind. The rest is in the hands of God, or Allah, or whomever you believe is our spiritual guide. Believe me, I am not being overly optimistic. We Kombonians know this country and its history, which is a major attribute. But only the election will tell us if we have been successful."

———

At 10:30 the next morning Duwango called Adam and Yusuf into his office.

"I have just had a difficult phone conversation with the minister of the interior. He has now focused on our planning for a Quick Count. The minister is outraged. He says that we are attempting to usurp his authority, that we did not have the right to do this, and that he is going to take steps to shut us down."

Adam could not resist a "told you so" moment. "Well, sir, I don't think we should be surprised about this. Frankly, I was not comfortable with how we pushed under the rug the issue of whether, how, and when we should notify the government of our plans."

Duwango's response was brisk. "We could not afford to run the risk of the government learning of our plans any earlier in the process. If they had had time, they could have found a way to shut us down and not look responsible. Now KADD is too well known, especially after the debate. They won't stop us."

Adam glanced at Yusuf who was, as usual, keeping his own counsel. "I certainly hope you are right—if not we are all in trouble."

How to deal with this?

By this time, Adam had been in-country for nine months. He received an email from Mulcahy suggesting that it was time for a check-in and a conversation about his performance. Pissed off, Adam called Mulcahy.

"This is a hell of a time to be discussing my personnel evaluation. I have got a million things on my plate here. Can't this wait until after the election?"

"Listen, guy—I know that you think that Kombonia is the center of the world right now, but other things are happening. It just so happens that CDP is undergoing a USAID performance audit, and one of the ducks that has to get lined up is our personnel practices. Janet Ross is on my case to make sure that all the field office director evaluations are up to date. So we have got to do this. Why don't you prepare a list of positive aspects about your performance as well as some thoughts regarding, shall we say, things you might do differently, if you had the chance to do them again?"

Two days later in the evaluation Zoom call, Mulcahy began by asking for Adam's positive self-assessment. Adam opined, "Well, it is not the simplest thing to just be dropped into the Kombonian environment, hit the ground running, and establish good working relationships with KADD, the US embassy, and other folks on the scene here. OK, so there have been some hiccups along the way, but I think I have had a fairly good track record thus far."

Mulcahy was supportive but probing in his questions. "How confident are you that you—and we—have made the right programming decisions given the situation in Kombonia?"

Adam replied emphatically. "This is exactly what we should be doing. We are on the right track with KADD and it is clear that the political situation here is one in which our support for KADD and election monitoring is what is needed."

"How do you know that for sure, really for sure?"

Mulcahy's probing ignited a flicker of self-doubt in Adam. *Did my haste to show progress, and to respond to USAID and CDP regarding a programming decision, mean I made the wrong one? Had my decision been overly influenced by Duwango's pressure? By Marie's flattery?* Adam, however, made a split-second decision to stick by his guns. *In for a dime, in for a dollar.*

"Look, no one has perfect knowledge or a crystal ball. But it is absolutely clear that this country is in a crisis, that these elections are going to be the most contested, and potentially legitimate, in the country's history, and that there are many questions about the ability of the election commission to act independently from the ruling party's thumb. So if a project designed to strengthen the country's leading nonpartisan democracy organization, to help ensure the election is legitimate, gives the country a chance to embark upon a democratic and stable future, and keep this volatile part of the world peaceful…well, if that isn't a good use of the taxpayers' money, then I don't know what is."

"But really, what argument would you give to, say, American congressmen who may not know a lot about Kombonia and who have to justify funding for this project to their constituents?"

"Kombonia is important to US interests. To many Americans, Kombonia may be far away and of little seeming consequence. But I can assure you that other countries and groups are very much aware of this place; people are interested in Kombonia's minerals. There is a pipeline under development that is supposed to go all the way to Mombasa on the Kenyan coast within five years. The Chinese want that and access to other minerals. The Saudis, the Emiratis, AQIM, and a whole bunch of bad guys are interested in Kombonia. So we have a security, as well as a human rights and democracy promotion, interest here."

"OK, dude," responded a chuckling Mulcahy. "You have learned how to talk the talk. I was just asking. But now tell me about some things you might have done differently. Like that RMK rally, for example."

Gulp. "Look, I am not perfect. I thought at the time that it would be useful to learn more about the RMK."

"Well that certainly happened." At this point the Zoom decided to briefly freeze up and Adam was left staring at Mulchay's usually kind face host a flicker of sarcasm.

Ouch. "There's no way to sugarcoat it. I screwed up. But at least there don't seem to have been any follow-on ramifications."

Mulcahy's voice hardened. "I'd say it is still a bit early to be sure of that. And instead of trying to minimize what could have been a huge disaster, I'd like to feel more comfortable that you won't go down that rabbit hole again. I want to be comfortable that you have the judgement needed to represent CDP effectively."

Adam felt the flush of humiliation, but also of anger. "If you are so concerned, then why don't you come out here and see the situation for yourself? And if you have doubts about me—well there isn't much I can say about that except I understand what happened, why it happened, and that it won't happen again. I can't do anything else except to ask you to trust me on that."

"What I am hearing from you now is some self-confidence, but also self-awareness. That is what I wanted to hear. And no, I don't want to come out to Kombonia now and take your attention away from the work you are doing. I wouldn't want a visit by me to look like it was because of a lack of confidence in you. So, let's just stay steady on the course."

Adam breathed a sigh of relief when the call ended. But he tasted a touch of bile when he considered how Mulcahy would evaluate his judgement if he knew about Marie, his now-deceased PMLP galpal.

Chapter 18

The Election

The period after the debate was one vast blur for Adam; he was working eighteen-hour days helping to direct logistical preparations for the Quick Count, organizing training for the poll watchers, liaising with the USAID mission, asking for advice and responding to questions from CDP in Washington, and tracking the evolving political and electoral situation. He had time for almost nothing else, although ten days before the election, he did grab a late dinner with Sarah.

Over grilled pili pili chicken, she asked, "So Mr. Political Expert, who do you think is going to win the election?"

"If I had crystal-ball powers, I would be lounging around the infinity pool at my luxury house in Saint Lucia right now. That not being the case, I can only hazard a guess. If, and it is a big if, the wheels don't come off this whole thing and the country blows up, and if Mushi doesn't tell the government to do everything possible to ensure his victory, including cheating and fraud, then I think Ruwoyo can win this thing."

"So…tell me more. Why do you think this?"

"I think he can get a huge swath of the Ome vote. And I think he is a sufficiently reassuring figure that he will get some support from the Pohane and Tuyunu. A wild card is how many votes Obewame gets…he could siphon support away from Ruwoyo. By the way, one thing people aren't talking much about is the fact that legislative elections are also happening. It is going to be very interesting to see which party does well in them. How this shakes out will determine the extent to which the new president has support in the legislature."

"Obewame scares me. He is very shrewd but sometimes reminds me of Trump with his populist rhetoric. That is the last thing this country needs."

"Yeah, well, Trump was also the last thing the US needed. I hope our legal institutions are strong enough to withstand him, but his whole thing has been a close call for American democracy. Just think of how that would play out here in Kombonia."

"I don't want to. I prefer to think of other things. On a more personal note, how are you feeling, Adam? After that debate you must be pretty happy."

"I'm happy being with you right now. But what I am also right now is exhausted. What with this job and the situation here, I feel as if I am running a long-distance marathon but I have only passed the half-way mark, and I am beat."

Sarah fiddled with her napkin, took a second, and then looked up at Adam. "I am very proud of you. I know that you have had your ups and downs here in Kombonia, and I won't say you have always exercised the best of judgement, but perfection is not part of our human condition. And, it can be overrated. I…I am learning about you and I like what I see."

Damn she is looking good. And I think she has a new look in her eyes toward me. "And I like what I see in you. Maybe it is my rose-colored glasses, but I am a bit at a loss to see what your foibles may be."

A soft, nervous, feminine chuckle. "Ah, my good man, thee may not knowest me well enough yet."

"Well, you have me intrigued, fair maiden. Come on, give me a hint."

More napkin fiddling. "It's not easy to talk about this."

"Talk about what?"

"I…I have intimacy issues."

"Ok." *Wow. I wasn't expecting this.* "Care to share with me why?"

A long pause. "Not long after I arrived here in Kombonia, I was raped."

Holy shit. "Oh my God. I am so sorry." Instinctively, before he thought whether or not it was a good idea, Adam's hand covered hers. She did not withdraw it. "May I ask how it happened?"

"It was at one of these expat parties here in Kayemba City. I was new, wanted to meet people and fit in. I got to drinking and flirting a bit with an Italian guy who was here on a short-term construction contract for their government. Before I knew it, I was in his apartment and he was on top of me. It was not consensual."

Adam dazedly repeated himself. "I am so, so sorry."

"Yeah, me too."

"What did you do?"

"For the next day couple of days, I was in a daze. I didn't know how to deal with it. I wasn't sure what path to take. It's not like there is a book written on what to do when you are raped in Kombonia. Finally, I decided to tell Carol Adams, the deputy Peace Corps director here at the time…I had met her a few times and felt that I could trust her." A rueful grimace. "Ironic that I have her job now."

"And…"

"And she got on to the Italian Embassy. The deputy chief of mission there was horrified and wanted to be helpful. But the circumstances of the rape were murky from an evidentiary point of view, and who knows what would have happened if all this had gotten tangled up in the Kombonian legal system. And I wasn't sure if I wanted that publicity…I still wonder if it was the right decision, but I agreed with the Italian Embassy's decision that the guy would be called back to Italy, his employers be informed, and let events take their course."

"Oh my God. Do you know what happened to the guy?"

"No, and to be honest, I don't care. I have made peace with this situation. I took a couple of weeks' home leave, and then decided that I was going to face things head on. I wasn't going to run away from my Kombonia commitments. I came back. I am not aware that anyone outside of the Italian DCM—who has now rotated out of here—knows about it. I just want to live my life with integrity, hold my head up, and feel that I am making a difference in the world. I don't have to seek revenge to feel healed."

Adam took her face in his hands, said, "You are so brave," and kissed her. There is a treasured moment in human existence when the realization hits us, thunderlike and out of the blue, that we are really, truly, deeply in love; that we care about someone else more than life itself. Adam's moment had arrived.

The last few days before the election were a whirlwind of dusty cavalcades of vehicles, ranging from battered Hondas to Toyota 4Runners to SUVs with smoked windows, all decked out with campaign paraphernalia. Many carried loudspeakers interspersing the praises of various candidates with popular music, and were accompanied by excited kids running beside them, and much horn blaring. The local T-shirt industry received a boost, judging by the amount of Mushi, Ruwoyo, and Obewame attire festooning the crowded sidewalks and streets. Watching one such demonstration, Adam found himself wondering, not for the first time, where these campaigns got their money. Clearly Mushi's was the best financed, but those of the other two main candidates certainly seemed to have some resources behind them as well.

The scenes were typically good-natured, masking the tension coursing through Kombonian society, given the stakes at play. The day before the election, Adam found himself with Yusuf, once again in the packed and poorly ventilated KADD offices, redolent with the odor of sweat from dozens of volunteers.

"What a blessing it's been to not have any significant violence in the run-up to the elections," Adam observed. "A month ago, I would have bet that things would be different."

Yusuf took a bit of the wind out of Adam's sails. "Don't be fooled. The various protagonists could just as easily be storing up their energy and ammunition for Election Day or the post-election period, when the courts will be adjudicating any complaints. After all, who knows what happens then? Sometimes I think that we should have more of a strategy about how to handle a post-election period that is probably going to be full of tension, lawsuits, and demonstrations."

Not for the first time Adam ruefully thought of the parallels he could draw with the elections and politics in his own country. *And we used to think that we were better, different. I guess this is the way life really is. Maybe getting taken down a peg or two will make us Americans a bit more humble, less full of hubris. But that doesn't mean we can't still make a positive difference in the world. We can still be a special country, maybe even a better one than before, as long as we can learn and internalize these lessons.*

At long last Election Day dawned. Thankfully, the previous night had been relatively calm, with only a few bursts of sporadic gunfire echoing through the city. Lying sleepless in his bed, Adam preferred to think of the shots as being celebratory, marking the advent of Kombonia's first democratic election. And indeed, as the morning passed, long lines of voters patiently queued across the country, in big cities and rural areas alike, as the red-hot sun moved toward its perigee. One radio interview with an excited voter captured the spirit: "We, ordinary Kombonians, we are sharing a feeling of excitement and positivity…we are hoping against hope that these election results will usher in a new and unprecedented era of peaceful and democratic progress in the country." But then the interviewee's voice took on a more somber tone. "But at the same time we also fear what could happen as a result of the elections if the losers do not accept the results—more violence and bloodshed."

The voting process varied greatly across the nation. In most parts of the country, voting was calm and orderly. However, voting was marred by reports of irregularities in significant parts of the country, especially in areas known to be supportive of the opposition. At noon, the Ruwoyo and Obewame campaigns took the extraordinary step of issuing a joint press release citing a list of problems, including: a lack of a significant number of ballots, especially in rural areas; the disenfranchisement of many prospective voters whose names were not on registration lists; isolated cases of intimidation by ruling party supporters; and claims of vote-buying. The statement also warned against vote results mysteriously 'changing' on the way from individual polling places to district tallying centers. Two hours later, the KRP put out its own statement, alleging intimidation of their supporters in opposition strongholds.

As the day wore on, Adam became increasingly nervous. He spent part of the morning at the KADD headquarters, but found himself without anything to do other than nervously chewing his fingernails, a disgusting habit that he had difficulty quitting. He then visited a couple of polling places in Kayemba City with some KADD observers and found the voting to be proceeding well. He also stopped by a local police station; it temporarily housed a mixed group of policemen and soldiers on duty making sure there were no disturbances. Adam was impressed by the comprehensiveness of the briefing on the local situation given by the station commander; the security forces there seemed to be sincerely ready to stop any violence or intimidation, regardless of who initiated it.

Still, Adam remained strangely unoccupied and at loose ends. He had imagined that he would be frantically busy, running to and fro throughout the election day. Instead he felt as if he were in the eye of the storm; the winds were raging around him, but it was deceptively peaceful where he was. The clock seemed to tick very slowly. Restless and seeking to get a taste of how things were going outside of the city, Adam drove in the early afternoon to some polling places about ten miles outside of Kayemba City with Sarah and a couple of KADD observers. As always, Adam was struck by the brusque change from the city to rural life; after just a half-hour drive from the center of town, he felt as if he was in the bush.

The group visited one polling place in a school in a small thatched-hut village. They quickly attracted a large gaggle of wide-eyed Kombonian kids, eager for the diversion of a visit from a "*Nazaran* or "white person" in the local Omean dialect. Adam had once inquired as to the meaning of the word and learned that it was an adaptation of "Nazareth," referring to the Christian religion of the most white people with whom the Kombolese came in contact.

After watching the line of voters patiently awaiting their turn to cast their ballots, Adam, Sarah, and the KADD observers turned to leave the polling place. Before they entered into their vehicles, one boy of about eight years old stepped up and shyly said that he and Sarah looked like a good couple. Despite, or perhaps because of, the tension of the day, Adam laughed out loud with joy. *Could I really be so lucky?*

Celestin Obudwe, the minister of the interior met, with Mushi at 3 p.m. "Mr. President, we believe that by midnight we will be able to announce that you have an approximately eight-point lead over Ruwoyo with fifty percent of the vote counted. We further anticipate that by 10 a.m. tomorrow morning we will be able to officially publicize that with 75 percent of the votes counted, you will have an unsurmountable five-point lead. Furthermore, you will have over 40 percent of the vote, thus obviating the need for a run-off."

Mushi turned to face Obudwe directly, looking him straight in the eye. "Is that what you really believe, or is it what is being cooked up?"

Obudwe, shocked at Mushi's direct allusion to fraud, nonetheless returned the steely look. "It is what the people of Kombonia need, sir."

In the evening, Mushi would learn the result of the KADD Quick Count.

Late in the afternoon, Adam returned to his house to rest and have an early dinner. He knew that it was going to be a late night. At 9 p.m. he returned to the KADD situation room, which was filled with volunteers rushing to and fro. The atmosphere was tense. He found Yusuf in a deep conversation with Duwango and a couple of other KADD staffers. Yusuf motioned for him to come in and close the door.

Yusuf said, "Since the polls have closed at 7 p.m. we have received in reports from about 425 of the polling sites—about half of our sites."

"Oh my God," Adam replied, "that's incredible. The Election Commission just said that only about five percent of the vote has been counted so far. So come on—tell me—how is it looking?"

"You have provided us with the gift of this Quick Count process, and we are now going to reap its benefits. The total from the Quick Count so far indicates that Ruwoyo is in the lead with about 45 percent of the vote, followed by Mushi with 31, and Obewame with 20. Needless to say, if these results hold up Ruwoyo would win outright since he would be above the 40 percent threshold.

Also, Ruwoyo's people just called us. They say that they believe he has won the election fair and square. They asked what our results are—we of course said we couldn't tell them at this point, but they suspect we have similar information and are pressuring us to announce our results right now."

Adam's eyes widened. "Wow. What do you think?"

"It is premature. KRP areas are still underrepresented in the places where we already have results from, so we aren't sure how this will go."

Duwango chimed in. "But we must not wait too long before making our announcement. People will start wondering why we are so quiet. We will need to make our voice heard soon."

The atmosphere in the room grew tense. Yusuf grimaced. "I don't agree. We need to be credible. We need to be accurate. We don't really know the full picture yet. I think we should wait until the Election Commission announces their results, and then we can either corroborate them if they match ours or tell the true story."

It was rare for Adam to hear him directly contradict his boss. It seemed like the two were going to erupt into a full-fledged argument but Yusuf's assistant Ezekiel rushed in and whispered into his ear just at that moment. Yusuf surveyed the room with a hard glance and said, "Ezekiel has been told by a friend in the Interior Ministry that Celestin Obudwe, the new interior minister, has ordered troops to stand by and be ready to occupy these premises if we don't announce a victory for KRP."

Before anyone had time to digest this information Duwango's cell phone rang. He listened intently for what seemed to be a long time to Adam. He then replied, "Mr. Minister, we will announce the results when we deem it to be appropriate. We will not be intimidated. We will tell the truth. The people of Kombonia deserve no less." The call ended. Duwango announced to the half dozen people in the room, "Typical autocrats. They want to tell us what to think and do. That was the minister of the interior. You heard how I responded. We shall see what happens." A nervous quiet enveloped the room.

The clock ticked on. The atmosphere outside of Duwango's office continued to be hyperactive. Volunteers rushed to and fro, relaying messages from field teams and other reports, which included news of some polling places being closed early for lack of election materials, while others had stayed open past the 7 p.m. cut-off time to accommodate the many voters who had waited hours to cast their ballots. Around 10 p.m. news came in of a polling place in the Pohane region that had been attacked by unidentified assailants, and the counting operation was suspended until security forces could arrive. But there were thankfully no reports of widespread or serious cases of violence.

The ten o'clock hour came and went; the Quick Count team rushed to assemble an updated set of results, but they weren't finished yet. Duwango flitted about issuing orders and making statements that, to Adam, seemed a bit superfluous, perhaps belying a subconscious nervousness.

At 11:00 p.m. Yusuf asked Adam, "Why do you think we haven't heard from the Election Commission yet? I would think they would seek to get out in front and shape expectations of results in Mushi's favor."

"I agree. Perhaps they are in fact playing it straight, and the tabulation of results is going slowly. Or maybe Buwemu and the Commission know Mushi is losing and aren't sure about how to deal with it—whether to try and cheat or not. Maybe they are arguing with Mushi and his people about what to do."

Around 11:30 p.m., the Quick Count team finally produced updated results, with 50 percent of the targeted polling place results counted. Adam, Yusuf, and Duwango, along with several Quick Count team members, huddled in Duwango's office. The air was stale, and the room was packed. Duwango read off the numbers in a quiet, strained voice.

"Ruwoyo's lead has increased—he has 49 percent of the vote, Mushi has 32, and Obewame has 15."

Adam surveyed the room. "This thing is real. Ruwoyo has won the election."

Duwango's response was quick. "We should put out a press release now."

"No!" Yusuf exploded. "If we do this, Mushi and Obudwe may order the security forces to shut us down. We must wait a while longer."

Duwango thought for a minute, and then, uncharacteristically, agreed. "All right. We will wait two more hours to see what happens. But if by then the Electoral Commission hasn't issued results that track with our Quick Count, we will go ahead and issue ours."

At 1:15 a.m. Yusuf took a call on his cell phone and moved out onto the office balcony to avoid the continued office cacophony. In a couple of minutes, he came back in and reported to Duwango and Adam. "I have just heard from one of my contacts at the Election Commission that Obudwe is planning to release results showing Mushi in the lead."

Duwango looked at Adam. "In that case we have to release our results, now." His normally stern visage softened. "You need to leave. I suggest you go to your embassy. We could be arrested at any minute. It wouldn't look good for you to be with us—they would use this to make a false narrative that we are the pawns of the Americans. For both of our sakes you should leave now."

Chapter 19

Dealing with the Crisis

The minute they left Duwango's office, Yusuf, who in Adam's experience had never been physically demonstrative, grabbed Adam by his arm, dragged him into an empty office, and slammed the door shut.

"Ignore what Duwango just said. The minister is ill-informed, or more precisely, what he is saying is premature. I didn't say this in front of Duwango because he would be offended for not being in the loop, but during the call with Ruwoyo's people, Ruwoyo himself came on the line and asked for help in brokering an agreement to keep the military from intervening. I said I would try. I have just spoken with my RMK contact, and Mushi's chief of staff. I suggested to them, and they have agreed, that you should mediate a resolution to this crisis."

Adam's head spun. "What?? What are you saying??"

"We are asking you to work with the three parties and candidates, and especially the KRP, to create a solution whereby the government and the military does not simply declare victory and shut down the whole election process, including KADD and this Quick Count. If there isn't some kind of understanding quickly, and I mean with an hour, then what Duwango heard from the minister will happen. We will be arrested, if not killed, and this country will erupt in full violence. We need you because there is a lack of trust between us Kombonians. We cannot work this out ourselves; there is just too much distrust and anger. We need an external mediator—we need you. Just think of it! If you succeed, then the election count can proceed."

What is going on here? Do all these different candidates really see me as someone who could successfully mediate this situation? Oh my God that would be so incredible…I'd be a hero! But wait a minute…maybe they all see me as a patsy. Maybe each side thinks that they can manipulate and intimidate me into ending up supporting their claim to be the election victor. Well, you know what? Screw them! I could do this.

So, in a flash, Adam felt two contradictory impulses. First, he wanted to go ahead and solve this problem; whether to justify the candidates' faith in him, or to prove them wrong, just to show that he had the guts and intelligence to midwife a lasting and just outcome. In a liberating feeling, he felt up to the task. The self-doubt that had plagued him for much of his life evaporated. It wasn't that he had lost fear—that was still there—it was that he had gained a certainty that he could handle it.

But he saw and felt one truth even stronger than that. Throughout his time in-country, he had learned that he could help, advise, be a friend to the people of Kombonia. But ultimately they had to be the ones who made the decisions at this point in time. Quite simply, it was not up to him to determine their destiny for them, nor should it be.

"Yusuf—I am so, so sorry. But the right thing is for me to take a back seat here. You guys have to figure this out."

Yusuf raised his voice, a rare occurrence. "But we need you right now! You cannot betray us!"

"You need yourselves right now. You would pay a higher price in the long run if this crisis was seen to be resolved by a foreigner —a young white American at that. My stepping in now would be the real betrayal of Kombonia. We need to think beyond the short term right now. I know how difficult that is. But you have to be the one to do it. And by you, I mean you, Yusuf. I have come to know and to respect you deeply. You can get them to trust you."

Yusuf was quiet, in contrast to the commotion outside the office. The air, and the moment, hung heavy as he gazed steadily at Adam. Adam couldn't tell if Yusuf was making up his mind, about to completely blow up at him, or was silently congratulating him for making what Adam knew was really the right call.

Yusuf then let out a sigh. "OK. You may be right. May Allah save us all if you are not. I accept your decision. I will go and see Mushi."

By midnight Simon Mushi saw that the handwriting was on the wall. He was aware that the optimistic reports that he had received from his intelligence service masked the reality of the situation. He knew in his heart that the Quick Count numbers, which had been quietly passed on to him from Isodore Samtu, the deputy minister of foreign affairs who was both a childhood friend and a KADD sympathizer, were much more accurate than what he was hearing from his own people. The telling manner in which the minister of the interior had responded to his question about the election said it all: to stay as president, he would have to cheat his way through the compilation of election results.

Is this what I really want to do? Is this what I want my legacy to be? That of a longtime president who held on to power ad infinitum?

Do I want to stay president of a conflict-wracked country, if in doing so that results in more polarization and divisions? Or, is it that by staying in power I could bring peace to the country?

There were another set of more personal considerations. *There are many who would see my concession as an act of betrayal. What would happen to me and my supporters? Should I stay in the country? Would I be arrested by Ruwoyo? What would my role be as a Kombonian ex-president who leaves power after losing an election? Would I be seen as a hero or a traitor? After all, there aren't any precedents…*

Mushi knew that the answer to the last question would depend on who was asking it—his supporters, or others? He decided to place his faith in giving democracy a chance. If it could result in a stable and possibly prosperous Kombonia, then his supporters, over the long run, would come to realize that his decision to accept the results was the correct one, even for them. Mushi thus felt a sense of relief and peace as he answered his own questions. He would not attempt to subvert the results of the election. Like Senghor in Senegal, Kaunda in Zambia, Rawlings in Ghana, and a number of other of his predecessors on the continent, he wanted to be remembered as a president who did much for his country and respected the will of the people.

Yusuf's request to meet with Mushi had been readily granted. He swallowed repeatedly to moisturize his dry throat as he walked into the presidential palace. He was ushered into President Mushi's office. Mushi remained seated behind his desk. He was joined by his chief of staff and military aide-de-camp.

"I am pleased to meet you Mr. Abwangou. This is the first time that we are seeing each other in person, but I believe I have known some of your family, who live in Pohaneland. They are very good people."

"Thank you Mr. President. My family and I are very appreciative for all that you have done for the country."

After a few more pleasantries, Mushi turned to the issue at hand.

"I had thought I would be speaking with Mr. Edwards, but I am prepared to deal with you. I have followed the work that you and KADD have been doing. So, I am glad that we can speak in person."

"Mr. Edwards was honored to have been requested for assistance, but he believes that this is a situation that should be resolved by us Kombonians."

"And so be it. Now, I understand that your projections have me losing. I frankly do not understand how that can be. But the issue is now what to do about it." He glanced over at his military aide-de-camp.

"Mr. President, I realize that this is not what you expected or wanted to hear. But the reality is that our Quick Count, which we have tested and know to be quite accurate, shows the margin of Mr. Ruwoyo's victory, and the distribution of his vote throughout the country makes it impossible for you to win. I should also inform you that we are preparing to release a public statement to this effect within the next two hours."

Mushi let loose a flash of anger. Despite his resolve to concede, it was hard to let go of being in charge of the narrative. "I do not appreciate being pressured in this way." He took a long look at Yusuf. "Tell me, what are your results saying about the legislative elections?"

"We do not know for sure as our Quick Count is only directed at determining the results of the presidential vote. But, assuming that most people who voted for you also voted for the KRP legislative candidates, it would seem that your party may be winning 35–40 percent of the seats, with the KDPR winning a few more and the RMK about 15 percent."

As Mushi considered the implications of this information, Yusuf cleared his throat and continued. "Mr. President, I must inform you that we also have a serious problem. We have reason to believe that the KADD headquarters could be stormed at any moment by military units whose leadership does not wish to see a truly democratic election. We are certain that you do not share this perspective. As such, we are asking you to send an SPB detachment to protect our headquarters."

The thought flitted across Mushi's mind that this was a ruse designed to aggravate the situation and sow mistrust in his camp. But he dismissed that quickly, because although he had no personal knowledge of such a planned military movement, he knew that it was all too possible. He spoke to his military aide-de-camp. "Colonel Manzingwe, please order two hundred men from the SPB to protect the KADD headquarters immediately."

"Very good, sir."

Yusuf recognized the courage of such an action, since such an action reduced the number of Mushi's own bodyguards at a very volatile moment. He quickly responded, "Thank you Mr. President. I need to call President Duwango right away to let him know that the SPB units that will be arriving are there to protect KADD, not attack it."

He placed the call to Duwango and explained the situation. Duwango, who was already fuming that Yusuf had been in contact with the country's political leadership without seeking his approval, reacted angrily. "How could you have done this without asking me? How do we know that the SPB will really protect us? How do we know that they won't either arrest us or otherwise keep us from doing our job? They could, for example, forbid entrance into and out of our offices."

Cupping his hand around his phone and speaking softly, Yusuf replied, "Sir, you have to trust me. Mushi won't let anything bad happen; I believe he understands that he has truly lost. If I may make one suggestion, it would perhaps be a good idea to have Adam communicate with the SPB commander to ensure that there is no confusion about the SPB's role here. They would think twice before taking action against an American."

Realizing that he didn't really have a choice, Duwango replied, "Well, I don't like this situation, but I will agree to it."

Mushi had spent the time Yusuf was on his call weighing his options, given the information Yusuf had provided. *I wonder how much of a difference there is in public attitudes toward me specifically, as opposed to my party? Am I more or less popular than the KRP? The answer to that would affect the KRP's share of the national assembly vote. But it is impossible to be sure how much. But the KRP's legislative representation will certainly be over 25 percent, the needed amount to veto constitutional amendments. Thus, the KRP will still have the power to veto any constitutional legislation that could be against our interests.*

Mushi let out a long sigh. "I am prepared to accept the results of the presidential election. But I need some assurances from Ruwoyo."

"I am willing to communicate any reasonable requests from you to him, Mr. President."

"I want to know that he intends to promote unity within the country. To be blunt, I need assurances that he will not initiate any unfounded investigations or witch hunts against myself or members of my government. I am not asking for blanket immunity because we have nothing to hide. But I want to feel confident that the legal and investigatory powers of a future government will not be abused, and subverted against the cause of justice."

"Sir, I could go right away to meet with Ruwoyo to convey this message. But please allow me to make a suggestion. Perhaps it might be best if you speak with him directly. His people told me that he is only a phone call away. I have reason to believe that they would be very receptive to your taking the initiative here."

Yusuf had an ulterior motive in trying to move this communication process along as quickly as possible. He feared that any delay engendered by his shuttling back and forth carrying messages between the various camps could be exploited by others around Mushi to convince him to take a harder line, or to even attempt a last-minute coup. He wanted Mushi's concession to be locked in as soon as possible.

It went against all of Mushi's instincts and experience to make such a phone call. To begin with, as the president he should be called, not the other way around. And the painful message that he would have to convey. He was reminded of Emperor Hirohito's statement to the Japanese people announcing their defeat in World War II. "We must bear the unbearable." Mushi felt as if the ground was almost literally shifting under his feet. *I will have to concede defeat. So I might as well start acting like an ex-president and sip the bitter brew of humility.*

His mind was made up. Referring to his personal assistant, he called out, "Alexander, could you please place a call to Ruwoyo?"

There was an embarrassed silence, followed by his aide's reply. "Mr. President, I am not sure that we have his phone number readily available."

This is unbelievable. I remember the story of the American assistant secretary of state for Latin America who, in 1983, having been summoned to the White House and given orders to invade Grenada, could not find a taxi to take him back to the State Department to start that short-lived war.

Mushi was about to tell Alexander to find the damn number when Yusuf cleared his throat, and said quietly, "I actually have his number here on my cell phone."

So Mushi made the call. "Good evening Ignace. How is your wife?"

"Thank you for calling me, Mr. President. She is fine, praise God. How is your wife?"

"She too is doing excellently and in good health, as I hope the rest of your family is."

"They are all well."

"That is very good, very good. Now, Ignace if we may, we should speak of what is happening."

"Indeed we should, Mr. President. Perhaps I could ask what your perspective is of the election?"

"Well, it certainly is far from perfect. There are many legitimate grounds for complaint. The question is whether whatever irregularities we see are sufficient to impact the overall legitimacy of the election. I am not sure we know that yet."

"I actually agree with you, although I suspect that the irregularities to which we are referring may be different ones. Still, I would suggest that we must act as if the current trends hold up."

Unlike that deranged would-be tyrant Trump and other autocrats,

I am not going to go down the road of alleging election fraud and claim that I had actually won the election. Mushi got down to the brass tacks. "I agree. But were I to accept that I have lost the election, I would need some assurances that my family and supporters would not be subject to arbitrary and unfair investigations or prosecutions."

"Mr. President, in many ways your presidency has been enlightened, and has led to a point where we can have a peaceful transition of power, which as we both know is unprecedented in our history. I can assure you that while we of course believe in the rule of law and prosecution of illegal acts, we do not have any overriding interest in or need to focus on whatever errors may have occurred in the past. I am certainly prepared to differentiate between mistakes in policy choices and the application of these policies, and illegal acts."

"Well, this is reassuring," Mushi began to respond.

Ruwoyo, however, had more to say. "Excuse me, sir, but there is one other thing I need to stress. Mr. President, we not only have no interest in pursuing the past; rather, as we move forward we see your voice as being an important one in promoting reconciliation and national unity. We understand and welcome that we will need your help in the future."

"In that case, let me be the first to address you as 'president-elect.'"

The ambiance was very different in Obewame's headquarters. Sullenness and anger permeated the air. At a meeting of Obewame and his chief lieutenants, his campaign director pounded the table and yelled, "This is a theft! We are being cheated out of our rights.

The whole process has been stacked up against us!"

Obewame's chief of staff was no less enraged. "Our people have not been able to campaign. We have had materials and supplies stolen. We haven't been able to get our message across enough in the media. For all we know, votes are being stolen from us as we speak. This must not happen!"

Obewame was more measured. "Thank you all for sharing your views. But I have decided. I am going to set an example of peace and reconciliation. We are not going to choose a course of action that could plunge this country into war. That will not benefit us nor our people; it would mean more suffering for them. We must play a longer game. We will take up our seats in the legislature and form the real opposition. We have to broaden our appeal and do a better job of reaching out to other political forces with whom we could ally. We will never get a majority of the people behind us if we only stand for Pohane rights. We must push more for a decentralized form of government. We must make the Ome and Tuyunu believe that supporting our party can mean development and stability. Not secession and chaos. This could set the groundwork for us to be the natural party in power.

"We have to find a positive sum solution to this problem. Yes, we have been tricked and betrayed by participating in this election. But the way forward is not to turn our backs on Kombonia. We have never spoken openly of this before, but secession would be a fool's errand. We would not be successful. The international community would not support us. We don't have the man power or resources to fight a war against the central government. We do not want to go the way of the Biafrans in Nigeria's civil war. Or lead all of Kombonia into chaos such that it becomes a failed state, such as Somalia."

"But we could fight a guerilla war of secession, a war that would wear the government and military down," argued one militant in a piercing and anger-laden tone.

Obewame shook his head in sadness. "So, let us imagine that we could win somehow. How prosperous could an independent Pohaneland be? We are landlocked. All of our transportation routes are at the mercy of Kombonia or neighboring countries. Our natural resources are limited.

"No, I believe that our best way forward is to trace out a path within the framework of a democratic and decentralized Kombonia. This election tells us that we have to redouble our efforts in this regard. But we must start with energetically promoting our interests in the new legislature. We can be the kingmakers, as neither the RMK nor the KDPR will have a majority. We will have to test Ruwoyo, and see if his words of national reconciliation and openness to considering our interests are for real or not. If not, we would have to be prepared to consider an alliance with the RMK. Either way, we will be in a position to promote our interests. Are you with me, or not?"

The session concluded with the participants grudgingly accepting his position.

Duwango called Adam into his office. "The SPB is arriving at any moment. Yusuf foolishly asked Mushi for them to come to deter any attack by others in the military. Mushi agreed, of course. This is a gift-wrapped present to him as an excuse to shut us down. They are supposedly coming here to 'protect' us. I want you to deal with them."

Adam swallowed hard. This was stretching to the limit his commitment not to interfere in the Kombonian election. *But I am damned if I am going to let the military stomp on this effort at democracy. And I care about KADD and these people here. We are all in the trenches together. These are my people, too. And I have to believe that the security forces will not want to kill an American.* "OK, I will head downstairs and wait for them."

He raced down the two flights of stairs and stepped into the hot and humid night. The street was quiet, although he could hear some horns honking in the distance. Adam breathed a brief sigh of relief that he was not hearing gunfire. He guessed that the honking was prematurely heralding election results; he wondered for whom they were celebrating.

Despite the elements, a chill swept through him as he stood on the dusty sidewalk. He felt both nervous and vaguely foolish, awaiting the SPB's arrival. *I wonder if they will be friends or enemies?* He suppressed the desire to take an urgent leak.

About fifteen minutes later Adam heard the approaching sound of sirens. Soon five SPB transport trucks arrived loaded with troops and equipment, including a number of light machine guns. A captain emerged from the cab of the first truck and approached Adam. "Who are you? What are you doing here?" he demanded.

"I am Adam Edwards, an adviser with KADD. I am here to welcome you."

The captain let out a noise that sounded like a haroomph. "And we are here to protect you. Please go back inside. Do not let anyone else out."

Adam returned inside and reported back to Duwango. "Well, they are here. They don't want us to leave the building."

Duwango grunted and went to the window where he could see by the dim streetlights soldiers setting up positions around the building housing KADD.

Not long thereafter, they heard other vehicles headed toward them, including the ominous clanking sound of a tank. Those vehicles halted around the corner, out of sight from the KADD offices. The captain and a small detachment of soldiers headed around the corner. Soon thereafter Adam and a number of his colleagues gathered around the windows, despite the warnings of one KADD staffer who urgently pointed out that those locations would not be the safest from gunfire. They heard elevated voices and then yelling. Duwango ordered people away from the windows. A heavy quiet permeated the offices.

After what seemed to be an interminable period of waiting, they then heard the tank revving up its engine and moving away. Nervous breathing was replaced by sighs of relief. It seemed that the SPB had been on their side, after all.

Chapter 20

Resolution

The next day, the news spread that Ruwoyo had won. At 4 p.m., Mushi made an address to the nation. "I thank the people of Kombonia for allowing me the privilege to have served as your president. I believe that the policies of my administration have put this country on the course for a brighter future. And I wish to explicitly congratulate President-elect Ruwoyo on his victory. I repeat, he is now president-elect of Kombonia.

"My government and I will cooperate with the incoming administration. I have spoken with the president-elect, and we have agreed that he will be sworn in immediately after the Constitutional Court has certified this election. While I believe that there were some irregularities in the electoral process that benefitted my opponent, I do not anticipate any major contestations of these election results. We have thus tentatively agreed that the swearing-in will occur ten days from today."

Widespread celebrations immediately erupted throughout Kayemba City as Mushi spoke these words. Excited citizens danced on car roofs and in the streets, horns blared, and church bells rang. The "pop pop" of fireworks startled many, reawakening fears of some sort of military action. But no such events occurred. For the moment, at least, Kombonia was at peace, thrilled and dazed by the prospect of a peaceful and democratic transfer of power.

Adam and Yusuf watched in wonder from a television in the KADD headquarters. Adam turned to Yusuf and exclaimed to his friend and colleague, "This is incredible…this has never happened before in the history of your country!"

Yusuf was full of awe and questioning, as if he barely had the capacity to be hopeful. "I wonder—what are we celebrating more here; Ruwoyo's victory, Mushi's defeat, or just the simple fact that one president will be replaced by another democratically?"

"How important is why this is happening? The fact that it is happening is just incredibly historic enough. How has this come about? What do you think? It's your country."

"I don't know for sure, but I do know that anyone who thinks that Kombonia has become, presto, a democratic nation is being very, very foolish. How will the defeated political forces react to this? The military? Other countries which benefited from instability in Kombonia? How will ordinary people feel six months or a year from now if their lives have not improved appreciably? Will the Pohane feel like they have a seat at the table in this new democracy, or will they continue to push toward secession? How will the new government pass its legislation if it doesn't have a majority in the parliament? How supportive will the donors be of this new government? Can it rule without being corrupt?"

"Wow. Good God, Yusuf, can't you enjoy the moment before getting all wrapped up in what may or may not happen in the future? Chill out, man!"

Yusuf exhaled slowly as he contemplated his response. "I can't help but think of these things for the simple reason that this is a very dangerous time. A lot of people are facing the loss of power, money, and even their freedom now. Do you really think they are all going to just lie down and take this change as a matter of course?"

"Maybe yes, maybe no. But I guess when you put things that way, the situation is pretty sobering. Now that I think about it, it is true that Kombonia has never had a truly democratic government before—I guess this means that there aren't many precedents, or established practices and rules upon which the new government can rely. That does kind of underscore all the challenges this government will face. But listen—maybe it will all work out. Can't you see how happy the population is now?"

Yusuf gave a wry grin. "Think of Kombonia as a sort of rocket launch. For us right now, the most dangerous moments are immediately after blastoff. Trust me, what happens in the next few weeks and months will be of the utmost importance."

Two days after the election, Adam had his first sound sleep in days. He woke up refreshed and wondered what the future held. There was obviously going to be a lot of wrapping up of loose ends and report writing to fulfill various aspects of the project—he was behind on the reports he was supposed to file every quarter to US-AID. And although he wasn't sure how much money the project had left to spend—things had been pretty fast and furious the past few weeks, and he had sort of lost track of the spending burn rate—Adam was pretty sure that there was still $30,000 to $40,000 left in the cooperative agreement with the USAID, which could perhaps be reprogrammed through a no-cost extension if Adam could come up with a good idea on how it should be spent. He had a long and mutually self-congratulatory WhatsApp call with Charles Mulcahy back in DC.

"My man," Mulcahy exclaimed. "You pulled it off! Way to go! I want to sic our communications people on you to get the word out about this success! God knows that the region needs it, and if the CDP gets a sliver of credit, all the better!"

Adam was a bit uncomfortable taking credit for the whole thing, but he was happy to lap up the obvious professional respect that he had rightfully earned. "Well, somehow the needle did seem to get threaded. A lot of things had to go just right, and thank God they did. But there is a long path ahead. We are going to have to do some thinking about where CDP goes from here in this country. We have built up some credibility and capital; we need to figure out how to use that wisely. I wonder how we can help Kombonians navigate the future."

———

Adam had dinner that night with Sarah. *I feel so at peace with this woman, and excited by her at the same time.* They went back to his place and played cribbage. After he beat her soundly, she looked up at him with sparkling eyes, and asked, "What would you like your prize to be?"

Adam didn't need a second invitation. They kissed, with his tongue running over her full lips. She returned the kiss with passion, and they found themselves on his sofa, laughing and moaning as they explored and discovered different parts of each other. Afterward, Adam felt a deep sense of contentment that had long eluded him.

They spent much of the next morning together in bed. Just before they bestirred themselves to start the day, Adam asked, twirling a stand of Sarah's hair, "How would you like to take a trip to Namibia with me?"

Pushing herself up on an elbow, Sarah took a minute to look at him in wonder. The she laughed, and said, "You want us to take a trip together?"

"Duh."

"Whatever made you think of Namibia?"

"I've heard that is an off-the-beaten-track country that actually works and is incredibly beautiful. We could rent a four-wheel drive and spend time looking up at the stars; that is, when we are not watching rhinos, springbok, giraffes, and elephants. Or doing other things."

"Mmmmm…sounds delicious. I like doing other things… and to experience this, all I would have to do is to put up with you for the length of the trip?"

"My dear, there is no such thing as a free lunch. Yes, you'd have to put up with me—but just remember, the opposite would also be true."

"Well, why don't we see if we can arrange it?"

With that, Adam began nibbling and tickling her throat and earlobes, brushed his mustache across her mouth, and kissed her. He then looked at her face, placed a hand on her cheekbone and whispered, "A person much wiser than me once said that, 'the eyes are the window to the soul.' I love what I see." *OMG I love this woman.*

Adam had been wondering when he should return to the States for a badly needed vacation and also consult with Mulcahy and others at the CDP about next steps for the future. He hadn't yet made up his mind on how to proceed when he received a call from Jonas Biringa, Ruwoyo's chief of staff who had participated in the CDP training in Melinda. "Adam, my friend, as you know, the inauguration will take place nine days from now. The president-elect is requesting your presence at this ceremony as a guest of honor."

Adam swallowed hard. He made up his mind on how to handle this on the fly. This wasn't going to be easy, but it had to be done. "Jonas, I would love to be there. It would, as the president-elect has said, truly be an honor."

In reality, Adam had learned his lesson the hard way about the need to avoid being front and center at Kombonian political events, but he did not want to appear to be insulting Ruwoyo, so he decided to honey the pill. "But I have already made plans to make a visit back to the US. I have personal reasons for needing to be there. I will, of course, be here in spirit on that very special day."

"Well, that is very disappointing, but we of course understand. But please do not be telling us that you will not return to Kombonia."

"Absolutely not! Your country has gotten under my skin!"

Sarah saw Adam off amidst the bustle of Murife International Airport. Their farewell kiss, at the concrete blast barrier outside the airport terminal and surrounded by would-be porters, food hawkers, and fume-spewing taxis, was not exactly the stuff of romance. But Adam made Sarah laugh as he summoned his inner Humphrey Bogart and said, "It's OK, baby—we'll always have Kombonia." Walking toward the terminal, he glanced back and saw the love light in Sarah's face. Glowing inwardly, he checked in for his flight as the happiest man in the world.

And the return trip to the US did not disappoint either. He flew business class on the overnight Air Kombonia plane to London. The champagne tasted superb, and he reflected, not without a measure of self-satisfaction, on how much had changed since his flight to Kombonia the previous year. He then accomplished something that had heretofore eluded him, and had a restful sleep as the Airbus A330 cruised over the Sahara, North Africa, the Mediterranean, and France before beginning its descent into London's Heathrow Airport as a new day dawned.

On the connecting United Airlines flight into Dulles, Adam was pleasantly surprised to recognize Raymond Bearson onboard. "Raymond—how great to see you! How are you?"

Bearson gave him a welcoming smile. "Adam—it is super to see you, too! I am, as they say, alive and kicking. I'm on the way back to the US after my Fulbright year in Burundi."

"So…what do you think of all the events in Kombonia??"

"I must admit that I find them amazing. Call me a cynical, old codger, but I never thought that I'd see that day when Kombonia would have a peaceful and democratic transfer of power. I do wonder, though, what will happen next, and whether Ruwoyo will have the skills to—and if Kombonia will let him—pull this thing off."

"I know, I know, I have heard the same thing from some people in Kayemba City. But don't you think it could work? With support from the international community, a stabilizing regional situation, good weather for the crops, and a population tired of conflict and tension; wouldn't it be possible?"

"Well, as Cole Porter once said, 'One never knows, do one?' But yes, if the stars line up the way you suggest, I do think that

Kombonia could become a success story. The country deserves it."

"I think Africa deserves it, and to be honest, we deserve it too. No one has ever explained to me how people's human rights can be respected in a system other than democracy. And no one has explained how a democracy can be lasting if it doesn't reflect the will of the people. We all know it isn't easy, but a liberal democracy, with its system of checks and balances, is the future if humankind is to prosper. No other system solves the problem of how to ensure stability with respect for human rights over the long term."

"Amen to that. But the sharks are still in the water, in Kombonia, and elsewhere."

It was just about a year previously when Adam had first visited the Kombonian embassy in Washington, DC. As he again entered its grounds, this time to celebrate the presidential inauguration, Adam reflected on the irony of how similar the embassy and its garden looked, but also how much had transpired since his previous visit. And now the embassy atmosphere itself was so different—festive and celebratory. People were drinking champagne despite the early hour of 10 a.m. A large TV screen was set up in the garden and, notwithstanding a fuzzy connection, the assembled guests were able to view the inauguration ceremony live.

The event was replete with emotional moments, such as when President Mushi was introduced as the guest of honor. The single most powerful moment, however, occurred when the chief of staff of the armed forces bowed in front of the newly inaugurated President Ruwoyo, symbolizing the subordination of military to the new civilian power. The approximately 50,000 people in the crowd were at first stunned into quiet, and then erupted into applause.

Adam caught snippets of conversation that echoed his concerns about the future, including: "I wonder how long the Pohane will give this new government to respond to their needs—or demands—depending on how you look at it."

"And how will they address the issue of retribution for the human rights abuses that occurred under Mushi? Will they form some sort of Truth and Reconciliation Commission, such as took place in South Africa?"

"And what about the fact that Ruwoyo doesn't have a majority in parliament? What does that spell for future executive-legislative relations?"

Wow. Seems like the election was just the beginning.

Chapter 21

Afterwards

A few weeks later, Adam whisked Sarah off to Namibia. They met at the airport in Addis Ababa, and took a connecting flight to the capital of Windhoek. On the drive into town Adam and Sarah marveled at the kudu and springbok, wildlife that existed even by the sides of the road. Sarah was particularly struck by the landscape, exclaiming at one point, "Oh my God, this looks like an Ansel Adams painting of the Southwest—such stark reddish orange colors. And the horizon seems to go on forever!"

Adam gave a chuckle of contentment. "You know, this country is roughly the size of Turkey, which has 85 million people. There are fewer than 3 million inhabitants here. Lots of open space. This place puts the Big Sky country of Montana to shame."

They spent the first two days in Windhoek. The German colonial heritage was manifest in the architecture and even street signage in Windhoek, which struck Adam and Sarah as rather ironic given the bloody heritage of the German rule. One evening, in their hotel bar, they struck up a conversation with a hefty white Namibian named Michael, who was of German descent. He explained that a controversy had recently arisen over a decision by the German government to provide over $1 billion in aid to Namibia.

"Oh, sounds to me like the Germans are making reparations," Adam noted.

Michael grimaced. "Well, the Germans didn't want to call it that as they were concerned that it could open up all sorts of legal liabilities against them. So the deal was called a 'Reconciliation agreement.'"

"Cute," Adam responded. Then Sarah interjected with what Adam was learning from experience would most likely be an insightful observation.

"Excuse me, but I believe the current Namibian government is mostly made up of Ovambos. So they will be getting the money. But didn't the Germans mostly suppress the Herero and Nama peoples?"

Michael looked at Sarah with amazement. "Well, I can see that you know your Namibian history. What you say is true, and this has proven to be a rather controversial aspect of the Reconciliation Agreement. The government has promised that much of the money would be directed to the Herero and Nama communities. But we shall see."

Adam added a note of optimism. "Well, we have just come from Kombonia where there has been much ethnic tension, but things seem to be working their way in a positive direction. So maybe that can happen here. Let's drink on that."

The next day Adam and Sarah rented a Toyota Land Cruiser outfitted with all the necessary gear for a ten-day sojourn through the Namibian landscape. They first headed south, along a seemingly endless ribbon of highway, which bisected the country. It was easy to see how traffic accidents could occur, as the countryside was at once starkly beautiful and monotonous. After several hours they left the main road and embarked upon a secondary road, which took them towards the Fish River Canyon, the second largest canyon in the world after the Garnd Canyon in the US. The next day they marveled at this natural wonder, and remarked on the absence of both tourists and protective fencing. Adam suggested that the latter would never be allowed in the litigation-happy US. They then headed north for six hours, during which time they saw exactly four vehicles on the road, to a lodge located near the largest conservation area in Africa, the Namib-Naukluft National Park. The area is famous for its large, red sand dunes, which are some of the tallest such dunes in the world.

At the park they shared a lunch table with an attractive woman who turned out to be a South African journalist based in Windhoek, named Elizabeth Tshiwala. She was well versed on African politics, and they got into a conversation comparing Kombonia and Namibia. Adam started it. "We are really impressed with Namibia. The streets are clean, there doesn't seem to be much petty corruption, kids are going to school, the place seems to work well. I may be wrong, and this may just be a first impression, but I don't sense many of the underlying stresses that we have seen in Kombonia. Can you explain this? Could you perhaps shed some light on why Namibia looks to have a better track record than Kombonia?"

Tshiwala laughed. "Don't fool yourself. There are stresses within Namibian society. There are serious income inequalities. Perhaps you are familiar with the gini coefficient, which measures the level of economic inequality. Namibia has the second highest level in the world, behind South Africa. This should not be surprising since Namibia was ruled by the white government in my country for decades, and thus was infected with the apartheid disease, which in turn results in huge income disparities."

"So why does Namibia seem to be doing so well, compared to other African countries?" Sarah queried.

"Partly because South Africa did build up an infrastructure here. And, while the country had an eventually successful liberation struggle in the last years of apartheid, this war was fought largely in the bush and did not destroy the fabric of society or the economy.

"If you ask me, though, there are other, more fundamental, reasons. Namibia's pre-colonial history of governance had some elements of democracy to it. The largest ethnic group, the Ovambo, had kings but their power was constrained by a group of counsellors, a sort of senate, called the *omalenga*. And there were instances of unpopular kings being replaced.

"There is, however, more to Namibian's governance story than that, a reality which is uncomfortable for some of my more anti-imperialist and anti-Western African colleagues. You see, Namibia's political culture has been highly influenced by that of South Africa, which in turn is in many ways a product of the British colonialists. While it is true that for blacks this was an authoritarian system, it was less so for whites and, to a lesser extent, people of mixed race and of South Asian descent. So certain traits related to democracy have been passed on. These include the concept of an independent judiciary, the importance of elections, the role of a free press, and the concept of a loyal opposition in parliament. Somehow these ideas have found their way into the system here."

"Far be it for me to be either a contrarian or an expert on Namibia, but I don't believe the ruling party has ever been voted out of office," Sarah noted. "How democratic is that?"

"That is true. But if being voted out of office is a requirement for democracy, then postwar Italy under the Christian Democrats and Japan under the Liberal Democratic Party would not have been considered democracies. And also, remember, the ruling party, SWAPO, has much support within the Ovambo community. No one has ever seriously claimed that elections here have been rigged. And corruption seems to be at a relatively low level. You may know that a leading global anti-corruption group, Transparency International, has developed a widely cited metric called the Corruption Perceptions Index—Namibia has one of the five best scores in Africa."

"Hmmm. Doesn't sound much like Kombonia," Adam mused. "I guess it hasn't had some of the advantages of Namibia, or for that matter, of other African countries such as Botswana. Still, Kombonia may be on a good track now."

Sarah then shared an insight. "Hillary Clinton is famous for her 'It takes a village concept.' When I was up-country during my Peace Corps service in Kombonia there was a saying: 'Wisdom is like a Baobab Tree; no one individual can embrace it.' It seems to me that developing, and then really embracing, a democratic system of governance requires a huge collective effort. It can't be just a few people to decide and implement it. It requires a lot of wisdom throughout society, of people linking hands to circle the Baobab Tree."

The last night of their trip Adam and Sarah had an outdoor candlelit dinner at the lodge restaurant, on a hillside, immersed between boulders but still with a breathtaking view of the rolling Namibian landscape. As she savored her "sundowner" gin and tonic Sarah fell into her own, deeply happy thoughts. *We have been so compatible during the trip. More than compatible—in love.*

I would marry this man. He may be a bit goofy, sometimes totally off base with his thoughts, but only on the small stuff. He can be a bit irreverent at times, but that is OK. And I know how much he loves me. I could spend my life with him.

"A penny for your thoughts."

"Oh, no you don't. You'll need to spend a lot more than that."

"Well, my dear. Maybe I will do just that. Let's take a walk."

Mystified, Sarah acquiesced. "As long as I can take my drink with me."

Adam grinned. "Actually, I know that ordering you to do something, anything, is a non-starter. But perhaps I could strongly suggest that you will have no need for it."

All the more curious, Sarah agreed. "OK. But you usually are more informative than now. I smell some kind of rat."

Adam took her hand and they scrambled up through the boulders to a particularly commanding promontory. Along the way they laughed as they heard the chatter of a troop of monkeys that they displaced. After five minutes, and as the sun's setting rays illuminated the red hue of the Namibian mountainsides, they reached the top of a boulder jutting over the grassland. Nestled at the foot of the boulder was a chilled bottle of Veuve Clicquot.

Adam knelt down on one knee. The rock hurt but he didn't care. His heart racing, Adam spoke words that would define his life. "Sarah, will you marry me?"

Sarah flung her arms around him. "Yes, yes, a thousand times yes."

About the Author

Edward McMahon has spent much of his career focused on the promotion of democracy and human rights in Sub-Saharan Africa. He has worked directly for and as a consultant to a wide range of international aid agencies including the US Agency for International Development, the United Nations Development Program, the World Bank and non-and for-profit organizations active on the continent. He is also a former US diplomat, focusing on African affairs. Since 2000 he has taught international development at the University of Vermont. He has also been a professor of political science at Binghamton University and Middlebury College. McMahon lives in Shelburne, Vermont, with his wife and Bernese Mountain dog, and is currently working on a sequel to this book.